HOT & BOTHERED 2

HOT &
BOTHERED 2

Short Short Fiction
on Lesbian Desire

Edited by
KAREN X. TULCHINSKY

ARSENAL PULP PRESS
Vancouver

SECOND PRINTING: 2001

ARSENAL PULP PRESS
103-1014 Homer Street
Vancouver, BC Canada V6B 2W9
www.arsenalpulp.com

The publisher gratefully acknowledges the support of the Canada
Council for the Arts and the B.C. Arts Council for its publishing
program.

The publisher gratefully acknowledges the support of the
Canadä Government of Canada through the Book Publishing Industry
Development Program for its publishing activities.

Typeset for the press by Robert Ballantyne
Author photo by Dianne Whelan
Printed and bound in Canada

CANADIAN CATALOGUING IN PUBLICATION DATA
Main entry under title:
Hot & bothered 2

ISBN 1-55152-068-0

1. Lesbians' writings. 2. Lesbians-Fiction. I. Tulchinsky, Karen X.
PN 6120.92.L47H67 1999   808.83'108353   C99-910950-2

Acknowledgements

Many thanks to Brian Lam, Blaine Kyllo, and Robert Ballantyne of Arsenal Pulp Press for editorial support, administrative assistance, encouragement, and for taking care of all of the millions of details it takes to publish a book. It is always a pleasure to work with Arsenal Pulp, and an honour to publish with a press that produces such an impressive list of progressive and engaging titles. Thanks to James Johnstone for ongoing support, administrative assistance and friendship. To Dianne Whelan for the gorgeous cover photography. Thanks also to Val Spiedel for once again designing such a beautiful book cover. To Richard Banner, Margaret Matsuyama, Trish Burleigh, Frances Wasserlein, Victoria Chan, and Victor Aker for computer advice and assistance, and bailing me out of countless technological nightmares. Thanks to all of the small, independent, gay and lesbian, feminist and alternative bookstores that against great odds stay in business providing the widest selection of gay and lesbian literature for readers, and a venue for writers and publishers. *Arigato* to my fiancée, Terrie Akemi Hamazaki, for inspiration, love, keeping me hot and bothered, and driving me crazy with desire. And to Charlie Tulchinsky-Hamazaki for unconditional cat-love.

To Terrie,
the woman who continues to keep me
hot, bothered and in love

Contents

Introduction

This is a book about lesbian desire. After all, it is our desire for other women that defines us as lesbians. It is our desire that gets us through the hard times of coming out (to ourselves, then to our families, straight friends, co-workers, neighbours, the world). Gets us through the hard times of breaking up with lovers, lures us out into the world (or the dyke bar) with promises of new love (or lust). Makes us happy. Brings us hope. Keeps us sane in a world that often misunderstands, even hates us because of our desire.

This is not a book of erotica. The theme of desire is broader. Desire is not always about consummation of the act. Making love doesn't always end in orgasm. Chasing a girl doesn't always mean we will have her. There isn't always a happily ever after (although thankfully, sometimes there is). Some of the stories in the book will turn you on, while others will make you angry, sad, contemplative or amused. The stories in *Hot & Bothered 2* cover a wide spectrum on the topic of desire between women. The stories are about romance, lust, fantasy, betrayal, grief, hope, and love.

This is a second book in a series. The first was released on Valentine's Day in 1998 to an incredible response from readers. The initial printing sold out before the first book launch and the book has currently gone through three printings after finding its place on numerous bestseller lists. That's a strong statement which, I think, points to the popularity of writing about our desire.

Lesbians need and want to read about our love, our lust, our attractions, our desire. Though there has been some progress in film and television in realistic, positive portrayals of lesbian lives (Ellen coming out in primetime, for example), it is still rare to see ourselves depicted in popular media. Most lesbians watch films and television programs that feature heterosexual characters. It is not uncommon for us to change, in our minds, the gender of the male love interest into a woman (a butch?) so that we can relate more personally to the story. We all derive comfort, recognition, joy, and self-confidence through fictional representations of characters who remind us of ourselves. Unfortunately, in film and television, the pickings are still rather slim. In the sparse moments of lesbian life that are visible in mainstream media, there is not much diversity. If one were to put together a composite lesbian from what one might see on television or in film, she would be white, middle class, gentile, tall, with blonde hair and blue eyes, and she'd live in a fabulous apartment in a large American city.

In putting together this book, one of my goals was a diversity of voices. Lesbians are not all from the same culture or class or geographical area, and I wanted the book to reflect that. The authors are from various countries, from both large cities and small towns. They range in age from their early twenties to their late sixties. They are Asian, African-American, African-Canadian, Caribbean-Canadian, South Asian, Jewish, European, North American, Latina, and Francophone. Some of the authors are being published for the first time; others, such as Lesléa Newman, Joan Nestle, Shani Mootoo, Jewelle Gomez, Carol Queen, Jess Wells, Persimmon Blackbridge, Elana Dykewomon, and Cecilia Tan, have published many books. There are stories about femme seduction, lost love, homophobia, penetration, long-term lovers, sex between friends, blind dates, gynecological fantasies, sex in a bookstore, in an alley, in a car, in the shower, on a bus, before a wedding, the first time, the last time, getting together, and breaking up.

What also strings these stories together is their length. One thousand words or less. Stories distilled down to their finest, most elemental states. Perhaps a fitting format as we cross the millennium and our lives grow increasingly busy and fast-paced. These short short stories can be read on the move—while standing at the bus stop, or doing your laundry, or waiting for your date to arrive. They can be savoured in the bath, in bed with your best girl, or by candlelight should the electricity go off on January 1. Wherever it is you like to read, I invite you to put your feet up, crack open these pages, and share in the experience of getting *Hot & Bothered*.

—Karen X. Tulchinsky
Vancouver
August 1999

PERSIMMON BLACKBRIDGE

The Real Thing

You don't understand how it was with her and me. There was something between our magnetic fields: when we were in the same room, clocks stopped working. The whole space/time continuum went haywire. Days drag-raced by in the space of a second, the moment between almost-orgasm and screaming her name slowed into years. Cars crashed into lamp posts when we crossed the street, panhandlers gave us money. Jehovah's Witnesses followed us for blocks yelling about flesh and sin.

Lying between her thighs, I understood the universe and my place in it. "This is my place," I whispered, "here. I lick, therefore I am." In her arms I was heroic, reckless beyond all sense. "Tell me what you want, anything, I'll do it for you. I'll blow up Dow Chemicals, buy you a house, kill your father."

"Cook me dinner," she said, and I learned how to cook right then, made the most magnificent macaroni and cheese anywhere, ever. She told me so.

When she touched me, the earth moved. Mountains reared up in the middle of wheatfields, threw themselves at each other and fucked shamelessly, Pre-Cambrian thrusting into Paleolithic in geologic ecstasy while farmgirls watched in wonder. When she kissed me—oh god oh god, there are no words.

She sang and played accordion in a bar band. This was the late sixties, so the accordion was considered a geek instrument and geeks were not yet cool. But she squeezed such sighs from it, fingered each tender button till it howled and the bar-drunks howled too. Her voice was big and low, vibrating in my bones, filling the bar like smoke, opium smoke calling visions into the strobing light. The band boys had a competent flash that disappeared in the meltdown of her presence. They hated her, loved her, needed her. Ignored me trailing behind her, gig after gig, carrying her accordion case.

Gig after gig I carried her case, sat at the bar drinking draft whatever, drowning in her voice, taking her home at dawn to drown some more.

Until the inevitable guy from L.A. showed up one night with a contract and a one-way ticket. The band-boys kicked her name around town: "Bitch." "Sell-out." "Gone commercial." I drove her to the airport where she kissed me, cried, promised to write, checked her bags, and disappeared.

She did write, pages of desperate loneliness day after day, becoming irregular updates on record company intrigues with love and xxx's, becoming silence.

The next time I saw her, it was thirty years later and she was walking into my office saying, "Hey girl, I saw your name in the paper, followed it down and here you are." And asking for my help. The kind of help it's my job to give but oh god, I would have done anything, blown up Dow Chemical, killed her dead-by-now father, it was still the same. My hair was shorter, greyer, my heart hard with old scars, but when she touched me, office towers danced through the streets of downtown Vancouver.

I'm not saying she was the one true love of my life, give me a break. One-true-love, it's like alien abduction, you read about it in the *National Enquirer* but it doesn't actually happen to people you know. Maybe someone says this is It, the Real Thing, but two years later they've broken up. The Real Thing is a Coke ad, I know that, but when she walked into my office, my entire life uprooted itself from everything I had so carefully built, and threw itself at her feet. She walked toward me and my case notes tore themselves to bits, scattered in her path like rose petals. She reached out her hand and my electric pencil sharpener sang "Only the Lonely." She touched my cheek and my computer clock sped straight to Y3K and died in the crash. My Jones of New York suit tore itself from my body and jumped out the window. My adjustable office chair flung me into her arms, my carpet tripped me, and I fell between her thighs: abducted.

JOAN NESTLE

The Bathroom Line

Dedicated to the Lesbians of the Fifties

We had rituals too, back in the old days, rituals born out of our Lesbian time and place, the geography of the fifties. The Sea Colony was a world of ritual display—deep dances of Lesbian want, Lesbian adventuring, Lesbian bonding. We who lived there knew the steps. It was over thirty-five years ago, but I can still peer into the smoke-filled room, feel the pressure of bodies, look for the wanted face to float up out of the haze into the circle of light, the tumult of recognition. "I wondered how long it would take you to come here," the teacher welcomes her adoring student, and then retreats into the woman-made mist.

Because we lived in the underworld of the Sea Colony, we were surrounded by the nets of the society that hated us and yet wanted our money. Mafia nets, clean-up New York nets, vice squad nets. We needed the Lesbian air of the Sea Colony to breathe the life we could not anywhere else, those of us who wanted to see women dance, make love, wear shirts and pants. Here, and in other bars like this one, we found each other and the space to be a sexually powerful butch-femme community. We entered their nets with rage, with need, and with strength. The physical nets were visible, and we knew how to side-step them, to slip by, just as we knew, holding hands in the street, clear butch-femme couples, which groups of straights to stay away from, which cars flashed danger as they slowed down at the corner of the curb. We knew how to move quickly. We had the images of smashed faces clear in our memories: our lovers, our friends who had not moved quickly enough. It was the other nets, the nets of the righteous people, the ones that reached into our minds, that most threatened our breathing. These nets carried twisted in their invisible windings the words *hate yourself because you are a freak, hate yourself because you use your tongue, hate yourself because you look butch and femme, hate yourself because you are sexual.*

The powers of the mainland controlled our world in some obvious ways. The cops would come in to check their nets, get their payoffs, joke with the men who stood by the door. They would poke their heads into the back room to make sure we were not dancing together, a crime for which we could be arrested. Of course, the manager had flashed the red light ten minutes before the cops arrived to warn us to play our parts. We did, sitting quietly at the square tables as the cops looked us over. But if they had looked closer, they would have seen hands clenched under the tables, femmes holding on to the belts of their butches, saying through the touch of fingers: don't let their power, their swagger, their leer, goad you into battle. We will lose, and they will take pleasure in our pain, in our blood.

But the most searing reminder of our colonized world was the bathroom line. Now I know it stands for all the pain and glory of my time, and I carry that line and the women who endured it deep within me. Because we were labelled deviants, our bathroom habits had to be watched. Only one woman at a time was allowed into the toilet because we could not be trusted. Thus the toilet line was born, a twisting horizon of Lesbian women waiting for permission to urinate, to shit.

The line flowed past the far wall, past the bar, the front room tables, and reached into the back room. Guarding the entrance to the toilet was a short, square, handsome butch woman, the same every night, whose job it was to twist around her hand our allotted amount of toilet paper. She was us, an obscenity, doing the man's tricks so we could breathe. The line awaited all of us every night, and we developed a line act. We joked, we cruised, we commented on the length of time one of us took, we made special pleas to allow hot-and-heavy lovers in together, knowing full well that our lady would not permit it. I stood, a femme, loving the women on either side of me, loving my comrades for their style, the power of their stance, the hair hitting the collar, the thrown-out hip, the hand encircling the beer can. Our eyes played the line, subtle touches, gentle shyness woven under the blaring jokes, the music, the surveillance. We lived on that line; restricted and judged, we took deep breaths and played.

But buried deep in our endurance was our fury. That line was practice and theory seared into one. We wove our freedoms, our culture, around their obstacles of hatred, but also paid our price. Every time I took the fistful of toilet paper, I swore eventual liberation. It would be, however, liberation with a memory.

JEWELLE   GOMEZ

Ounce of Charm

Okay, deal the cards. Like I was saying . . . what you mean
we all got to be at the table? Shiiit! All right, lemme finish
the story. I can't believe y'all ain't heard this already. She musta told
it a thousand times. Like I said, I shouldn'ta been surprised. I mean
how many times can you count on scientists really knowing what
they're doin'?

The way she tells it she was basically happy with how the world
was turning. A regular nine-to-five at the Department of Human
Services, which was a joke since any time a city employee acts
human, or like she's helping another human obtain some services,
the wall of bureaucracy falls on her like the old ton of bricks. But
you know government really is about the only place a black woman
gonna find a job in this town. Don't get me wrong, Juanita is good
at the people thing. You know when you hear about folks goin' in
and shootin' up city workers 'cause somebody wasn't acting right
around their cheque or stamps, whatever? I personally seen Juanita
short-circuit two or three of them massacres all by herself.

Anyhow, she does the church thing every once in a while just to
check in with the ancestors, house party now and then, visits from
relatives back in Texas. What's missing? Romance, of course.

Her friends kept telling her she was good lookin' and smart. They were as puzzled as she was about why she couldn't find a man. She got that round, brown look anybody would snatch up quick. But they shoulda known that when it comes to a woman searching for a man, smart cancels out good-lookin' like a sixteen-wheeler splats a possum.

Hey, Juanita is not a depressed kind of woman, you know that yourself. Opposite. When she meets the brambles, she makes a new path. That's her all over, always has been far as I can tell. Yo! Can't we deal the cards? Y'all disrupting my luck.

All right, all right. So it wasn't like she didn't meet men all the time. There's the middle management at work, the guys at church, the guys who volunteered at the food delivery project she works for a couple hours a week. Then there's...well, hell, it don't matter now.

It was kind of a joke at first. They had these ads all over the radio. You couldn't get away from them. Juanita listened and didn't listen. She wasn't the type who was what you call "on the make." But she found herself at a perfume counter at Target and there it was: Charm. Just like she heard on the radio. Really expensive—an ounce set her back as much as that leather bag you carrying. But there it sat. Charm.

How am I supposed to know? She went for it, that's all. She sure got enough goin' for her on her own. I knew that soon as she come to work in the building.

On the radio they kept saying it made you irresistible, you know, to the opposite sex. Some kind of gnomes. Pheromones . . . something . . . mixed in it. Like a smell you can't smell that you supposed to have anyway. And it 'sposed to trigger something in somebody else and they can't help themselves. A dash behind the ear and they after you. Yeah, I always been partial to musk myself.

Anyway, she tries it. Ounce of Charm, to go. Well, from what I can get out of her she dabs a speck of Charm on her neck and before she can finish putting on her pantyhose she felt her heart flutter. She checked the mirror, wondering if she was lookin' sick. But there she was—bronze amazon in the pink, so to speak. Her breasts were heavin'. The swell of them in her bra just captured her attention. She smiled at herself, and next thing she finds she's sitting on the floor in front of the mirror.

She touched her nipples and they were hard, like little candies. Well, girl, she leaned back and opened her legs. Her thatch of curlies was already wet. First, she rubbed the lips, and then, when she touched the hard button, she knew she'd hit gold. Back and forth she went, like she did this every day. Those fingers found places she had not even thought about. Neighbours must have wondered what was goin' on up in her flat, 'cause she called in sick and spent the day exploring. Exploring her body, I mean. You gonna deal?

Hell, that wasn't the best of it. First she didn't think it was connected. To the Charm stuff. She thought maybe she was just hot, hormone shifting, who knows. But the next day when she goes to work, just to be sure, she waited till she was getting ready to come in the building.

You know the building. Looks like a fancy warehouse. I sit there all during my shift, in my security uniform, trying not to scare the folks to death. I hate wearing that thing. The pants never fit right and that badge, umph. Don't mean a damn thing, 'cept to people already too vexed as it is. So I see her come and go every day. This time I notice she stopped just before coming through the door. I wondered what she was doin'. Then she come on like she always does. Says to me, "Mornin', Idell," just like usual and goes on up in the elevator.

Well, let me cut to the chase. Right. It works, like a charm, so to speak. But of course who falls for her first? You got it. See, they kept saying it would make a person of the opposite sex fall for you. Hell, scientists don't even know what the opposite sex is!

Juanita, being Juanita, didn't even bat an eyelash at the invitation. Danced the night down to the nubs like she always been hanging out 'cross the bay with the girls at the SisterSpace. They thought disco was dead! Not Juanita. It was like she was possessed by Sylvester and the Weather Girls.

Then, after hours, she was still lively as a tiger on visiting day.

You ain't telling that story again?

Yeah, Juanita, I am.

Idell, why you don't let me tell my own story?

Well, go ahead. They waiting to deal.

So I go dancin'.

I already told that part.

Oh. Well, she asked me to come back to her flat and I said yes, 'cause I hadn't figured on BART being closed down at that hour. I couldn't even tell what I was saying yes to. But she was something. Turns out her people from Texas, too. So there we went and she kissed me soon as the door was closed. I thought the top of my head was gonna fly off. We went into her room quiet, 'cause she had roommates.

I was a little nervous, so I kinda looked out the window. Child, there was this view! I mean I've seen a view, but there was something about the night and all the lights. Many years as I've lived here, how many times you think I looked out and thought, This is my city? Not many, I'm a tell you. It was like I was seein' a city I ain't never seen before.

But girlfriend wasn't into sightseeing. She was busy taking off all my clothes. I think that was what got me, too. Nobody ever did that before. I was laying on the bed, on top of a kind of gold comforter, and she start kissing me at the bottom, working her way up. I couldn't catch my breath. She was licking my knees and rubbing my thighs and I closed my eyes at first. Then I wanted to see what was going on. When her lips touched my breasts, child! And started all over again. She bit and nibbled on my breasts until I wasn't sure they were part of my body. I watched her get up then and take off her shirt and slacks. I realized I had never really looked at another woman's thing before.

Thing...you know. I was hypnotized. She was so dark down there, yeah, down there. Like a pool I could sink into and never return. But I didn't see too much of it right then 'cause she laid down again. On top of me. Something about the weight of her took my breath away. I don't mean she was heavy! Just made me want to stop breathing and pay attention. She kissed me on the mouth this time. Her lips were like sucking on a fruit pie.

My mind was completely taken up with them, so when she touched me I jumped. Her fingers smoothed the hairs inside my thighs, then around . . . you know. I was scared I was dripping onto the pretty gold comforter. Funny the things you think about, ain't it?

She didn't say a word, just plunged right on in, like she knew I was waiting. Her finger became two, then three, moving in and out. And my hips moved to meet her. I wrapped my arms round her back. I was digging the way her muscles rippled, and then her butt! Girl's cute, round mound. But mostly I just opened up to take her in.

I was ready to holler. She pushed deep inside, then out, touching the edges, pushing in again. I felt her hand swell inside me, filling me, taking me to the top. And I screamed. At least I started to. Her hand clamped down over my mouth like it was a stick-up. Set it off!

Girl, she held her hand over my mouth and my eyes popped open. She said ooh, baby and kept moving inside me, hard and fast. One hand pinned me to the bed and the other worked like a Texas oil drill—slick, deep, and steady. Harder, harder she pounded, and my scream kept coming into her hand.

Damn, Juanita, you love to get graphic, don't you?

You the one started telling it, Idell. Five years, and she still blushing over a bottle of perfume.

Come on now, just deal the cards.

How come you always get so shy when the story gets to the part with you in it?

The woman just asked me what I give you for our anniversary.

And what was you gonna say?

I was gonna say Juanita always had all the charm she needs, baby. That's why I always give you lilac water.

Okay, deal the cards.

Betrayal

I'd like to say at the outset that Pruitt drove me to betray her; I'd like to explain here how she was disappearing into something else, no longer giving me that easy laugh, the way she did in our first months together, standing in the park grass barefoot, fists on her wide hips. She'd long since stopped sitting at my piano, letting her short fingers dance over the keys, all the while encouraging me to sing the words to the old show tunes. At the time I betrayed her, I'd like to say, there was no more talking late into the night as we lay in bed together in the streetlight that came through her open summer window.

But the truth is, I was no better than anyone, no better than Lizzie back ten years ago when she stepped out on me, certainly no better than Pruitt. I lied to her, and kept my secret inside me where I kept telling myself I'd tell her when the time was right, and the time was never right, and then it was too late, and I hadn't told her, I'd kept the lie in my chest, where it rusted like a thin metal wire.

Here's how it happened: Kamal handed me a mimosa in a beautifully frosted glass, a sliver of lime lisping along the rim. He sat beside me in the other kitchen chair we'd brought out to his tiny tarpaper porch. All around us, Boston was sinking into a blue autumn evening.

"To the unpredictable human heart," he said, lifting his glass, and I said, "May it somehow keep pumping," and we smiled at each other and drank.

"And how is Moody Prudy?"

"I just don't know what to do anymore," I said, setting my glass down and pulling Kamal's sweater around my shoulders. "It's gotten worse the past week."

"Is she still inhabiting another planet? Or some new thing?"

"It's mostly that. Still. She's working late again tonight, she told me. I don't understand..." I broke off, letting my hand finish the sentence for me, a gesture of my inarticulate fumbling.

Kamal was leaning forward, elbows on knees. "What *I* don't understand is why she won't talk to you about these things, Krista. You don't live together. It isn't like you're exactly demanding an overdose of intimacy from her."

"Oh, you know how it is. Wasn't Kevin like that with you, dodging your best attempts at some semblance of actually being close?"

"I *do* know." He reached for my hand, and his was cold from the iced glass. "I'm sorry, Krista. I wish I could be more helpful to you."

We sat for awhile, thinking about Pruitt, about Kevin, about the seeming impossibility of two people knowing one another, and I watched Boston go salmon-rose in the evening air. Just as I thought it was getting a little too chilly, even with Kamal's sweater to warm me, he took my empty glass and said, "Let's go in—I have a beautiful dinner planned for you."

But the betrayal part came later, the betrayal I've never admitted to anyone, not Pruitt, not Ana, not Billi. Not anyone.

We ate sitting on Kamal's rug, the greens and blues like an ancient map, the colours so faded they bled into each other. Our mimosas gave way to a bottle of Burgundy and a supper of hummus and baba ganouj, the likes of which I haven't tasted since, smoky and dark, followed by a piece of sticky rosewater candy, the rosewater like a Lebanese breeze from the Mediterranean. We watched the lights of Boston come on, and Kamal took my hand again, as he had many times before.

But this was different. His touch was illuminated with a current I'd only glimpsed in him before, and I took his hand in both of mine, as I had many times before. I looked up, and he was looking at me with his eyes so dark they appeared floodlit. I slowly traced my forefinger along the silhouette of his hand, for the first time noticing that his hands were as delicate and well-kept as a woman's. I remembered his stories of the travelling manicurist who came to his mother's house in Beirut every month, how the neighbourhood women would gather in the living room, gossiping and giggling as each had her fingertips dipped in rosewater, and her nails carefully filed and polished, while Kamal half-hid behind a chair, listening.

I ran my fingertip along his palm and his fingers.

I looked up, and he was still watching me, his face calm and serious, desire there as I'd never seen it before. Even though I'd seen him with various boyfriends and lovers, watching the men in the bar or at our little parties, I'd never seen his desire so fully apparent. I'd never seen him so calm, and expectant.

Until then, I still hadn't betrayed Pruitt. Kamal and I had held hands many times, had sat on his Persian rug after a meal together, had waltzed at his cousin's wedding. This was nothing new. But then, still looking him in the eyes, unflinching, I lifted his palm to my mouth and pressed my lips against the soft centre, and in that singular gesture changed everything—between me and him, certainly, but we would weather it—more importantly, I changed everything between me and Pruitt, irrevocably. And maybe most importantly I changed everything in myself. Not that I was changing from being a lesbian, but in that gesture I recognized where everything with Pruitt was. I saw the map of our intentions, our mistakes, our miscommunications, as if a grid sheet of clear tracing abelene were laid across Kamal's palm. I saw the crooked path of my love for Pruitt, the steep contour lines, the dangerous cliff faces, and I knew then that the spring of feeling she and I had for one another wasn't ours alone, but that it led into an underground lake that I could swim into without her. I could see that the silt and sand and mud between us had seeped up, that Pruitt, in her "moods," her restless rants, couldn't really lie with me at the pool's edge, looking in.

I let Kamal's hand, in mine, drop onto my lap. The light of

Boston filled his living room with a clean orange glow, just enough light for me to see the familiar few objects of the room: his piano, his one wing chair, his microscope on a plant stand.

I looked back to him then, leaned over, and kissed him on the mouth, as I had before in greetings or goodbyes, his lips pursed like a little boy's, but this time his lips were soft as moth wings, and I kissed him and his lips parted as easily as a skinned orange unfolding, and we sat there on his old Persian rug, in the city lights of Boston, kissing, and then, bewildered, sad, happy, making love.

I left the next morning. Kamal and I never talked about it, about what happened that night, and I never told Pruitt. It was my secret against her, my weight to balance against her moods, against the way she elided away from me slowly, like tendrilling smoke curling up from a desert fire.

But after she left, after I lost her for good, I kept thinking about that night, as if that secret I harboured in my heart's cove had proved our final destruction.

That Boy

I love my daughter and she hates me. I don't understand why she moved out. She waited till the day before to tell me. All she asked for was the double bed. I threw together some towels, a pillow, and other linens for her. Went and bought a bed cover, too. I felt afraid. At night, she was never at home. I don't know where she slept. I never knew where she was. When she was at home, she'd be on the phone constantly with someone. I could tell it wasn't just a "friend" by the hushed tone in her voice. When moving day arrived, I decided she couldn't have the double bed. I didn't want her to use it. Why should I support her to sleep with someone else, especially another woman? I'd seen that other one, come driving up in that big car. I thought it was a boy. It wasn't. It was a woman.

She was probably moving in with that *boy*. Going to sleep in the double bed with that boy. My daughter is a lesbian. What happened to her? I protected her from the world. I protected her from my husband. I would die for my daughter. She is my eldest, my right-hand person, as I was to my mother. I remember when she was born, after such a long and painful labour, holding her in my arms and looking down at this creature that was my daughter. There was no question of what I would name her. Akemi: bright beauty. The

name that was to have been mine. She could keep herself enter-
tained for hours. But would never keep anything on her feet. I
would put socks and shoes on her, and she would kick and kick till
all were off her feet. My mother told me that if she kept that up,
she'd insist on going barefoot when she was older, too. She was
right. Akemi doesn't like wearing anything on her feet, nor anything on her body, for that matter. Less is more, seems to be her
motto.

I have never understood Akemi. She's so secretive, hiding
things from me, not answering my questions. They're living
together. That boy and my daughter. Like boyfriend and girlfriend.
I haven't told anyone. I can't tell anyone. Not after what my hairdresser said. She told me stories about lesbians on Commercial
Drive, where Akemi's moved to. I told her to move back home.
Kaette kinasai!

It's dangerous around there. Had to warn her to come home to
me. Where she's safe. My hairdresser told me about how these lesbians walk around and feed each other right on the street! Putting
food into each other's mouths. Disgusting. Right on the street! I just
want her to be careful. Not show it out in public where my friends
may see her. Am I strong enough to protect her from people talking about her behind her back? Like they talked about me when I
divorced her father. Talked about me being a bad wife for not staying with that abusive man. I couldn't have him in the house anymore, beating me, humiliating me in front of my children. I had to
protect them from him. He was a bad man. Such a bad man.
Drinking, smoking, chasing sexy women. Akemi takes after her
father. She drinks, smokes, chases . . . well, she likes to have fun.

She even looks like him. Those big eyes, thick hair, eyebrows,
high cheekbones. I hated her for growing up and away from me. I
couldn't keep up with her. She was always ahead, running away
from me. I didn't have time to teach her about things. You know,
about sex. What could I tell her about sex? That it was painful,
smelly, and always ended up in pregnancy? That the man, your husband, would want it constantly? All the time? No matter how tired
I was, no matter how upset I was. I couldn't talk to her about sex.
Maybe that's what went wrong. Because I didn't talk to her about
sex, she became confused, thinking sex could be with anybody.

Disgusting. The whole thing.

Okaasan-ni kikankatta kara.

My mother was right. She told me over and over, *Sonna toi tokoro ikan-ya.* Don't go to such a far-away place. I left my mother. And Akemi has left me. To live with a woman who looks like a boy.

You scare me, Akemi. Remember that story I told you? I quit school when I was a teenager so I could help support the family. It was so painful. I loved learning, the books, having the right answers, doing my homework. Feeling smart for once in my life. I also knew we didn't have money. There was never enough to feed everyone. There were six of us kids. I was the second eldest. Mom's right-hand person. She never asked me to quit school. I just did it. One day I didn't go back. The teacher came to the house to talk to me and my mom. To ask me, beg me to return, because I had so much potential. I said I didn't want to. Told her I was bored and it wasn't doing anything for me.

It hurt. Because I loved school. But we needed to eat. We needed to eat.

I moved away to a dorm which was connected to the candy factory. There were over 200 of us girls, all who had quit school and come to work there. We shared bedrooms, chores, and the boring repetitive work of wrapping candies. An assembly line of young women, all lined up, in our blue uniforms, wrapping candy, one after the other. All of us strangers, from different parts of the countryside, all from poor families. I was afraid to be there. I felt lonely. There was one woman . . . she was smart, beautiful and quiet. She would go about her work. Minding her own business. Answering only when spoken to. Carried herself with a kind of sureness that the other girls didn't. I thought she was . . . tough. I would think about her constantly, watch for her. Hope that when break time came, we'd see each other. I never said two words to her. Was too shy. Too afraid that she'd know what I was feeling.

And what was I feeling?

I felt longing for her. Wanted to know everything about her. Wanted to touch her. Wanted to hold her, protect her. Wanted her. I never told anyone. It wasn't the first time I'd had these feelings for another girl. But it was the last. I couldn't do anything about those feelings. What could I have done? I would've brought so much shame to my family. We were already so poor and had no standing in the village. My family would've been the laughing stock of Kagoshima. And where would we've moved to then? Ridiculous. There was nowhere we could move to. We could barely keep ourselves together where we were.

I'm not a lesbian, Akemi. You are. You carry that desire in your blood. I passed it on to you. It is my fault. I couldn't get rid of that longing, that wanting. And I passed it on to you. Forgive me. *Gomen*. Forgive me for not having been stronger.

Under the Samaan
Tree

The dry clay earth is creamy brown, like their bodies. Underneath them a thick wool blanket, lime green, like the long thin leaves of the bird-of-paradise surrounding them, softens the ground. Their clothing is concealed in a straw bag a shade lighter than the earth. Like a fan, the edges of the densely broad-brimmed samaan dip and sway overhead, evaporating the fine beads of sweat off their bodies as fast as they form.

Kamini props herself up on her stomach and reaches a hand out to part a couple of branches of the bird-of-paradise, so that she can glimpse the house a little way off in the distance. She can see the back of the house, the top of the back stairs outside the kitchen, where she often stands looking over in this direction. (One can only find this spot if one knows where to look—behind the fence, down the steep hill with tall razor grass, a little beyond the edge of the forest to the vined, spreading samaan. From the house one can see only the top of the tree, nesting ground of hundreds of noisy parakeets.) Just behind that is where they lie.

After making love, she always parts the branches and pensively looks over to the house.

She feels Anita's palm touching her, feeling her damp skin, the shape of her arched back, fingertips skirting her bony shoulder blades. Looking at the fenced-off house in the distance, she is unable to respond like she had minutes ago to the slightest coming together of their skins. Anita sits up slightly, beginning a firmer rubbing, a more intent massaging. Kamini knows that Anita has sensed her worry.

Even though there is no one in the forest to hear them, Anita whispers, "What's happening?"

Kamini lets go of the branches, which spring back up, blocking out the house and the hill. Looking into the wall of bush, she remains silent. The fermenting smell of rotting wild fruit floats over them in a wave of a cooling breeze, sharp and sweet. Anita turns to lie on her stomach and puts her arm around Kamini's back.

"What's wrong, what's going on?"

Kamini looks down at the dusty clay earth just beyond the blanket. Reddish brown leafcutter ants with young, bright green leaves in their mouths, hovering over their heads like umbrellas, march in single file back and forth over the cool ground. Black ants scurry erratically, frantically. She looks at them but does not really see them.

"He says that he'll kill us both if he ever finds out about us."

"What! Both? What do you mean? What made him suspect?"

"I don't know"

"What did you say to him?"

"Nothing."

"Do you know what made him say that? Do you think he means it?"

"I don't know. I don't know why he suspects. He just does."

Anita turns over and flops back down; her head hits the blanket with an exaggerated thud. She clasps her hands on top of her stomach and forcefully expels a breath and the word "fuck!"

Kamini looks down at Anita's face, which is oddly bright, a smile taking shape on it. "What are you smiling about?"

Anita unclasps her hands and reaches up to touch Kamini's cheek.

"He's always so arrogantly flattered that those men he works with and parties with would like to have you, and so cocksure of himself that they never could. And now he's worried about me!"

She grins shyly, which makes her look much younger than she is, and stares up into Kamini's face. "I just sort of like the idea that he's jealous of me, squirming about whether he has you or I do. He's probably anxiously wondering right this minute if we're somewhere making love."

"It's not something to joke about, Nita. I don't think he is joking. He would kill us if he found us together, you know! I'm really frightened that he might come looking for us."

"Does he suspect about this place?"

"I don't think so."

Anita extends her arm on the blanket, an invitation Kamini accepts, resting her forehead on Anita's shoulder. They lie still for several seconds, then Anita pulls Kamini to rest on top of her. Their chests, stomachs, and thighs are still damp. Their bodies become slippery with sweat, but gentle breezes cool them in the shade of the big tree. The branches of the samaan shift and part to reveal a thin, pale blue sky. Anita looks up distractedly, trying to catch the blue. She turns her head and whispers into Kamini's ear, "Kam, I have to ask you something. Did you sleep with him last night?"

Kamini is still.

"Tell me, Kam, did you? When was the last time you slept with him?"

Kamini lifts her head and, without looking at Anita, turns to face the bird-of-paradise bush. Anita is spurred on by Kamini's silence.

"Kami, you slept with him last night, didn't you?"

"No."

"Well, when was the last time? You did, I can tell that you did. God! I can't stand the thought of him touching you, kissing you, going and coming inside of you. How could you!"

Kamini pulls away, off onto the blanket, stiffening her body.

"What's wrong with you?" Her voice drops, sounds defeated. "I am his wife, you know! What am I supposed to do? Say no all the time? I am married to him. I can't always say no every time he wants to make love. . . ."

Anita, hearing her sadness, tugs at her to pull her closer. Her eyes are full of tears, and Anita sits up and says coyly, "You and I make love. He and you have sex, and even once a year is too often for my liking."

"Cut it out. You make me feel as if I'm sleeping around. If I keep saying no, no, no to him, he will suspect even more strongly. You don't know him. I wouldn't put it past him to. . . ."

Anita reaches out and touches Kamini's lips with hers, taking in the smell of skin, lips, mouth. She slides her lips around to Kamini's cheek and leaves them lightly resting there, her tongue anxious but holding back. The earthy smell of the forest, alive with decaying fruit, subsides for a moment as Anita feels herself suddenly awakening again to the familiar warm lemon scent, blunted by the evening heat, sharpened by the closeness of Anita's breath, hovering between their faces. Kamini feels Anita responding to her smell. She lies back onto the blanket as her lover's mouth follows hers. Her fingers take time curling over Anita's shoulders, drawing her closer down as she curves her pelvis up toward Anita's. She lets Anita nestle her body between her thighs.

Kamini glances up momentarily to the top branches of the darkening samaan, bristling with lime green parakeets beginning to land for the evening, ruffling themselves, hopping around, shifting their positions. Responding to Anita, she bends her knees and gradually slides her feet up on either side of Anita's body.

The blue of the sky has turned warm yellowish white.

Desire Beyond Gender

She stands in the doorway, watching as her naked lover fills a syringe with a colourless liquid. He shifts his weight onto his left leg then pushes the needle in, breaking skin before penetrating his taut thigh muscle. Their eyes meet, one demanding, one pleading.

He throws away the used needle and looks into the mirror searching for changes. His hand traces his face for signs of hair, smiling as he locates the fine blonde bristles, which are barely visible. Eager to begin the ritual, he reaches for the soap and brush and lathers the frothy suds onto his cheeks, as if he'd been doing this all his life. The razor, a gift from a friend, removes hair and soap, leaving his face pink and soft like a woman's.

Returning to the bathroom, she turns on the taps of the shower, keeping her gaze inward, as if not seeing might equate not happening. It used to be that she was the only one who used a razor, removing hair from legs and underarms as she does now without thinking. Her cleansing complete, the steam evaporates into the silence. He slides back the shower curtain. Tentatively he offers her a towel. She wrings the last drops of water out of her hair. Says nothing. Without turning to face him she takes the towel, wraps it around her slight frame and steps out of the bath. He moves behind her to rub her back dry. She closes her eyes, leans back into his body.

Gently he guides her around to face him, removing the towel, letting it drop to the floor. Face to face she holds his gaze as her hands tiptoe up his body, fingertips cautiously circling the outline of his breast, then edge toward his alert nipples. Impatiently he takes hold of her wrists, bringing her arms up around his neck. Her body sinks. She goes to move away, but he pulls her closer, tightening his grip on her waist as he bends to kiss her, pushing his tongue through the barrier of fleshy tips and sharp teeth.

For a minute she pounds his chest with her fists. Then her hands come to rest on his shoulders as she surrenders to a desire beyond gender. He presses up against her damp body and reaches down to her cunt, feeling heat before being enveloped into her warm wet layers. She falls back against the cool surface of the sink, lifting her pelvis up to meet each thrust of his hand, as he goes deeper and further inside her until she gasps, hears her breath escape, feels her legs quiver. She does not wait to taste herself on him. Already on her knees she is opening him with eager hands followed swiftly by her tongue, teasing his female body to release its juices into her open mouth. Satiated, she wipes her lips with the back of her hand and rises to her feet.

"Will we lose this, too?" she asks.

He shrugs, then reaches for her hand. She pulls away. This time he doesn't try to stop her.

Left alone in the bathroom, he stands quietly. Slowly his hands move his soft, creamy breasts toward his chest bone, spreading out their fullness. He steps back to get a better view of what will soon become permanent and the corners of his mouth begin to curl up toward his eyes.

His hands quickly drop to his sides as she joins him in the bathroom. She picks up her toothbrush and squeezes the pure white paste onto the waiting bristles, careful not to make a mess. Looking up, she catches his reflection in the mirror and sees that he is now binding his breasts across his chest with an elastic bandage, which he pulls tightly, securing the end with tape. She winces as her breasts fall freely.

There was a time when touching him was like touching herself, only different. Loving his body when he was more woman than man helped her love herself. Now that is gone.

Later, both dressed in gender-specific clothes, their queerness has disappeared along with any signs of his female form. Out on the street they will surely be seen as man and woman, killing her coveted lesbian identity with a single silent shot. As he steps into what feels to him as his rightful place in this world, she is sent reeling into obscurity.

In the bedroom, his overnight bag lies open on the tousled sheets of another restless night. He places his wash bag on top and zips the two sides together with finality. She lowers her head and her unruly red hair escapes, falling around her face. Her hand moves to wipe away a tear, careful not to smudge the recently applied mascara. A woman is dying here and she wonders if it is her.

Backstage Boys

Tom B. is my stage name. It's short for "Tomboy," which is how everyone has referred to me since I was old enough to shock the housewives on my block by delivering their morning papers sporting only shorts, sneakers, and an assortment of Band-Aids.

Standing backstage, I watched Ernie Tulips perform, studying how his hips rocked slightly as he belted out his signature swing dance tune. He was one of the best drag kings in the Midwest, and as impatient as I was to perform, I was relieved not to have to follow his act.

There were two numbers left before mine, which meant I had about fifteen minutes to kill. I hated being ready early. I never knew what to do with myself while I waited.

Ernie moved into the dance portion of his number and I imitated his smooth moves, trying to make them my own. It felt awkward. He was a crooner, k.d. lang meets Tony Bennett. I was Melissa Etheridge and Bruce Springsteen's love child, and Ernie's moves didn't match my jeans and white t-shirt. Still, there was nothing else to do. Step, cross, step-step-step . . . I was getting the hang of it . . . step, cross . . . I felt a hand on my ass.

Probably another drunk fag confusing me with Rob, one of the bartenders. Rob and I are about the same height and build, and we both have short black hair. Unless they were coming at us from the front, in a well-lit room, people regularly confused us, although as far as I knew, none of my buddies ever accidentally grabbed his ass. I couldn't say the same for his friends, whose greeting of choice seemed to be a five-fingered inspection of the right buttock. I turned around.

"Hey . . ."

"Keep your hands to yourself?" a fat butch woman suggested playfully. I hate being goosed, but I like women with big grins. "Danny," she said, extending her hand. She smelled like Ivory soap and leather.

"Tam, but I go by 'Tom B.' for the show. It's short for 'Tomboy.' What about you?"

"Just Danny," she replied, looking me up and down. I could feel her body heat.

"Oh." I'm so eloquent under pressure.

I heard applause, and turned to see Ernie leave the stage. The emcee announced Ricky Rick, and a Latin beat started up.

Pretending to glance around, I snuck another look at Danny. Thirty-something, about 250 pounds, a little taller than me, probably five-foot-seven. Blonde buzz-cut, sea green eyes, worn leather pants, and a long-sleeved black t-shirt. Leather pants and green eyes were two of my favourite things, though I typically liked the pants on myself and the eyes on a sultry femme with long, wavy hair.

I turned away before Danny could catch me looking at her. I didn't want to give her the wrong idea. As a general rule, I don't go for other butch women. It's not like I haven't slept with a few of my butch buddies, but it's always been equal parts wrestling and orgasm, the kind of sex where you have to flip a coin to see who lies back and takes it first.

"He's really good, but I bet you're better," Danny said, her voice low and close.

My heart started to beat faster. The crowd, and Danny, joined Ricky in the chorus. My temperature rose. The performance must have been affecting me. An arm wrapped around my torso, pulling me back into a warm, pliant body.

"You're irresistible, Tomboy," Danny whispered into my ear.

My heart skipped a beat. I wasn't used to being on the receiving end of butch pick-up lines. She was smooth. Was I that smooth?

On stage, Ricky took off his jacket, then slowly unbuttoned his white shirt to loud catcalls and whistles. Danny's mouth brushed my neck, spreading goosebumps across my back. Her lips were as soft and gentle as those of the femmes I usually dated, but her arm kept me firmly pinned to her chest. I felt light-headed, so I leaned into her, glad for her size and strength. Her free hand found its way to my stomach, where it rested as she nibbled my ear. I was wet. So this is what the other side of seduction felt like.

"I'm going to take you, Tomboy," she said quietly.

Heat rushed through me. My legs felt weak and my clit was aching. I was suddenly drenched in sweat.

"If you don't want it, just step away now and we'll forget it," she continued.

I stayed put, rooted to the spot by my throbbing cunt. My ragged breathing prevented me from speaking. Her hand moved down to where my jeans met damp skin. I closed my eyes. Fingers entered the gap in my boxers. The Latin beat was replaced by a synthesized throbbing.

"Spread your legs," she commanded.

I complied willingly. She opened my labia and entered me slightly. I pushed onto her fingers.

Her strong, fleshy arm continued to grip me tightly as she bit my neck, hard.

"I'm marking you, Tomboy. You're mine tonight." I shivered involuntarily.

She pulled her fingers from my cunt and circled my clit slowly, her fingertips barely brushing me.

"Harder—please—more," I begged softly.

I was rewarded.

A moan escaped my lips, and her touch got feather-light again. Just when I thought I could take it no longer, she stroked me hard.

"Come for me," she ordered.

I hadn't realized it, but I'd been waiting for her permission. The release was sudden. It was all I could do to remain upright as

I shuddered against her chest. When I was done, she turned me around and enveloped me in a hug. I sunk into her arms, my scent mingling with her soap and leather.

"Sorry you missed your act," she said.

My act! Damn! I missed my cue. I guess fifteen minutes wasn't so long after all.

LISA   SHERIDAN

Birdwatching

North Sea foam froths onto a thin line of visible sand. The
wind, born on the coasts of Norway, careers its icy edge onto
Scottish soil. Cheryl notices from the blue of her hands that she is
finally home. One year of self-imposed exile has eroded her memory. Four years of shared space, shampoo, toilet paper, saving the
world and bodily fluids . . . squeezed into a Pandora's box, whose
hinge had sprung and which had all come tumbling out, the day she
phoned.

"Surprise!" Cheryl looks up and Sunni is standing there holding
two ice cream cones in her gloved hands."

"Ice cream? It's freezing!"

"Don't be ungrateful. Anyway PMS, low blood sugar. My
monthly indulgence!"

She smiles. The cyclical ritual, Sunni's Menstrual Madness, how
could she forget?

They demolish their cones in silence, looking out beyond the
coast to the outline of a trawler heading toward the harbour mouth.

"I'm glad you phoned," Cheryl says. "I meant to write from
Europe, but . . ." Sunni carries on watching the boat and says nothing. Cheryl decides some things are better left alone.

"It is freezing," Sunni says finally. "Come on, I'll give you a lift. Why don't you pop around for dinner tonight? You can tell me about Europe."

Two hours and four outfits later, Cheryl wonders if she should take a bottle of wine. No, too easy to misinterpret. Playing safe, she picks out a melon at the supermarket and suppresses the lesbians and melon jokes that spring to mind. She catches the bus to Sunni's.

Sunni opens the door. Cheryl is thrown off balance by a sense of déjà vu.

"Great! Come in."

Cheryl's eyes flick from one corner of the apartment to another. Sunni had decorated, but so much was familiar. . . . Should she stay, or bolt for the door? Jesus! Europe was just a Band-Aid.

"Thanks."

Over dinner, Cheryl recounts anecdotes and adventures, mostly hairy moments with the gendarmerie of various European havens. Sunni updates her on the antics and gossip of mutual friends and ex-lovers over the past year. They cut open the melon, lapsing into hedonistic muteness as the juice runs over their lips and tickles their tongues. In a desperate attempt to switch wavelengths from sensual, melon-induced fantasy, Cheryl spies a new pair of binoculars perched on a pile of books on birds.

"You've taken up birdwatching?"

"Don't laugh! I did for a week. There was this woman at work, very straight, but so cute . . . she goes birdwatching every weekend. I said I had always wanted to, and she asked me along. I bought the binoculars, borrowed the books . . . only to find she goes with her birdwatching boyfriend, and spends more time glued to his lips than she does to the bloody binoculars! I've always had bad luck with blondes."

Cheryl fingered the binoculars tentatively. "Does that young blonde with the cute bum still live across the street?"

"The one with the boyfriends. Monday, Tuesday, Wednesday girl?"

"Meow! I always said you were jealous."

Sunni laughed. "Yeah, she's still there . . . Cheryl! What are you doing?"

Cheryl is kneeling by the window, binoculars poised on the opposite high rise. "She's in, she's watching TV."

"Well, whoopee."

"Wait, there's someone coming in . . . a guy in a bathrobe."

"I'd never have guessed!"

"She's getting up from the sofa. She's kissing him and slipping her hands inside his robe, pulling at his nipples. She's kissing his neck, running her tongue down his chest, licking, biting, nibbling. She's working her way down to his stomach. . . . Now she's taking his dick into her mouth."

Sunni doesn't say a word, but Cheryl hears the rustle of fabric, of skin against denim, the sound of a zipper coming slowly, quietly down. She knows Sunni is touching herself. She imagines she can even smell the familiar aroma of her juices, sweet and funky. Inside her own jeans her cunt throbs long and slow. Curiosity and a hard clit push her back into the narration.

"They're going over to the sofa. He's taking off her sweater, she's wearing nothing underneath. Her breasts are beautiful, her nipples are large and dark. He's rubbing them hard. She likes it, she's holding her head back, her mouth open. He's working her jeans down, now her panties. She's opening her legs wide."

Cheryl doesn't notice Sunni leave the room. When she hears her coming back in, she doesn't turn around. Sunni's hands reach round from behind and find Cheryl's breasts. Cheryl moans. Sunni pulls Cheryl's top over her head and starts on her jeans. The guy and the woman are still going at it on the sofa as Sunni's fingers slide over her clit.

The binoculars fall to the floor and Cheryl slips slowly forward onto all fours, baring her cunt to Sunni's every manipulation. Cheryl starts at the clank of a belt buckle. Sunni is naked and she never wears belts, but confusion melts into pleasure as Sunni draws aside her lips and Cheryl feels the tip of a well-lubed dildo slide inside her. They begin to move, together, Sunni fucking her again and again. By the time Cheryl goes down on her, Sunni is a furnace in meltdown. Cheryl's juice runs down her legs as she buries herself deep into Sunni's cunt. Small tremors, hot, sweaty, sticky bliss. . . .

As the sun rises, one sleepy eye opens, and a hand gently caresses a slender thigh.

"Sunni, I never knew you were into strap-ons!"

"You never asked," she grins mischievously. "But then, I never knew you were into birdwatching!"

Social Skills

It wasn't till later that I wondered how high she'd been. At first I was just having fun talking to her. But that's how some of my best sex and worst sex has started: chatting animatedly, or looking into someone's eyes while they tell me something intimate, or working up a really good theory. Then they touch my breast or thigh and it's either perfectly right or a huge interruption of what had been a fine conversation. I wish more people could tell the difference.

She'd introduced herself to me and was very tall and lovely and mentioned the name of a mutual friend. And she had good social skills, it seemed—social skills just get more and more important to me the older I get. (If I could find the formula for easily instilling them I could make a million.) She had long, dark hair, beautiful thick shining hair. Strippers take such good care of their hair—one of the erotic elements that can set them apart from the many other micro-bikini-clad beauties looking for a lucrative lap-wiggle at the club. Her hair could have been used as pony reins during a raging fuck. Did I telegraph that thought to her somehow? I wonder.

Usually women err on the side of caution. I certainly do, so when in the middle of a sentence she leaned in and got my slightly-parted lips in an other-side-of-friendly kiss, I admit it took me aback. But I decided to go with it. I don't get kissed by enough beautiful, rangy, raven-haired pony girls. Who does? And she kissed very nicely; she moved rapidly from lips brushing and catching, that tiny friction that shows a kiss could get much deeper, to—well, much deeper.

I remember thinking, "I really honour women's desire when they're this direct in expressing it. So few women are comfortable doing anything like this. And a femme! This younger generation of dykes has it all over the women I came up with."

Kissing was nice, so it took me aback again when she broke away and breathed, "Ohhh, I've just got to fuck you, I've got to feel your hand inside me." That didn't seem immediately possible. We were at a party, and not one of those sex parties, either. Still, this proved no deterrent. She left me for a second and asked around. No one was carrying gloves, but she scored a condom and some lube. Did this mean the guys were ready for anything, but not the women? Hmmm. And shouldn't she, in fact, start carrying such gear in her own purse? This surely couldn't be her first experience at spontaneity.

On that warm night there was no need for us to disturb the party. She pulled me out onto the deck, where only a few people held mixed drinks in plastic cups and chatted quietly.

"Here, I want you to be comfortable," she said, taking off her shirt to make a pillow for me.

And it was a good thing, too, because she nearly ground me through the oak planks, positioning her clit against my pubic bone and swiveling her hips in tight, thrusting circles. I love it when turn of the century writers discreetly and romantically call this position "playing the tribade," but they must be talking about women with soft beds at their disposal.

After just a few minutes of this, which made me wish some loud, rhythmic music were playing, she rose up, stretched the condom over my hand—all the way over so my fingers were pressed tightly into that position all fisters know intimately—and then she poured lube in a steady stream—who'd had a whole bottle of lube, I wondered? Maybe the host—until my hand was covered and the lube threatened to sensuously, slowly drip onto my bare arm.

Her short little skirt hiked up to her waist, her panties off (if she had even been wearing any to begin with), she lowered herself onto my hand, then began to do some of those moves that got her tips at work, from men mesmerized by any woman whose hips could swivel. Of course, there she did the moves without assistance. Here, my hand was a pivot, a dildo. "Wow," I thought, "this is really an adventure," and apparently several people at the party agreed. When I looked up and away from her dervishing, sunfishing body, her flipping veil of shiny hair, quite a crowd had gathered.

The host, however, came outside to urge her to stop. "Look there! That next house! They can see right over here! The neighbourhood association! Please!"

Indeed, there was a lad leaning dangerously out the window of the neighbour's house, looking as though he might be starting puberty right that very minute.

"Nooo! Let me come first!" she wailed.

I felt badly about it, but I really didn't want our host to have to explain it to the police. Personally, I wouldn't have bought a house in such a conservative neighbourhood—but asking us to stop was certainly his prerogative. And my wrist was starting to ache a little.

Her friends were waiting in a worried little claque to take her away.

"Wait! How will I get in touch with you again?" she cried. She wanted to give me her number, but for some reason there was no paper to be had in any of her friends' pockets. Undeterred, she grabbed one of my shoes and wrote it in that. With every step home my sole kissed her name and phone number.

By the next day her number had worn off. I could only make out two digits. There was an inky smear on the bottom of my foot, but I couldn't read it. If she wonders why I haven't called, that's at least part of the reason.

Morning Girl

Pamela ran around the park, chuckling to herself. Sure, the light was soft and the birds were out—there was even fog settled on the soccer field this morning—but after the first five minutes of her run, when she established her pace, Pamela started thinking about sex. Lap after lap, running until her legs burned, she plotted the seduction of Sandra, lying unawares under a crumpled down quilt.

Sandra had no idea that Pamela ran for erotic reasons: she thought she was into health—and she was, but she was also devoted to her morning strategy sessions. Today she sprinted up a small hill, steadied her pace and cruised behind the pump station, bright with graffiti. The first of the cross-bay buses were pulling out of the garage. She'll be lying on her belly and this morning, well, I'll start with the basics, she thought, the lips in her mind kissing Sandra's ankles.

Sandra would flinch and pull away. Pamela would grab her ankles and pull her toward her.

"Baby," Sandra would laugh sleepily, "baby, stop," grabbing for her disappearing pillow. Pamela, her body slick with sweat from her run, would move up over her lover's buttocks and back and lie full length on Sandra's warmth.

"Morning," she'd murmur and nestle her face in Sandra's ear. She'd slip her hands under her lover's ribcage until Sandra, arching forward, offered breasts that were warm with sleep.

Pamela ran the straight-away beside a line of eucalyptus trees. She would press Sandra's breasts against her chest and part her fingers for the nipple. Moving in circles, she would knead and caress her nipples until she saw a reaction in Sandra's eyes, pinching, then releasing, to turn her lover onto her back.

Pamela stretched her arms out and increased her pace. Her muscles were still tired from her push-ups of the day before. She liked the idea of throwing off her clothes and climbing under the comforter from the bottom up. She liked the idea of holding a reluctant ankle with one hand and with her palm against Sandra's cunt, nibbling and kissing the long expanse of fleshy calves and thighs.

The idea of Sandra struggling against her grip pleased Pamela, and she thought perhaps she wouldn't say a word and wouldn't let Sandra see her, but would slowly push Sandra's legs apart until she was spread to her limit and then lick and bite her legs in circles and lines of pleasure, her pumped-up arms and wakeful hands strong against the woman's protests.

"Ah, woman, you're..." Sandra would murmur against her pleasure and her sleep, but Pamela would only move forward, to blow warmth against her cunt and slide her nose into the slit of her body, nostrils gliding along the rippled folds. She would gently part Sandra's lips and curl her fingers into her black hair, pulling her labia up and open, kneading them down to expose the clit.

Pamela ran through the eucalyptus grove unaware of the trees. She thought of how her mouth would come down slowly, how she would moisten her lips and prepare Sandra's clit for the tongue that would sit for just a moment before it circled and began to vibrate. She thought of how Sandra would moan and turn over to press her face into the pillow, tangling her black hair. Sandra's cunt would wet Pamela's face as she lifted her hips and ground herself across Pamela's chin, then the tongue that teased her hole by trapping then darting inside then trapping, to slip up to her clitoris again.

Pamela ran the curving path between the children's swings and slides. Perhaps she would try a different tactic. Maybe this morning she would take her clothes off outside the bedroom door, slip in without a sound, and climb onto the bed, straddling Sandra's head. With her cunt just above her lover's face, Pamela would part her own labia.

"Kiss me good morning, baby," she would say. She knew her cunt would widen from the noise Sandra would make. She would lower herself to Sandra's lips and then pull herself away, just out of reach, as her lover woke and strained forward.

"See how wet I am from my run," Pamela would say, caressing her own thighs, stroking her hands upward into her cunt and wiping the wetness across her lover's cheeks. "I'm drenched, baby."

Pamela ran behind the pump station again. Perhaps she would sit on Sandra's face and let her float between the half-sleep of sex and the bliss of half-sleep.

Or maybe she would hold herself aloof and, reaching behind to grasp Sandra's nipples, tease and play and pull until she felt like muffling the woman's cries with her cunt.

Now which would it be? Pamela wondered, as she pounded through the eucalyptus trees. She looked at her watch. A full thirty minutes of running. Her heart was pounding and her lungs felt full. She could see her nipples through her soaked t-shirt and her legs were burning. She looked across the park at the Bay Bridge and Oakland in the gentle morning fog. Plan A, or Plan B, she wondered with a smirk, as she tore down the steps and headed home. Either way, it was a morning well begun.

Fire Alarm Theory

Rockets of colour tear the fabric of the sky and dissolve to a ballet of stars. Ketley looks with wonder at the air decorated with bursts of flame.

"You can imagine the birth of the world all over again," she says as streams of colour splatter the sky.

A Superman curl falls across her forehead and I brush it back, taken with Ketley's child-like delight. Her face tilts upward, mouth open, completely engaged. As the rhapsody of whirling light continues, I'm held by the thread of her breath, scented like cocoa. A pool of desire laps at my vagina and sexual energy swirls between us.

"That light show was worth staying up later for," Ketley says as the July 4th crowd disperses.

We walk toward her room at the St. Anne's Cottages. I should simply return to my cabin and spend the remainder of the evening listening to music, my bribe for sleep, but I can't rest from this prowling frustration. An eagle of desire has been long homing in on Ketley.

"You sure liked those fireworks." I smile to disguise how I feel, like a moth haunting her flame.

"All that light and colour was the gurgling of a baby universe," she says, opening the cottage door.

"Then it disappears to heaven leaving stars, planets, and other miracles," I follow close behind.

Ketley tosses her keys to the bureau, leans against it, hands pocketed in her khakis. "I love any kind of flame. If it weren't for the heat and the neighbours, I'd have a great time in hell watching things burn."

I sit on her bed as if invited and pick up the Aladdin's lamp-shaped candle.

"I like this for light." When I put a match to the wick, the orange globe immediately sweats soft wax.

"Put down your cap and stay awhile," I say, but Ketley fastens her hands across her chest, sending me a look of warning.

"You know, Beryl," she says, "I'm feeling it, too, but us having sex won't cure what ails me. Maybe we should just pass on this vibe."

Caught by my libido, I speak without thought. "Well, let's fake a deal."

She laughs. I'm amusing her, that's a good sign.

"Sit and I'll show you something." I smooth the bed and turn out the table lamp. The only light in the room is the candle's single stroke. We're attentive as it performs an operetta of flame and flicker. I dip my finger in the pool of melted wax and it clings to my skin.

"Umm. Better than kindergarten glue. Give me your hands," I say, and hesitantly, miraculously, she does. I pour a little melting wax into the bowl of her palms. It forms a spongey coating that I spread with my finger.

"Don't crack the wax," I say. She holds her hands steady in her lap. With my fingers, I draw imaginary patterns on her wrists and up each bare arm to her biceps where veins pulse and glow in the shadowy light. At her shoulders, I play my fingers across her sternum, up her neck to trace around her lips.

Her eyes are on the alert, questioning me, but allowing this to happen, so she's not surprised when I lean across to kiss her.

"I have a lover, Beryl. I can't afford any more problems."

"I am not a 'problem,' Ketley. I am a free and easy love affair."

53

"Sex for me has never been easy or free. The real stuff is being able to trust someone, to work it out with her."

"I agree, Ketley."

Her expression warns against even one false move, but she keeps her hands in her lap to follow my strange command. Not sure where I'm headed, I move the candle to the table and push her down to lay on the bed. Now I know I'm home free.

I get her shirt unbuttoned and set my mouth on each of her breasts, which have the texture and weight of Spanish onions. My tongue kneads the bulb to sprout florets at the tip.

Soon her pelvis arches and recedes. She lets me undo the buttons of her khakis. When she makes to pull them down, I scold, "Mind the wax." Her arms retreat and she lays back, legs now fallen apart.

I inhale the incense of sex—the scent arising once the body is lit. When I've finished peeling the fabric away from her skin, I push my tongue through her pubic hair and roam through her folds of flesh.

I put questions to Ketley's body about attraction, caring, and meaning in life. The air is lit with the slightly sacred smell of burning as Ketley squirms against my mouth's wordless conversation. The long flickering shadows tell me the candle is melting close to the wick.

She orgasms from my mouth like a newborn waylaid and wailing, having no idea what caused her world to turn so inside out. Tears begin to curl from her eyes, a sorrow that has nothing to do with me.

As I cradle her, lights brighten outside the window and I see Ketley's skin as the shifting colour of cider. She sighs like wounds pulsing blood. I'm waxed and silky between my legs, underpants sticky against my vulva. Something has been satisfied. The candle flickers one last time and I see a flare of colours rip across the sky, but the room light is still and gone.

HEATHER MITCHELL

What Took So Long

For two years now, my best friend Gwen and I have gotten together every Sunday night, with her girlfriend Maggie and whomever I'm seeing at the time. It's become something of a tradition—dinner at my house, a movie, and generally enough wine that Gwen and Maggie have to take a cab home.

Tonight, however, Gwen showed up alone. When she handed me the bottle and video she was carrying, I noticed a pale band on her ring finger—skin that hadn't seen sun in years.

"She left a few days ago," Gwen said before I could ask. "For one of her yoga students, of all people."

"You don't seem too upset," I responded, walking with her into the kitchen where I uncorked the wine.

"I'm not. It's been over for a while. She was just waiting for someone else to come along before she left me for good. You know, she hasn't been alone for more than a week since she was seventeen."

"Serial monogamy strikes again?" I asked.

She laughed, slinging her leather jacket over the back of a chair. "Where's what's-her-name?"

"Who, Stacy?"

Gwen nodded.

"She decided she wanted to move in with me. Said she felt like we'd known each other forever and were meant to be together. After two weeks? No, thank you. So we're both solo tonight." I poured the wine and toasted her. "To the single life!"

We had almost finished the bottle when the oven timer rang. In a mellow haze, we ate and talked about our lives.

After dinner, Gwen stacked our plates in the sink and opened a second bottle of wine. I waited in the living room, curled up on the sofa as I fast-forwarded through previews. Our fingers brushed when she handed me the glass. The unexpected contact made me blush. I told myself I was reading too much into things when she shifted closer to me and stretched out, resting her head on my thigh.

"More wine?" I got up so quickly I nearly pitched her onto the floor. I didn't wait for her to answer, just grabbed our glasses and headed for the kitchen. Deciding more alcohol wouldn't be in my best interest, I poured a glass of water and leaned against the counter, trying to clear my head.

"Sarah?" Gwen stood in the doorway, back lit by the flickering television. "I have to tell you something."

I put the glass down and turned to her, watched her walk across the kitchen, felt her hands on my hips. I tasted the wine when we kissed. She tightened her grip on my hips, holding me hard against her, our bodies pushing back against the fridge. When she pulled away I was wet, radiating heat.

"What was it you wanted to say?" I asked, trying to maintain my composure. She slid her hand under my sweater and twisted her fingers around my nipple.

"I want to fuck you. I have for years."

"Why didn't you say anything before?" I slid my leg between hers, pressing my cunt against her thigh through the layers of denim, knowing she could feel how hot I was for her.

"Never seemed to be the right time," she answered, kissing me again, hard, until my hips rocked into her.

"And now?"

"I realized that there's never going to be a right time, and I don't want to wait another five years." She pulled her shirt over her head and let it fall.

My breath caught. I'd seen her shirtless before, but never like this. Never with her back pressed against my fridge and my lips swollen from kissing her. But when she reached for me again, rationality came back. I stepped away.

"Hold on a sec. Is this one of those too-much-wine-after-a-break-up things? Do you want me, or am I just a convenient warm body?"

She looked at me for a moment, then slipped her hands into the back pockets of my jeans.

"I told you, I've wanted you for years. I just never had the guts to do anything about it before." She kissed me. I believed her. When she pulled my sweater off and bent to take my nipple in her mouth, I grabbed the waistband of her pants. Walking backwards, I led her into my bedroom and pushed her onto the bed.

"You sure about this?" I asked, reaching for the box of latex gloves I kept on my bedside table. She answered by unzipping her pants and kicking them onto the floor.

We fucked as though we'd been lovers for years. My fingers slid easily inside her. I could feel her heat through the glove as I moved deeper and deeper until my hand was enveloped in her cunt. She came, hard, her back arching as she rode my fist. When she finally opened her eyes, I pulled my hand away from her, took off the glove and tied it.

"You okay?" I asked.

"Very okay," she answered, sitting up and kissing me. "I was just wondering why we didn't do this a long time ago."

"Well, there's no sense in wasting any more time," I said, sliding down on the bed.

Gwen smiled her agreement and unbuttoned my jeans.

Sex Hall

The hallway is narrow. I had expected it to be less bare—there are no pictures on the walls, which have all been painted dark reds, slick mahoganies, and purples. I laugh to myself. The coloured girls must have had fun checking out swollen pussies when they were painting this. The lights are sunk deep into the ceiling and turned down low so it's lit like a club. A house diva is wailing through the P.A. system, backed up by an insistent fuck-me-baby, fuck-me-baby tempo. I feel as though I am in a peep-show.

Brown, bronze, and various sun-kissed women move past me, some with their eyes straight forward, nervous, others whose eyes seem to burn a path before them. I can feel their heat as they pass. There is a steady pulsing below my skin as I move forward, the current stopping and starting and me feeling the blood push-flow-push-flow through my neck and fingers, my heart growing, forcing blood into my breasts. I pass the first doorway and hesitate. The door is open but I am suddenly afraid to be caught looking.

Someone behind me stops to look over my shoulder, and her fingers inquire at my leg. I can feel her questions all the way up my thigh into my stomach. I almost jump into the room, and there is laughter behind me. I catch my breath, surprised at my confusion. This morning I was so sure of what I wanted, what I felt, but now. . . . Excitement? Pleasure? Fear?

Didn't I want to be fucked from behind, anonymous?

A voice in my ear saying, "Look forward, baby, or I'll leave."

And, "I know you're wet."

And, "When I remember how you look I'm going to think about parting your bush, how you almost reached behind to guide my hands. But I told you not to move. *Don't move.*"

Hiking up skirt, pulling down panties, the snap of a glove and a hand between my legs. Fucked in a doorway. Fingers up my cunt, feeling the space in my flesh, pushing deeper and rubbing till there's this cross between a sharpness and pleasure, my muscles filled with blood, taut, filling and pressing until I think I'm going to pee on the floor.

My mouth is filled with stars and they're burning their way through my vagina. They hurl through my chest and I can't breathe, sweat collects in the band of my skirt. They light up nerves, sending shocks to my clit and behind my eyelids. I hear myself salivate as she works her hand in further, I pant, my cunt pants for her and the feeling of stars.

I am high, nipples sharp from the sound of her inside me. I am straining against damp fabric, pores fucked alert, open, wanting to feel air on sweat and oil-steeped skin, as I brace myself in the doorway.

Bodies passing by us go quiet as another finger goes in my puckering ass, tilted to receive, and lips circle my neck, her tongue leaving a trail that ends with a mouth clamped on the back of my throat, kissing, sucking hard, until a half-moon appears. I wanna come bad, but I could stay here forever.

Can you fuck too much? Can you feel too good? Can you be so ripe that you keep bursting and swelling, bursting and swelling until a mouth bites you open again? Her teeth burn into my ass, she whips the hand out of my cunt and I feel the air leave my chest, my breasts suddenly get heavy and full. Her hand spanks my ass, my skin wet and hot, and enters me again like horses. I swear I'm gonna drop to my knees as the finger in my ass moves back and forth, teasing the rim of my anus. I feel myself coming, raging against the horses, grasping them, expelling-thrusting them out as they lunge-push further inside. She holds onto me; "That hand isn't going anywhere," she says.

I feel cum like hushed spurts, warm like blood, flowing out of me. I'm on my knees, my unconscious fingers take her horse hand, arching as I pull her out of me, and rub her against my lips and clit. I feel like a dog, mouth open and bent over writhing against her hand, I'm not thinking anymore, just doing what feels good. She doesn't pull away. I come again, air passes through my throat and I hear a sound like the last breath as you break the surface of water. Doubled over, breathing hard, I pull away from the finger in my ass and pass her other hand from between my legs. I lick my juice from her glove, and pull the latex off. My tongue dives for the skin in between her fingers. This is how I will remember her, by her hands. She helps me up from behind, pulling up my panties stretched and tangled in my boots, her fingers spread wide feeling me up as she pulls my skirt down.

She bites my neck and says, "It's too bad you came early," and rubs her pelvis against the crack of my behind. I can feel her packing. Well, I'm sorry, too.

"Next time," she says, her hands firm on my hips, teasing, pressing into, circling against me, slowly. "It's underneath my black vinyl shorts, it peeks through a little cause they're short-shorts like the ones the reggae dancehall queens wear. Zippers up the sides, I only wear them here."

"How do you know you're the only one?" I ask. She can't see me smile.

"Well, if I'm not, we'll find out soon enough," she laughs, and bites the half-moon she left before. I listen to her walk away.

Boots, I guess, with heavy soles.

L . M . M C A R T H U R

A S u d s y A f f a i r

I open my eyes to the sound of birds singing outside my window on an early Sunday morning. Another weekend has come and gone, ending all too soon. I think about trying to go back to sleep, but with the symphony of birds in the background, I decide to get up and do one of the thousand and one chores I have neglected for the past few weeks. I glare at the pile of laundry accumulating that threatens to take over the closet.

I sort clothes, grab the laundry basket and head downstairs. On the elevator ride down, my mind wanders to the image of a woman I caught a ride with the other day. The smell of her perfume—was it Halston? Tresor? I breathe in deeply, trying to remember. The way my luck's been going with women these days, I probably won't run into her again until one of us is ready to move out. Being dumped twice in the last six months, my eagerness to be the suave dyke isn't so forthcoming these days.

In the laundry room, all is quiet. I start jamming laundry into a washer when I hear the jingling of keys and the sound of the door opening. I just about drop the coins on the floor when I see who is walking in. Five-foot-five, auburn hair cut shoulder length, deep blue eyes I could get lost in. Legs and curves I'd like to spend a lifetime going over every inch of with my tongue. We hold our exchange for several seconds, devouring each other with our eyes. We smile. I can hear my heart beating faster, the palms of my hands are sweating. She walks over to the washer beside me and sorts laundry. I watch out of the corner of my eye as she pulls out a black lacy bra, silk underwear, and a satin nightshirt. I feel a trickle of moisture between my legs as she places each item in. I continue stuffing my washer when I hear, "Oh shit, you stupid thing." I turn to see her fighting with the coin slot.

She looks over and says, "It's jammed."

With a smile on my face I say, "Let me try."

I walk over to look at her machine. She reaches from behind me, pointing. "See, it's stuck, here."

Her scent is delicious. I try to concentrate on the coin slot, but from behind I can feel her breath on my neck, her breasts against my back. I try to take a step back, but she doesn't move. She stays in her spot, and places her hand on my neck, and glides it down my back. I stand, startled by her touch. I slowly turn around and we gaze into each other's eyes. Feeling unsure, but willing to take the risk—what could possibly happen? A slap in the face? One of us never doing laundry again?

I cautiously lean into her and we gently kiss. The sensation is overwhelming and my body reacts, with no thought of the conse-quences. I want to feel my hand inside her. I reach down, caress her thigh as she leans into me and nuzzles her face in my neck and hair. I stare into her eyes, blue like ocean waves. We grab each other and kiss, hard and demanding.

I push her toward a washer and lift her up as we continue to kiss. I reach down and feel the fullness of her breast in my hand. Reaching for a nipple, I squeeze it between my fingers, feeling her hardness. She has no bra, only a shirt. I move my hands up and down her body, feeling every curve as we explore each other's tongues. I taste the salt on her lips, the softness of her tongue, I glide to the side of her neck and drift to the soft mound of her breast, I start to suck her nipple through her shirt, hear her moan.

"More," she says.

I lift her shirt up over her head and suck on her nipple, lightly at first, then harder. I cup both her breasts in my hands and suck from one nipple to the other, flicking my tongue on each nipple until she cries out. I free one hand and gently move down her thigh, slip my hand between her legs. I move my hand up through her shorts. She is not wearing underwear. She responds to my touch immediately. She bathes my fingers with her silky juices as they slide across her clit, and welcomes me by opening herself up even wider. I slip one finger, then two, then three inside her. She grabs and moves with me from within. Thrusting in and out slowly, then faster and harder while I flick my tongue on her nipples. She gasps, wanting more and matching each thrust with her hips. Pulling in and out, using my thumb to slide up and down her clit, matching the rhythm with my fingers. Plunging deeper and deeper, I hear her cries from deep within.

She arches her back and grabs for me, holds me tight as she comes. I can feel her clit throbbing under my thumb. Holding my fingers inside of her, we become as one. I'm not sure where she begins and I end.

I hear water running. I look down. My hands are immersed in warm water, soap bubbles everywhere. I glance over as she puts the last of her clothes in the wash. Could she possibly know what I've been thinking? I take a deep breath, let it out and shake the bubbles from my hands. I close the lid of my washer. I hear, "Oh shit, you stupid thing." She is struggling with the coin slot. She turns and smiles at me. "It's jammed."

I return the smile. "Let me try," I say, moving closer. "Maybe I can help."

The Bottom

There's a tunnel that ends at solid rock. It's dark. It's always dark in there. People dream of this tunnel all the time.

Some say it means sex, some say fear, some say death, some say tunnel, tunnel, tunnel, and to hell with you symbolists.

One year, in December, we were hiking, both sick. I had just stopped wearing the eye patch, but my muscles were still stiff and twitching, and I had a cold. She'd been rear ended, may still have been wearing a neck brace. My feet were bad, and I was using a cane. Our house was two sizes too small to hold our complaints. So we took them outdoors: Pinnacles national monument, the middle of California. We had a certain kind of mid-thirties dyke pride in challenge. And of course, we hoped for desire (nothing can damage us enough to keep us from the cornucopia, the bounce, cool startle and hot joy).

The path is beautiful—green in strips running between round red boulders, rocky pools wearing collars of late wildflower, some kind of seed pod thick in places on the ground.

We have flashlights, for the cave. First the trail leads into a narrow corridor, funneling through stone until we think it is the tunnel and we turn the flashlights on. Water drips down the wall, water is always dripping down the wall in these stories, in tunnels and caves.

Because it does. Caves are mostly wet places. We think wet dark places are sex but maybe they're just caves. It's hard to tell geography from biology. I was always such a good student that it's strange now to be mixing up the subjects.

Are dreams psychology or literature? Is memory physiology or the history of film? Is this the advanced course?

This cave isn't so impressive, she says. She kisses me before we leave the tunnel and bump into sunlight. Before I can say it, she does, poking fun at me, You always want to kiss me in beautiful places.

But this is not exactly lust's good season, so I turn to poke my cane at the trail ahead, scouring boulders with my good eye. Suddenly it isn't clear which way to go. Not well marked. We scout up, down, around a rocky slope, not wanting to go back. She has a goat nature and can scramble up and down better than I, even recently injured. I have a good, slow sense of orientation, of which way is next.

Between us we find a descent. Should we really be going in here? A hole, and no light showing. Slippery, hard, too dark, unmarked. The park service couldn't mean this—it's too obscure. The park service is not supposed to let you do anything dangerous, is it? The park service is not allowed to scare you. We pay taxes for clear signs, for trail guides.

But down we go. The flashlight bounces off walls, all of them grey, thick, hard; I dislodge a trickling avalanche of pebbles. Too quickly we are in over our heads. I don't know if I can climb up the way we've come down. I let the flashlight lick up the incline for a minute, and know I can't. Maybe she could. Maybe she could go for help. Stop. We don't need help, do we? Not us. But then we hear how our breath catches in our throats. What else is down here, in the cave?

Insect, animal, skeleton, gas, the souls of trapped miners, journey to the centre of the earth, snakes, monsters? They poke our soft ribs, snicker in our hair: who told you to come here? Who said you could?

Look for water. I told you, there is always water in this story.

ELANA DYKEWOMON

Follow where it goes. The ground has a long stain in a deep streak below our feet. I pull the light along the string of water, clenching my jaw. Someone panicked in a labyrinth, I remember, but it's not going to be me. She, my lover, breathes shallowly, and her cheeks have gone cold, which I know, although I am not touching her, and her stiff back is in front of me.

As the beam follows the water, it finds daylight in a crack forty, sixty, two hundred feet from where we slid down. Hard to measure distance when you're scared. There, she says, and we transport ourselves across the dark, pressing out into another green canyon bottom, surprised and delighted with ourselves, the trail beneath us clear again.

That wasn't so bad, was it? No, I say, filling with regret that I'd been so frightened, that I hadn't spent another ten minutes, another hour, pressing my palms against the walls, turning the flashlight out, finding something beyond fear to run my hands on in the cave. Holding my love's body, rubbing the bones of her neck in the dark, listening to the peculiar flutter of our organs stretched to sense our selves again. If you let anxiety awaken you until you stop trembling, can recognition come back in? Could I have found her again? Would she have known me there? Now we amble on, companionable and quiet, both in our memories of being in a bottom we did not recognize until we left.

The trail back is much longer and steeper than we expect, and we meet no one except a young woman, the park ranger, who says, yes, it wouldn't be any fun if they'd marked the cave too clearly, would it?

NILAJA MONTGOMERY-AKALU

High Noon in the Middle of Spring

I love the sun. Sometimes it feels like a warm, wet tongue licking the length of my body. Outside the sliding door of my apartment I have my own private patio. I keep my little garden out there. Every day around noon when the sun is at its peak, I like to go out there with a glass of something cold to drink and lie out in the sun.

On this particular day, during the middle of spring, the sun was beating down hard. I went out onto the patio, closing the door behind me. I laid out my over-sized beach towel, propped a pillow under my head, and soaked in some rays. I closed my eyes and enjoyed the sound of the noises below me.

From below, I heard a car drive up. It was my next door neighbour's. She was a hottie. She was about five-three and had boobs all the way to China. Ms. Big Titty, as I liked to call her (not to her face of course), was married to some old man. He was a mean-ass geezer. There's only one reason she was with him. It was the oldest in the book: money. Old dude was mad loaded. Anyway, Ms. Big Titty always got my motor roaring. She was a big flirt, too. Whenever I saw her, she was always bending over to pick something up, and I would get a good look at her juicy booty. I just wanted to get her naked and hump that ass. Just thinking about her being naked got me wet. These were the times when I wish I wasn't single. I missed having someone to cuddle up next to.

I sat up and looked around, checking to see if anyone was watching. Seeing that I was alone, I pulled the top half of my swimsuit off and laid back down. Since I had a fairly small chest, my tits didn't fall into my armpits. I had always wanted bigger breasts, but didn't want to spend all that money on the surgery. I compensated my lack of boobage with my taste in women, I never dated any woman smaller than a 'D' cup. I love big tits. I love sucking them, biting them, squeezing them. I don't care what anyone says, more than a mouthful is not a waste.

As my hands played with my nipples, I found myself thinking of Ms. Big Titty. I'm pretty sure her tits were a gift from the old guy. I've never been all that attracted to fake boobs (another reason why I won't have the surgery), but *her* breasts could make a gay boy come in his pants.

I found my hands leaving my breasts and pulling down the bottom half of my swimsuit. I slipped out of the thong, kicked it aside, and stroked my kitty tenderly. A quiet moan escaped my throat as my middle finger slipped inside. My pussy was soaking as my finger slid deeper up my hole. I moved my hips in a circular motion as my finger pushed against my clit. My other hand was rubbing my breast. I slipped another finger in, then another. I spread my thighs wider to accommodate my hand.

Ms. Big Titty kept coming into my thoughts as I fucked myself on my private patio under the hot sun. I closed my eyes and pinched my nipple harder. I pictured her grinding her body into mine, imagined myself on those fake nipples like a hungry newborn. I could almost feel her tongue replacing the fingers in my cunt. I spanked my kitty faster at the thought. I bit down on my lip to stop the scream trying to escape my throat. My hips gyrated faster as I fucked myself harder, dreaming of Ms. Big Titty eating me out. I flipped over onto my stomach, my butt high in the air. I pushed down on my fingers and fucked myself deeper.

I came hard and fierce. I rode my fingers like a cowgirl riding her bronco. My body jerked around on the patio floor, and I screamed into my pillow as my orgasm ripped through my body. Even with the noises below, I could hear my heart pounding. I rolled over on my back and sucked on my sticky fingers. Now this is relaxing, I thought, as the sun beat down on me and warmed my naked body. I love the sun. Especially at high noon.

Femme Seduction

We snuggle longer in the night because it is unusually cold for San Francisco, and we don't sleep with the heat on. I wake early and go downstairs to turn on the thermostat. By the time I return to the bedroom the heat has kicked in. As I approach the bed I can hear Tony snoring a dull roar, in a sound sleep.

Watching my caramel chocolate Butch with her curly, mixed grey hair, my heart starts to flutter. I gently pull back each blanket slowly and methodically so I don't disturb my honey. Tony is sleeping on her back. She does not sleep in pajamas now, a habit she started shortly after I came into her life.

As I continue to pull the covers away from her body, her silky mound comes into view while my heart pounds hard and fast. I pull the covers down to her ankles. My thoughts and emotions race as I view the brown skin of my lover. I become obsessed with eating her pussy. I want to devour her at that moment, my butch lover, my man-woman. I want to feel my face nestled in her pussy juices while she caresses me with her pleasure liquids. I imagine my tongue playing on the tip of her clit and darting in and out of her pussy hole simultaneously, alternating my fingers as a love toy to continue caressing her silky hairs, then using the palm of my hand to caress her private place in its entirety.

Tony, Tony, I whisper, inaudible. I need to make love to you. My happiness spills over, my feelings of love, caring, and joy are overwhelming. I am in lust.

As I fling the covers over the edge of the bed, I straddle your legs and caress your hairs which feel like silk to my touch. You move slightly.

I continue on my journey, loving you so tenderly. I caress your hairy mound with the palm of my hand, then I slide my palm over your clit. I continue these motions until you open your eyes. You smile, stretch, and reach for me.

My head moves toward your right breast, licking and sucking you. Your response is a low moan. I let my tongue massage your chest as it moves toward your left breast. I lick and suck your breast while my juices flow from my pussy.

I massage your leg with my juices, that rush like a waterfall. They come from my excitement during the heat of my passion for you. You continue to moan. I move my tongue and centre it on your navel, let it descend to your hairs and onto your clit. I lick you like a kitten lapping milk from her bowl. My tongue darts in and out of your love hole. I lick slowly. At intervals I suck your clit and flick it with my tongue. I feel your clit start to throb. I stop. I bury my face in your wetness and wash my face with your juices many times, very slowly.

I stop. Taking your clit in my mouth I begin sucking you even slower. I sense your heart racing. Your moans escalate. Your clit becomes harder. I can feel it throbbing in my mouth as you gyrate leisurely, then faster, your voice growing louder. Words and sounds come together.

A loud scream, then quiet; your release is explosive. I'm happy. I move beside you so you can lie in my arms. Tony my butch lover is not so butch she can't receive my goodies.

"You are the best," Tony chuckles deep in her throat.

My best femme seduction.

Henna Me Wet

It started with her tongue on my navel, soft sweet kisses on my stomach, waking me up. She was a new lover, an artist. I had fallen for yet another artist. I should have learned my lesson by now but here I was in her studio naked and waiting for more of her.

She is a photographer. We met at a reading, a friend of a friend had introduced us. She was beautiful . . . no, she was sexy. Sexy in the way that makes your head turn to take another look at her. Sexy in the way she looked comfortable in her big, strong body. Sexy in the way she stared directly into your eyes when she talked with you and sexy in the way when she left a room you could still feel her presence on your skin.

Last night we fucked. No "making love" or "having sex" or "doing it," but pure, raw, limitless fucking. We were totally immersed in each other. Fingers, lips, tongues, legs intertwined, pelvises pressed against each other, hot bodies, flesh on flesh.

Now her morning caresses feel tender in contrast to last night's activities.

"Are you awake?" she asks, her voice rising from my hips, her hands stroking the curve from my waist over my hips to my belly. I don't want to respond. I just want to be in that warm and cozy place before I fully wake up.

"You are awake, aren't you?" she asks, her face now above mine.

"Yes, but I don't want to move, I just want to stay here."
She looks at me with her mischievous brown eyes. I know she has plans for our day.

A hot bath together, the smell of lavender, mint, and rosemary floating through the steam. My back against her chest, her strong arms around my belly, between my legs, smooth and silky skin on skin, the oils in the water glistening on our brown bodies.

"I want to paint you," she whispers in my ear.

"Paint me?" I ask. "I didn't know that you painted."

"No, not a picture of you," she clarifies. "I want to use your body as a canvas."

Her breath on my neck, her words vibrate in my ear.

"My body as your canvas." I feel skeptical, but curious. "Exactly what medium were you thinking of using?"

"Henna," she says.

I had grown up with henna at weddings. Expectant Indian brides celebrating in bridal showers, surrounded by women who attended to their every need, while one or two women adorned the bride's body with traditional, detailed designs of henna all over her hands and feet.

"You want to henna my feet or my hands?" I'm confused by her request.

"I want to henna your whole body," she says. "I want to start with your back and go all the way down until I run out of skin." She smiles flirtatiously.

I agree to her invitation. My relaxed body, supple from the bath oils, my desire for her and my interest in being her subject, lead me to lie down on her studio floor, a mixture of silk and flannel pillows beneath my naked body.

She prepares her supplies: plastic cones filled with the olive green henna mixture, cotton balls, a damp face cloth, and a dish of clove oil. She starts slowly. I can feel the cold grainy texture of the henna touch the back of my neck. The rich earthy smell of the henna pours out with each delicate line drawn. She is naked, sitting with her legs spread over my back, one of her hands firmly on my shoulders, helping her balance, keeping steady. The other hand carefully, gently creates a unique series of curves and designs all over my flesh. The rhythm of her breath on my neck causes goose bumps all over me, small hairs rise up my arms. The pattern takes on a form that I cannot see, but that I can feel expand from the base of my neck across my shoulder blades. It is like an extended version of the "drawing on each other's back" game I used to play with my girlfriends as a child.

My body is now totally relaxed and with each breath I feel myself melting into the floor.

"How does it feel?" she asks softly, in my ear.

"Wond . . . er . . . ful," I manage, my voice muffled in the bedding underneath me.

My body had not experienced such attention in a long time, a very, very long time. The calm atmosphere makes me doze off, my mind fixed on her image, inhaling the scent of her body near mine.

The next thing I know I am awake, and hands are spreading my inner thighs. I can feel my back completely filled with henna. I do not move. I do not want to crack and chip the tapestry constructed on my skin. She knows that I am not going to move, so she teases and plays with me. Kisses instead of henna are lavished on my upper thighs, inner thighs, the back of my knees, and my calves. I want to turn around. I want to kiss her back, touch her, have her turn me over and continue on from last night, but this is only an artist's break. Soon the kisses stop, leaving me wet and unsatisfied. I can feel the henna being applied on me again. After hours of more work, she settles for having decorated the full back of my body. I wait patiently as she snaps photos, with her assurance that my name and identity will be disguised.

The rest of the afternoon is ours to make the most of, so we spend our time leaving a trail of henna bits and pieces all over her studio floor, on her sheets and finally in her shower. The design is stained on my back like the memory of her and that night in my mind.

Months later my new lover and I go to a local coffee house. As we sip our lattés, I look at the photos on the wall and there across from us is a naked body, my naked body. Although carefully shaded in

74

black and white, the photos reveal the most beautiful patterns, so fine and overwhelming, each piece linked with delicate precision. As my lover and I are about to leave I stop by a photo on the wall. The title is "Henna Lover," and as requested, the subject is "nameless."

Life Drawing

In life drawing there is an exchange. You are there, people look at your body. You pose. They draw. Your emotions shimmer on your skin: the artists see and reproduce them on the page. Between you, you make art. Sometimes the drawing touches you, as if the artist had reached to you directly and laid that brush upon your skin.

Your body is slicked down with sweat, warm and solid with hillocks and dales and aromas from caverns. This is your body, and you open it to them in this way, for them to draw you, to feel you without touching to stroke you with pencils, brushes and inks, crayons and charcoals and contes. You are their model and they are your artists.

There you are, all of your body out there, being seen, being drawn, in a still and vibrant dance. Life drawing. Would that life were spent so naked. How many lies could be told then?

On the posing platform, you are a warrior, an actor, a dancer. Gestures are your favourite, the fast, dynamic poses that allow you to flex, to stretch. Movement in stillness. The possibility of change.

There's a woman who comes to draw you sometimes. You've had a crush on her for five years. She's there now, with the others.

You watch her look at you as you pose; you study her face, her eyes, her mouth, watch her brow crinkle with concentration as she draws you. At the break you speak to her. You approach her, naked, and talk as though you were clothed. Maybe it is just before your period, and you are warm from the posing, and the smell from your cunt is earthy, sweet, pungent. You wonder if she can smell you.

"I like to draw you," she says. "Such strong poses, and so still, it's like drawing a sculpture."

"Thanks," you reply, and point to her drawing, "I like that line there, it makes the drawing almost move." You touch her hand as you gesture toward the picture. She looks at the drawing, then at you, then down. She blushes.

After the break, you take a pose: a half-hour standing, facing her, looking down, one hip out, your weight on your right leg, hands on your hips, head tilted. You try to achieve a look of enigmatic amusement. Cool. She uses charcoal. With it she describes your jawline, shoulders, collarbone. Your breasts are caressed onto the page. She draws your belly. A few strokes become the shadow from the hand that rests on your hip. There is an unbroken line of charcoal and desire between the two of you.

Your leg tingles. Your fingers are going numb. You watch her draw. Your body needs to move. She looks at you with an artist's gaze. She squints up at you, then at the page. She draws more lines, more curves, and there is a new roundness, a suggestion of heat.

There is the artist's gaze and the model's gaze and you have no way of knowing if the one upon whom you gaze returns your desire, you just suspect. Can she feel the tension vibrating between you?

Her gaze shifts. Your eyes meet. She sees you. Not the figure, you. She sees you and she wants you. Your eyes meet in mid-air like that. You want to leap off the platform and wrap your arms and legs around her and go toppling backwards over the blocks holding her paper and crayons and inks.

The gaze intersects. At the next break, you go to the machine room above the studio where the motors and pulleys and cables that run the elevator are housed. There's a small space there, beside the narrow opening for the cables, atop the trap door which opens into the shaft. In the thin beam of light, your skin glistens and whispers. She follows you. She carries the charcoal which she had been using to draw you.

She reaches for you and you stand waiting for her touch. She caresses your left breast with the charcoal she holds. The dark of your nipple enhanced by the line of black beneath. She slides the crayon along your ribcage. You reach for her belt and touch her belly through her shirt. She leans her hip against your naked thigh. She strokes your leg, your back, a shadow along your belly. You can feel her heat through her jeans. You place your hand inside her pants. You feel the curve of her hip, her jeans holding your hand, pressing her against your body. You slide your tongue along her neck and she takes your earlobe in her teeth and she draws her fingers to the small of your back. With the charcoal she traces the curve of your ass, feather light, and her other hand searches your face, holds your cheek. She pulls back, looks at you. And then she is kissing you, fierce, hot. You slide a finger around her labia. Her leg is between your thighs. You push your clit against the rough denim of her jeans. She runs her hand along your back, the charcoal leaving dark streaks running over your body. You can hear the others down the stairway, a laugh, a murmur, float up to you. Someone calls for the elevator, the motor squeals and the cables screech and move and the elevator shudders, and so does she. You hold one another and you smell one another and you hold your fingers up in the narrow light of the shaft and smile and take the crayon from her fingers and kiss it and give it back to her. It's time to go back.

In life drawing, there is an exchange.

Anticipation

My face breaks out when I wear make-up. My feet are too wide to wear heels comfortably, and in a dress I look like a bear in drag. But the day I met Jimmy Sue, I knew I wanted to be her femme.

I arrived at Blueoats Stables at eight-thirty in the morning on a cold, rainy Saturday in February. My friend Joyce was letting me work at her place in exchange for learning about boarding horses, something I was starting in the spring. When I walked into the barn on that morning like I had for the past three months, looking for Joyce, standing in the alley was this tall, stocky, handsome woman holding onto a bay mare.

"Have you seen Joyce?" I asked.

"She's gone to town," she replied. "I'm Jimmy Sue. Joyce said for you to help me groom this mare." She extended her large cal- lused hand toward mine.

"Marie," I said, meeting her grip. "Glad to meet you."

Her firm, warm hand was so comfortable that I didn't want to let go. I just stared at her and felt the colour creep up the back of my neck.

Her face was chiselled with laughter, her eyes the colour of amber. She was close to six feet tall. I had this urge to fold my soft curves into her angles and let geometry take over.

She handed me a curry comb and with, a small smile, told me to start on the mare's mane as soon as we had her tied out. I grabbed the tie out rope hanging from the wooden post between the stalls and hitched it to the mare's halter. Jimmy Sue was doing the same on the other side. We couldn't see each other's faces, but our legs and stomachs were almost touching. The mare snorted and her hot breath defined the area between. A warm tingle crept up my legs and I thought, this is going to be an interesting day. As I took a step back, Jimmy Sue looked over at how I had tied the mare and said, "Nice."

I laughed and started stroking the horse's mane with the curry comb, slowly and firmly. Feeling the warmth and life pulsating through the horse's veins, I thought about how I'd like to be stroking the back of Jimmy Sue's neck, running my fingers through her cropped, greying chestnut hair and outlining her ears with my lips. She came around the mare to show me how to get a knot out of the horse's mane. A radio was playing in the barn and Jimmy Sue was humming along as she worked. I could feel her body move to the rhythm, but like a country music guitar player, she was hardly moving. I began swaying in time to her voice. I imagined we were on the dance floor doing a slow two-step. Holding me securely in her arms, she used her legs and torso to guide me in twirls and twists. We moved like a cowboy and quarter-horse in a slow canter: one giving the commands, the other following and together forming a unified team. My breasts tingled and a sweet ache was spreading to my centre.

"Is she your horse?" I asked.

"Yeah. My first in four years. Used to raise them, was going to start a riding stable. But it didn't work."

"Why so?"

"My dad got sick. I had to leave and care for him. What about you? You got horses?"

"I'm hoping to be able to afford my own next year. Right now I'm learning to be around them again so I can keep them at my place. Do you know Joyce?"

"We've been friends for years." She stopped grooming, rested her hand on the mare's back, and smiled. "Joyce told me you'd moved into the area. Thought we might want to know each other. Small community. It's good to know who's who."

"And who are you?" I asked, looking right back.

"Stick around and find out." Jimmy Sue winked and went back to stroking the horse's back with the brush.

I looked at that strong hand and shivered. I wanted to know how those hands would move on my body. Where she'd want to touch and probe. Shaking off those thoughts before my knees buckled, I said, "I haven't seen you around here before."

"No you wouldn't have. I've been away for half a year with my dad. Now that he's gone, I've got time to get thinking about horses and women again."

"Horses come before women, do they?" I asked lightly.

"Depends on the time of the day," she drawled. " I was thinking about going for lunch and a beer later. Have you been to the Aikenhead Pub?"

"Love it. They have the best cider."

We finished up the mare and Jimmy Sue put her in the stall. Joyce arrived back and the three of us spent the rest of the morning mucking the stalls, watering the horses, and talking about events in the communities that we lived in. Every once in a while, I'd catch Jimmy Sue's eye and she'd give me a sly smile. I felt the pleasure of promise.

When we finished, I cleaned up and got ready to go. Jimmy Sue was waiting by the barn door. "Come in my truck," she said, leading me by the hand toward a silver Ford long box.

"You know, I never asked. What's your mare's name?"

She smiled. "Anticipation."

I hooked my arm in hers and walked in step with Jimmy Sue toward the afternoon ahead.

ROSALIND CHRISTINE LLOYD

Deflower

The Union Square Green Market has a certain nuance that cannot be found anywhere else in the city. New Age farmers gather there to hawk agriculturally sophisticated organic perishables and flora. It was early April and the sun was burning the New York City sky at an unseasonable seventy-five degrees.

A trough of wild orchids: their cups were tiny with colours so vibrant they seemed surreal. After selecting a nice bunch, while waiting patiently to pay, someone's elbow, sharp and swift, violently found its way into my left kidney. Now, I'm what's called a typical New Yorker. In other words, this rude, ill-mannered culprit was about to feel my wrath in the most scathing criticism I could hurl. I looked at the guilty party. Before me was a tight little ass squeezed into a pair of sinfully soft leather jeans. Bent over, this goddess stretched long golden arms sparkling with a thin film of sweat reaching over bouquets of flowers to retrieve her target. Choosing a wild rose a certain shade of pink so luminous it was almost fuschia, she raised the flower to her face, allowing the silky petals to caress her nose. Satisfied, she cupped the bulb within the palm of her left hand, her long dainty fingers tenderly stroking the external smooth petals. I wasn't exactly prepared for what she did next.

With her right hand, sinking her long finger into the pistil of the flagrantly pink rose, she penetrated the bulb while her left hand squeezed the silky petals. In a split second, every conceivable part of me capable of becoming aroused was demanding some serious attention.

Severely chiseled cheekbones cradled dark and sultry bedroom eyes that were opened only half way as if in a perpetual state of arousal. Her short, naturally bushy spirals were streaked in brown and gold hues. Her skin colour, glistening in the sunlight, reminded me of Grandma's hot buttered biscuits. Tall and thin, centuries of African royalty seemed embedded in her dignified posture. Full breasts were giving her ultra tight t-shirt a hard time.

Seemingly content with her selection that included the pink rose, she thrust the bunch at the farmer. I couldn't believe her nerve. First, she assaulted me, then she molested a defenceless flower, then she jumped in front of me while in line. Strangely, instead of feeling angry, her aggression was turning me on. The farmer handed the roses back to her, wrapped simply in a thin sheet of tissue paper tied with sisal. My gullibility expected eye contact with her when instead, she slammed her entire body against me; breasts, thighs, mounds of Venus all crashing together creating this confused exchange of energy so fast and hard it rattled me, making my head spin. The wind knocked from me, my orchids were tossed to the ground as "Leather Pants" marched on.

"I think she likes you," the farmer remarked, gathering my orchids and wrapping them for me.

"I don't think so. She practically knocked me over," I answered, attempting to regain my coolness because my body was vibrating with both pain and pleasure while I watched her escape.

"Well, she asked me to give this to you." In his hand was the fateful molested rose.

Lingering behind her at a safe but interested distance, I watched as she browsed through a few veggie stands before darting across the street and into the Coffee Shop, a trendy restaurant on the Square.

Once inside, I didn't see her. Where could she have disappeared to that quickly? With flower in hand, I followed my feminine instincts and went directly to the ladies' room.

The door of one stall was open. I could hear a steady tinkle penetrating the ice cold water in the bowl of the toilet. She stood facing the tank as I peeked in, the toilet seat up, her magnificent naked ass exposed like an epiphany. Her leather pants were down around her knees as she straddled the toilet bowl. Ms. Thing was peeing standing up as if using a men's urinal—a woman after my heart. As she finished, without turning around she said, "Don't just stand there, come in here and lock the door behind you."

Standing directly behind this insanely beautiful woman with her pants down around her legs, I slammed the door shut, dropping my shoulder pack and flowers on the floor. Seizing her from behind, I wrapped myself around her like a depraved fiend. One of my hands fondled a breast quite warm to the touch. Arousal swept over me like a wild fire threatening to burn me alive unless I found something wet to put the fire out. While brutally swirling a pouty pierced nipple between my fingertips, my other hand went between her legs, dipping caramel fingers in between creamy thighs, sliding inside her hot, slippery wet cunt. My fingers manipulated her inflamed, pulsing clit sheathed in silky moist splendour, causing her to grind her bare ass into my crotch in a very demanding manner.

Balling my hand into a nice grip, I gently buried my knuckles deeper inside her flooding sex, deftly and steadily, stuffing myself so far into her that she whimpered, saturating my hand with soft heat.

Her hands were spread out in front of her against the wall behind the tank as if under arrest. With her legs spread open over the bowl, I reached for the fateful pink rose. Gliding it across her divine ass, a trail of goose bumps appeared, inciting more of her groans. Tenderly sticking the tip of the long stem of the flower in between her cheeks, I guided the rose downward as if arranging it within the confines of her beautiful juicy ass turned exotic vase, thorns pricking her tender skin in its trail. She sucked in bits of air between clenched teeth before moaning sensuously as I continued to slowly slide the flower in between her buttocks until the bottom of the stem appeared from her ass. Carefully pulling the stem down from underneath her, the rose snuggled tightly between her ass cheeks. This rocked her, making her quiver and forcing her to whimper a little louder. I grabbed her mouth to muffle her. When she succumbed to silence, I licked the back of her neck with cat curls of my tongue. She tasted like salt, body lotion, and almond soap, making me wonder what her other wonders tasted like. My licking turned into fevered sucking which caused her entire body to slide around in my arms as if begging me for something. After wiggling the long stem of the rose from between the divide of her ass, I lightly brushed its petals along the pretty tiny red imprints left by the thorns, taking broad strokes that gradually developed into a brief round of light spanking. Her sighs provoked me to guide the stem forward in between her thighs, massaging the silky petals against the delicate flesh of her smooth shaven lips. We soon discovered we couldn't exploit the moment any further—someone entered the bathroom, going into the stall next to ours.

Gently removing the rose from between her legs, I got myself together, sticking the rose in with my orchids. Repressing the urge to take a playful bite of her ass, I allowed myself one final nibble of her luscious neck before picking up my shoulder bag, unlocking the door and disappearing, leaving her surrendered over the toilet.

In hindsight, I think she learned a valuable lesson about disturbing flowers.

Between Friends

We are just friends. You said so yourself, Sherry—that you were not searching, not ready to be caught. And me, my heart is on vacation, recovering from overstretching. I still have a suitcase of stuff waiting to be picked up at my ex's—I'm too scared to venture that near.

We are just friends. Yet the former house of loving has fallen down, and there's nothing left but a hole of boredom and restlessness. The cat next door eyes birds from her cushioned window seat, yawning while her senses automatically look for prey.

We are just friends. Of course there is the little matter of that kiss last night on the Chelsea Pier, that little tongue-on-tongue punctuation of our rambling conversation, the vaguest exploration of teeth, as if it were an accident, as if we had just fallen against each other and our tongues accidentally brushed, and it was not altogether unpleasant but not intentional, either.

And then it was time to go, big day tomorrow—Gay Pride Parade, queers take Manhattan.

I walked you to your subway stop. Ever gallant, pausing at the top of the steps I took you in my arms, tipped you back, and ravished your mouth thoroughly.

"Where'd you learn to kiss like that?" you asked, startled, girl-ish.

At a loss, I said simply, "Get home safe. See you tomorrow."

Next morn I slicked back my short black hair, donned a puffy white shirt, black leggings, and thigh-high boots. I poked a gold hoop through one ear, with an eye-pencil drew on sideburns, a thin moustache, a goatee. Last, I looped a plastic swashbuckler's sword through my belt so it dangled off my hip. And I went to meet you at 42nd Street.

I was not trying to seduce you. I simply like to dress the pirate whenever it's even vaguely appropriate. I feel prettiest when expressing my masculine side. Teetering in tight dress and high-heels, I feel awkward and ashamed, like a novice in drag.

We find each other amid the simmering crowd. You look me up and down and grin. "Hey, girl," you say, shimmering in your striped shirt.

I offer you a peppermint. Sun warms our cheeks, and we squint while sucking our candy. The procession is underway—flashes of colour as brightly clad fags and lesbians, bis, and baby butches strain to get at Fifth Avenue. Proud hookers jostle proud slaveboys who jostle proud grandparents with festive animals and children scissoring between. We forge ahead through disco-dancing stallions and gaggles of drag queens and floats and music and bands and fire-eating and garlands of rainbow balloons and octogenarians waving benignly from limo windows; fancy dancers, sword swallowers, people supporting all manner of banners.

On and off we hold hands. Emboldened by that intimacy—or maybe it's the pirate in me—I try to lift you up and carry you, but unable to, I stumble. Your sandy blonde hair is held back by a crimson ribbon that I attempt pulling out with my teeth and, failing that, too, at least I make you laugh.

As we approach downtown, the crowds of onlookers become denser and louder. Below 14th Street is a solid, euphoric cacophony of shouting and applause. Hunks in rainbow tanks hanging off fire escapes cheer and wave. We are drunk on the spectacle of ourselves.

We spill into Greenwich Village and are forced to disperse. I offer you my apartment, so near, for napping. After all, we will want to be fresh tonight, for dancing.

87

You accept.

I really meant nap. This has been fun, but we are just friends. My heart is on vacation—I told you that. But I am undressing you regardless.

"I'm very hairy," you warn shyly.

"That's because you're a wild animal."

You look at me, your eyes full of desire. Even as I am vowing not to love you too soon, nothing could be dearer than your responsiveness. For my ex had insisted on a tangled web of rules I ultimately could not abide. All sex had to be mutual and simultaneous, or else it just didn't count. What a heavy load her prerequisites became. My landscape shrivelled. I became a dust bowl.

So when the hot liquid trails I forge over your flesh make you buck and moan, I am so happy. My tongue writhes aimlessly over you, soaking in desire, then pauses cruelly before it nearly forces you to come with a shriek.

Suggesting toys to my ex had been like pitching a threesome, so it is not without trepidation that I reach under the bed and whip them out. Wrapping your hand around my dildo, I show you how to thrust it, when to swivel. Laying my topography bare, splayed across the pillows, pressing Magic Wand to my clit, I show you how I plumb my wilderness, get myself off. You help me get off. After I come, I collapse, breathing a raspy, "Thanks."

"You're welcome, I guess," you say flatly. "But that really had nothing much to do with me."

Sitting up abruptly, I feel my heart flinch.

What the hell is that supposed to mean? I want to blurt, but hold back. I can live without knowing if you can live without telling. Wherever that came from is not a pretty place and I don't want to go there, so I let the question die. After all, what's a little ambiguity between friends?

D E B   E L L I S

It Happens Like This

You're in the upper berth of a train crossing a piece of land that has no end. You look out the window while the world passes you by, and the rhythm of the train rocks you almost to sleep.

Then the woman in the berth below sticks her head through the curtains and asks you for a cigarette. You don't have one since you don't smoke, but she doesn't seem to care about the cigarette. She stays there a moment, leaning against your bunk. You're looking out the window but you can feel her there, her weight putting pressure on the mattress. You don't think she's looking out the window, you think she's looking at you. You hold still, you don't even breathe, and then she's gone, back to her bunk below yours. You think about the fact that she is stretched out below you, you wonder if she is thinking about you stretched out above her. You roll onto your stomach, press yourself into the mattress, and the rhythm of the train isn't putting you to sleep anymore. . . .

No, maybe it's like this. You are standing before the airport window, watching your plane taxiing into position. She comes up behind you, you catch the scent of her perfume, hear the jingle of her bracelet. You wish she would reach out her hand, you want her to stroke one finger through your hair, one finger starting at the top of your head and moving slowly down your scalp, brushing against your neck, the ridge of your collar, the centre of your back. You don't know what you would do if she did, you don't know what else you want, but you do want that. And you're so busy wanting it, you almost miss it when it happens, when you feel her one finger gently moving from the top of your head, brushing the ridge of your collar, down to the centre of your back, and all the sweetness there ever was is in that one gesture and you think your heart is going to break.

Or you could be on a Greyhound bus, rolling across the emptiness and it's nighttime, the bus is dark, you have a seat to yourself. You should be sleeping but there's a woman across the aisle from you, one seat up, and you can watch her without her knowing. The bus stops at a gas station and you get off to stretch your legs. It's three in the morning, in the middle of nowhere, and you and the other passengers are the only people alive on the planet. You look for the woman, you spot her, she looks like she owns even this desolate place. You watch her, she's standing alone, having a smoke, looking down the empty highway, a ray of light from the Sunoco sign falling just to the side of her. You watch her, and suddenly her head turns and she looks right at you. You back up into the darkness.

Back on the bus, you close your eyes, pretending to sleep. Someone sits down beside you. You open your eyes and see that the person next to you is the woman you've been watching for five hundred miles. She is looking right at you. She is not smiling, she is not extending her hand to shake, she is not revealing her name or asking yours. In her eyes is not quite a challenge and certainly not a plea, not amusement or longing, or anything but arrival, and you feel chilled all over, and want to get off the bus but you'd have to climb over her and that you cannot do. Your gaze goes all over, to avoid hers. You feel itchy and awkward, and you know that your hair has that three a.m. bus-ride look and you wish it wasn't so. Then, in the second before the lights go out on the bus, you look at her eyes again and you stop fidgeting, because what you see in her eyes is danger, a danger so great you can't move, then the bus rolls back onto the highway, and you discover you are right, her thighs and shoulders and the nape of her neck are just about the most dangerous places in the world.

Or it could happen this way. You're the one who decides, you're the one who enters the bar as if you own it, never mind that you're alone, you won't be for long, your confidence drawing others to you like a magnet. You are the one being watched in the shadows by women who wished they had the guts to approach you, you are the one the others are hanging out their desire for.

You swirl on the dance floor, the music seeks you out and nestles in your skin and muscles. You dance alone, feeling the others around you, enjoying their shyness, their need, their hesitation.

You draw a woman to you, dance with her, take liberties with the strand of her hair that keeps falling in her eyes. Another woman melts in. The three of you move together on the dance floor, you touch them lightly until their heat is combustible, but you are not teasing, this is not a ritual of power but of introduction. You draw the circle tighter, hands replace fingertips, you feel the torso of one woman and the hips of another, and all three of you feel the music that has settled into your skin and your muscles, and you know that this night will go on for a long, long time.

Or maybe it happens like this —

Clean

B ut I'm a dyke, I think guiltily. How did I get here?

My mother had made a generous offer. But her generosity always masks ulterior motives. She winces at the sight of my shaved head and pierced lip. She wishes I would shower a million times a day, and she hates the sound of my boots clunking around the house. So she asks me all casual the other day, would I like a facial and a skin care program? Naturally, I hurl back a fierce no. But I guess she won this round, because I am sitting in this chair of beauty care S/M with the mistress of make-up hovering over me. This woman looks ready to pounce, her crow's feet flexing under brownish guck. She is telling me how to scrape a tiny spatula in a small jar of wrinkle cream. I nod and smirk and wonder how its plastic flat would feel between her thumb and forefinger, tracing grooves beneath my eyes. She looks like she'd like to fuck—like she needs to fuck—if she'd ever let herself. She's probably a big top. How would she use the plastic corner to etch lines from below my eyelashes, up and around my cheek? She would draw it along the curve of my chin, pressing hard. Then she would trail the plastic edge down my neck and arc it around the flesh of my tit, spiraling red circles tighter and tighter until she marked me with a small, round brand—a make-up company copyright symbol.

"Tsk, tsk," she would say as she honed in on my nipple, "you should really pluck those hairs."

I suddenly snap out of my fantasy, realizing she would never do any of this. I remember where I really am. Me, a radical queer feminist dyke! I'm too butch for this. I refuse to shave or pluck. I refuse in my railing against the ways people like her try to turn women like me into girls. This is about power. And I won't let her have mine.

So why am I here? Why did I say yes?

She begins rubbing a creamy, white substance on my face, the pads of her fingers pressing hard as her black eyes. How could I let my mother do this to me? I need to check out of this bullshit. I close my eyes. I remember pre-school finger-paint etchings. We used our nails to pretend at writing stories, practicing our letters. My mind swims through the sticky colours. Paint. The scratch of nails against paint. . . . Nails. In this chair with this woman hovering. Her long nails. Her seizing my hand, showing me, guiding my fingers wordlessly through the milky mess of this stuff, drawing it down along my throat and around to my shoulders. Her standing in front of me, straddling my thigh to get a better angle on my arm. Her tits in front of my mouth, her settling finally all warm on my leg. Her holding both of my hands, pressing their flats against the round rise and fall of my belly, reaching, wet, warm, her hand guiding my palm to cup my cunt lips. Her sliding down my leg, crouching, watching square-jawed, her muddy fingers, her fingers, her fingers spreading me. Her lined face. Her mouth reaching to taste . . . to taste me all creamy white and moist. My wanting. Her face. Her eyes, demanding and black. Me, immobile, mute. Me, breathing heavy. Her reaching to taste. . . . Her lined face. Her terse mouth . . . .

Someone sneezes. The register jingles. I am fully dressed, and she is standing next to me, wiping her hands on a cloth. The mask has been fully applied, and I taste it bitter and real on the edge of my lip.

"Keep your eyes closed," she tells me, all cold and velvet and unaware. Amazingly, I obey as she adds, "Don't move. Not until I come back. I'll tell you when."

It is a command, and in this dungeon of beauty I do as I am told. Of course, we are in a store, in a suburban mall, but part of how I ended up here is about my mother and what I have to do to deal with her. Part of why I am here is about doing what I'm told, being a good girl to get her off my back. Even though I hate all this good girl shit. With my eyes closed in the silence, I am suspended in a middle place, weightless, a funhouse of lights and mirrors and painted clowns, a place of waiting without time or sounds beyond muffled shoppers. I am tied in this chair to the choke and pull of submissions so easy in a world of mothers and straights and models and femmes. It's like ropes.

Finally, she removes the dried mask, peeling away this tinny, hollow feeling I have like when I wake from strange dreams. She explains with the aid of a mirror and cotton how much dirt from my pores is now cleaned away. She explains how my skin is new again. Like a baby's. She uses a toner that burns my face and waters my eyes. I sit still and silent with the sting. "Be honest," she says. "I want you to tell me how this feels."

"Clean," I reply.

Softly she layers my forehead, nose and chin, my red cheeks, and my neck with cool moisture cream.

I buy all the products she has used on me. Even the wrinkle cream, though I don't think I will use it. I just don't want to tell her no. Besides, my mother is paying.

She hands me a business card with my receipt and tells me to keep her posted on how the products are working. Looking at her, unable to meet her eyes, I reply, "Yes, ma'am. I will."

MARLYS LABRASH

The Blind Date

Friday night and I've agreed to go on a blind date to make my best friend happy.

"I can't believe I'm doing this," I mumble as I climb the front stairs. I'm wearing my best suit, hoping to make a good impression. I even remembered flowers. I adjust my tie and straighten my jacket. Relaxing the choke hold I have on the flowers, I look over the bouquet, making sure I haven't squeezed the life out of them. It's now or never. I clear my throat and knock. The door opens and I find myself studying the flowers intently. A low, smooth voice says, "Hi, I'm Jessica."

I swallow, raise my head and oh my god I'm totally captivated by her overwhelming beauty. I stand not able to utter a sound, caught in her spell. I think it's love at first sight. "Are those for me?" she points to my hand.

I thrust the flowers at her. "Oh, I'm your date." Oh, good one, you dope. I silently kick myself. The tips of our fingers meet as I give her the flowers. Warmth spreads up my arm. My knees feel like rubber.

"I'll just go put these in some water, come on in." She turns and disappears into the shadows.

When she returns I am still standing, dutifully, right where she left me. Rooted. With a hint of a grin, she places the vase of flowers on the table.

"These are beautiful."

Jessica reaches for her coat from the back of a chair. I quickly step forward and help her put it on, but just as she slips her arms in, I lose my grip. The coat slides toward the floor and I lunge for it bashing my elbow on the jamb. My eyes cross. I bite my lip to keep from crying out. If Jessica notices, she says nothing.

We go to a small Italian restaurant on Commercial Drive. From the moment we sit down, it is all I can do to remember that I should chew, swallow, and breathe. I can't keep my eyes off her. I keep peeking over the top of my menu. She is nibbling on her lower lip as she reads. She looks up, catches me watching, and much to my annoyance, I blush uncontrollably. An easy smile plays at the corners of her mouth. Trying to regain at least some of my dignity, I clear my throat. "Are you ready to order?" I ask.

"Yes," she says.

Signaling the waiter, we order dinner and wine. Is it hot in here or is it just me? The sweat is trickling down my face. My gaze is drawn to her fingers as she traces imagined designs in the condensation on her water glass, then runs her wet finger across her pink tongue. She is so sexy. I am going to die.

The dinner arrives, our hands touch as we both reach for the bread. Every nerve in my body is on fire. I can barely catch my breath. I hastily withdraw my hand, and, flushing, I knock the salt off the table. I bend down to recover it and as I sit up I bang my head on the corner of the table. Jessica's brows arch mischievously as she stifles a giggle. Somehow I make it through the remainder of the evening without inflicting serious bodily harm.

On the ride home I convince myself there's no way she would go out with me again.

I walk her to her door wondering if I should kiss her good night, but I would probably only end up embarrassing myself again. On the porch, she moves in closer until there's no room left at all.

"I had a really nice time," she says. I search her upturned face and stare deeply into her blue eyes. Her gaze is as gentle as a caress. Melting into the softness of her body, our lips meet. My heart hammers in my ears. Leaving her mouth, I step back and let out an audible gasp, my voice a husky whisper. "I must go," I say, fleeing the porch.

Just as I reach my car, I feel her hand on my arm. I turn slightly, our eyes meet.

"Please stay," she says simply. Her smile is as intimate as the kiss we shared. Hand in hand we walk back through the gate.

I stop. Stuck. Frozen in place. Looking down I realize my pant leg is trapped in the closed gate. Jessica bursts out laughing.

Examined

I'll just tell you what I know, and I won't wax poetic about it. I hate eloquence and clinical terms for cunt and tits. Sometimes I say pussy, but never vagina or vulva. I'm making love to a woman, not giving her a Pap smear or some kind of pelvic examination. Although, that's one of my fantasies. Stirrups and latex and her.

My gynecologist, Samantha, or Dr. Morgan as her cheery name-tag indicates, is an absolute fox in white polyester. She takes my blood pressure and I'm wet down to my knees. Are gynecologists supposed to take your blood pressure? I dunno, but I don't care. The way she slips on those latex gloves over her long, slender fingers. She's twenty-nine and has the tits of a budding adolescent. Pert and taut, and what an ass. A sculptor could never capture those curves. Bend over, baby. Put your feet in the stirrups.

I never need any of that lube stuff for Dr. Samantha to glide her whole fist inside of me. I'm not sure if I should be embarrassed about that— you know, the fact that I get so damn wet with my legs spread wide in the stirrups. Jesus, my nipples get all erect and I know my clit swells up so fat, just like a goose egg, when she's examining me. I lay there with that little wax paper sheet just under my chin and absorb her every movement. She speaks to me but I can't respond. I'm imagining her tongue lapping up my sweet wetness. Her Colgate smile is between my thighs, nibbling my clit. Her hands are racing across my body and tugging at my hard nipples. She squeezes my breasts like she's searching for the ripest peaches in the bin. My tits are bigger than peaches, though, and I love it when she cradles them in her big hands. Well, she's not really cradling them, she's examining them for lumps I guess, but when she does it, she does it without the latex gloves. The feel of her warm fingertips prodding and poking and rubbing in circular motions makes my face flush redder than wild strawberries. I watch her perfect lips as she reassures me that I have no lumps.

Her hands are golden from the summer sun, like butterscotch. She checks my nipples with her butterscotch fingers paying careful attention for any abnormalities. She touches my areolas, and in my mind, I touch hers. With my tongue, though, because my fingers are elsewhere. Searching. Playing. Did I mention she's a redhead? I love redheads. She's not a *red*-redhead, she's more like the colour of leaves in autumn. Burnt sienna? Her *bush* is like the colour of leaves in autumn.

Beads of sweat form on my brow as my skin heats up with arousal under the thin wax paper sheet that I want so badly to throw to the floor. Then she could see me, all of me. She would notice the fine surface of my skin, smooth like pudding. My flat stomach and slender waist. The way my ribs stick out just a little and my navel dips in. She would see me naked and abandon her white polyester jacket with the little Dr. Morgan tag pinned just above her left breast and press her hot flesh against mine. Her autumn leaves pussy, her perfect pouty strawberry lips, rocking hips, butterscotch skin . . . all of her, lying on all of me. Feet spread in the stirrups so I could feel her wet labia gliding wildly across mine. Our bodies like warm pancakes, sticky with syrup.

I stare at the textured white ceiling, the self-examination breast chart taped on the wall, and the plastic model of the uterus. I stare at the crumpled wax paper sheet on the floor, my clothes hanging on the back of the chair, her white polyester jacket and skirt and shirt, lying in a heap by my steel-toe boots.

She wants to love me. Really love me, with her tongue and mouth sucking me in my most vulnerable spot. She slides down off the examining table and gets on her knees. She inhales my scent. The scent carries her away to fields of sunflowers and the warm July sun, she says. Sunflowers and earth and sweat on the back of her neck and behind her knees. And in the crook of her elbow, and between her legs. Her clit is swollen like mine and her heart pumps fast, pounding in her chest as she takes my clit in her mouth.

I leave my feet in the stirrups as she devours me with a deft tongue, licking me like her favourite flavour of ice cream. Sucking me and licking me like I was all of her favourite things. Chocolate fudge still warm from the oven. Sugary pink cotton candy from the fall fair. She covers my skin with that same careful attention she practices when examining my breasts. She touches me everywhere, inside and out. She doesn't use the clinical names when she whispers what she is going to do to me next. I lie on my back, my skin sticking to the black vinyl of the table, waiting.

Her skin would be like silk. Like velvet. Like butterfly wings. She wears no gloves this time as she enters me. Her whole hand slides into me, right inside me. I love that feeling of fullness. I watch her eyes, green like ripe avocados as they close and open with a smile. My muscles begin contracting in the stirrups, as though I am about to give birth. I forget to breathe. Muscles contract around her fist, holding it so tight inside me. *Stay inside.*

I push my purring pussy further down the table. Closer to her face. Closer to the wide breadth of her wagging tongue. I grab handfuls of her burnt sienna hair in my hands as I beg her closer. She pulls her fist out, wanting me to come in her mouth. She wants to taste my cum after the rush, to lick it from my soft pink flesh. The white walls disappear.

Dizzy, covered in delicious sweat, she returns to my breasts. Pulling at my nipples with her teeth like warm taffy on a wooden spoon. Then my body feels her swollen clit on mine. Rocking in the stirrups, she continues to suck my slippery nipples until my whole body clenches. I moan and fall back on the table, my body turned into a liquid mass.

My next appointment is in six months.

S O O K   C .   K O N G

Read My Navel

I can be so dense. You had been phoning me forever and I still had-n't clued in. Everytime you asked how I was, I would blab on about work, about how intense it was—you know, the big job of examining queer access barriers. On and on. Ad nauseam. It was amazing you never once said how boring I was in that bloody head space. Never once did you remind me that I kept forgetting to return your calls because I was swamped.

Finally, one Saturday, you said, "Aren't you going to take a break?"

"Yes," I said, "I'll be at the poetry reading tonight."

"That's what I was calling you about. To see if you would be there."

The café was filling up. I plopped myself down on a bench. The place swirled with people. Then *you* appeared. I almost didn't rec-ognize you. When I did, I realized that you had changed remarkably in the year you had been away. That evening, you were stunning. Even the way you wore your hair had changed. Gone were the girl-ish locks. Your long hair was pulled back to reveal the sleek glory of your head. You moved with supreme confidence.

You busied yourself, chatting with the writers, doing your job as

101

Searching for Vera

It is no great secret that Vera has disappeared. What I have not told you is that after six months, just this week, she called. She was at a payphone, she told me. We had an aborted conversation. Twice that week when I picked up the receiver and uttered a very perky, very promising hello, whoever it was on the other end, hung, albeit gently, as if not to be noticed, up.

I knew it had been Vera.

We talked a long time. It must have been nearly an hour. The conversation had progressed to a point where it seemed like we might try to meet.

"Where are you?" I asked. This seemed like a natural question. "Vera? Vera!" No answer. There was no sound, no click, nothing but the cushion of silence that marked her not being there.

"Damn!" I said.

So it was Vera was once again lost to me.

I should, perhaps, have more quickly agreed to see her. Where was it we got off? I ran the conversation over and over through my mind.

"Do you have privacy?" I had asked.

"No," she answered.

And later: "Why did you call me?"

Silence.

"Had you wanted to get together?"

"At least that," she said.

"Is that why you called me?"

Silence.

"Is that why you called me?"

"Many reasons," she said.

"Where are you?" I asked, more tenderly.

That's when she hung up the phone.

The conversation with Vera had awakened my yearning, re-kindled my desire. I had read and re-read *Lolita*; I had tried creative visualization; I had combed the city over and over, but still there was no Vera to be found.

Frustrated, upset, blocked in my process, I decided to visit Madeline Danovich, my therapist, in Denver.

Suddenly the physical distance between myself and M.D.—we had been having phone therapy for almost four years—the fact that she could only hear me but couldn't see me, grew unbearable. I could no longer stand talking to her on the phone. There was too much air and static. Everything, it seemed, was a vapour.

I would go there, I decided, and tell her about Vera. I would reveal all the gory and not so flattering details.

What happened though was not what I expected.

I wanted to talk about Vera. I wanted to describe to Madeleine Danovich exactly what happened, how one day Vera had been there, the next day she was gone. For some reason, though, I just couldn't get started.

I smoothed the cushion on the couch; I looked out the window and sighed. "I don't know," I kept saying. "I'm not sure where to begin."

"Why don't you let your unconscious go where it wants to," she suggested. She could see I was groping.

Madeleine Danovich was wearing this beautiful black-and-white print dress, with a midnight blue rounded collar.

"It went where it wanted to go and that's where it is now."

"Where's that?"

"At your breasts."

"Oh," she said, amused. "And what's it doing there, your

unconscious, I mean?"

"It's having a good time."

She laughed.

I looked at her breasts, the shape of them, tried to find the full contour of their roundness under her dress. Then I looked at her lap, down her legs and up again.

"Where are you now?"

"I've taken a little trip."

"Aha," she said.

"But I'm back—at your breasts, I mean. You look good in that dress."

"Thanks," she said.

There was a silence.

"What were you just thinking?"

"I came to talk to you about Vera." I shifted in my chair. "But actually, if you want to know the truth about what I was thinking, I wasn't thinking. I was undressing you with my eyes. I guess it's not really cool to do that or if you do it you're not supposed to talk about it but it's the truth. I wasn't even really thinking. That's what I was doing."

"And you think that's not PC to do that, you mean?"

"For a man. I don't know the rules for a woman."

"So you were undressing me with your eyes?"

"Uh-huh."

"And what did you find?"

"I found your breasts, as I told you. I started to feel a little uncomfortable."

"Anything else?"

"I was looking for the shape of you. I don't think I've ever really seen the shape of you before."

"And did you find it?"

"Not really."

"Why not?"

"I don't think you're very open to me, so I sort of see you and sort of don't."

"Why do you say I'm not very open to you?"

"I can feel it. Your body seems closed to me so I can't really see it."

"Hmm," she said.

"Is it closed to me?"

"It's clothed to you, but it's not closed to you."

She laughed and I laughed too. She smiled and shifted in her big brown leather shrink chair.

"If you're not closed to me, I guess that means you're open to me."

"I'm open to you, yes," she said.

"Then I'm making love to you," I said. And we looked at each other. We looked into each other's eyes. I looked her up and down. I could see the shape of her, her narrow shoulders under the shoulder pads of her dress, her breasts, the curve of her lap.

"How is it?" she asked.

"I think you're just letting me make love to you. I'm doing everything and you're just letting me."

"You mean you think I'm not responding?"

"Maybe. Are you responding?"

"I'm responding."

Again, we looked into each other's eyes.

"Do you do this often with your patients?"

"Do what?"

"Make love to them with words?"

Every word I have recounted here is true. If I didn't feel crazy before the session, I certainly felt crazy after. When the time was up, Madeline Danovich uncrossed her slender legs, moved effortlessly to the door and opened it, gesturing for me to leave. I was angry, bewildered and, admittedly, still slightly aroused. This was supposed to have helped me?

"Fine," I shouted. "That's fine. Just fine! And when you're looking for payment"—I was bitter, felt rebuffed—"like your advice, you can find my cheque to you signed in smoke signals against the sky."

At this, I slammed the door behind me.

Therapy? I didn't need therapy. How's a shrink supposed to help you find your lover who's disappeared? No, what I needed—and this was a turning point in my search for Vera—was a private eye.

The Game

Cin's head hung down on her chest. She felt Angel's glare rest on her. She chewed the inside of her lip.

Angel stood, hands on hips, feet shoulder-width apart. "You don't really love me."

Cin studied her hands.

"Look at me when I'm talking to you," Angel ordered.

Cin turned her eyes upward, not daring to meet Angel's eyes. She knew the gold flecks would be dancing in their hazel green background.

"While you're out playing all day I'm here. Waiting for you to come home. Do you think I enjoy being alone?"

Cin waited uncertainly. She glanced up. Angel crossed her arms. The muscles in her forearms rippled. This excited Cin. She shifted. The coarse fabric of the couch chafed against her bare skin.

"I'm waiting." Angel pushed thick black hair away from her face.

Cin's stomach tightened as she tried to remember what wrong she had committed. She knew the rules of the game. She knew what Angel expected—no, demanded. And she willingly complied. She looked fully into Angel's face.

"When you left this morning you forgot to turn on the coffee pot. I had no coffee when I got up."

Cin couldn't believe she had forgotten something so basic. Tears started to run down her cheeks.

"Oh, is the baby upset?" Angel scoffed.

Cin bit her bottom lip harder.

Angel gripped Cin's face with her fingers, forcing Cin to look at her. "You've been a bad baby, haven't you?"

Cin avoided Angel's eyes, staring instead at her full red lips. She longed to kiss Angel square on those lips. She felt her face glow crimson at the boldness of her thoughts.

"What do you say?" Angel's voice grew low and husky.

"I'm sorry." Cin's voice was barely audible.

"And . . ."

"I didn't mean to disappoint you."

"I can't let this go, can I?"

Cin shook her head. She tried so hard to get it right. But Angel was perfect. And she expected perfection from those who served her.

"Go. Ready yourself," Angel ordered. "Make certain you use hot, hot water. And the scrub brush."

Cin hurried up the stairs to the bath. She turned on the shower full force. As the bathroom filled with steam she climbed in. She soaped the coarse scrub brush and applied it gingerly to her skin. She checked to be certain there was no stubble. Angel liked her privates smooth. She clamored from the shower and dried herself. Angel would be waiting.

Cin padded down the long hallway, knocked on the heavy wooden door to Angel's room, then waited. "Enter." Cin opened the door and crept into the room.

Angel stood at the end of the four-poster bed wearing black leather chaps, a vest, and boots. Her skin seemed luminescent. Angel's dark fur patch glistened in the opening of the chaps.

Cin glanced around nervously. She didn't anticipate Angel's actions, never held expectations of their encounters.

"Here." Angel pointed to the floor. Cin knelt at Angel's feet. "I'll let you decide."

Cin's eyes flickered across Angel's face. Was this a trick?

Angel pulled Cin to her feet. "Choose."

On the bed lay a selection of whips and paddles. One she had never seen before. The whip was long and slender with a phallic shaped ivory handle. She shivered as she noted the thickness of the handle.

Angel ran her hand over the long thick handle. "Good choice." She hung the curled whip from her chaps. Angel inspected her, running her hands down her neck, across her shoulders. Her fingers burned Cin with desire. She hefted Cin's breasts appreciatively. Reaching into her vest pocket she removed two small clips. She twisted each nipple until it grew erect then clamped it tightly with a silver clip.

Angel pointed toward the bed. Cin turned. Angel pushed her down on the bed. Cin's nipples burned. She moaned softly. Angel shoved her leather-wrapped knee between Cin's legs, forcing them open. Cin knew her privates were exposed to Angel. Angel ran her hand down Cin's ass and pried open her nether lips. Cin grew wet with desire. Satisfied, Angel stepped back.

The leather strap cut the air with a whistle as it stroked Cin's bare ass. The whip snapped again and again. Cin cried then moaned, as her pain began to turn to pleasure. Angel ran her hand roughly across Cin's red bottom, squeezing and kneading her buttocks.

"I want you to please me," Angel cooed. She pushed her fingers deep into Cin's wet cave.

Cin whimpered as Angel pulled away. The leather strap found its mark again, then stopped. Cin felt Angel move behind her. She felt the cool ivory handle as Angel slid it down her slit. She tensed, then tried to relax. Angel plunged the ivory dildo deep into Cin's wet cunt, then stopped.

"On your knees. I want your ass." Roughly she pulled the dildo from Cin's pussy. Parting Cin's burning cheeks Angel spotted her target and plunged the wet dildo deep into Cin's ass. The pain pierced her.

With her free hand Angel reached around and found Cin's swollen clit. She pinched and pulled the extended knob as she pumped the dildo in and out of Cin's ass. She was ready to burst, but she waited. For Angel.

Angel pushed Cin to the bed and rolled her over, moving between her legs. Cin felt the wet roughness of Angel's furry mound against her clean mons. Angel pounded against her frantically. Cin felt the dildo in her ass and tightened against it. She felt Angel's hot breath against her neck.

"Come for me, baby," Angel whispered hoarsely. "Now."

Cin shuddered in release and felt Angel stiffen then fall against her, small shivers running through her.

In one quick moment everything was forgiven. Not forgotten. Never truly forgotten, only temporarily reprieved. Cin sometimes thought it was the forgiving that caused her to make the mistakes. She knew it was the forgiving that kept her in the game.

The Game of Love

I love being wanted, being desired. I love the dance we do when we're new. The buzz of the unknown, of potential, possibility. Being wanted so bad she can taste me before she's tasted me. I love the feeling of new hands on me, not knowing how they'll move, where they'll go. The smell of a new woman, familiar but unique. The fit of female on female. The slick slide of sweaty flesh. And the sounds she makes when she's about to come. The sounds that come from so deep down they seem to emanate from the core of her. I love new love.

It usually goes something like this.

I arrive at the bar late, when the place is packed. Why waste an entrance? I like it if the butches are starting to despair. One sweep and I've made my choice. I'll position myself so she doesn't have a good view of me, and I'll keep moving to stay just beyond her sight. Make her work for it. Of course, you know butches, you have to let them think they've discovered you. I love a sweet butch thinking she's pursuing me, the way she looks when she first catches me, catching her, watching me. The blush, the hesitation, and then the straightening up, the "I'm cool with this." And when she finally works up the nerve to come over and ask me to dance, or buy me a drink, or take me away from all this, I take a long, slow look up and down her, like it's the first time I've laid eyes on her. If she's too forward, or too fast, it's over. If you can't play the game, you don't win the prize. I want to be courted, seduced, adored. *She's going to have to work for me.*

I want her to try and talk to me. At this point, I don't care what she has to say. I want to see her mouth move. I want to see how she punctuates her conversation with her hands. I want to see her hands moving. I want her to have to lean in close to make herself heard. I want to see if her breath catches the first time she smells me. I want to see what she looks at when she looks at me. Does she talk to my breasts, my mouth, my eyes? What part of me does she see?

I won't hear her the first time she suggests we go some place a little quieter, a little more intimate. I'll just toss my head and look towards the dance floor and say, "We should dance." And I'll make her dance until she's *soaking wet, so tired but so pumped she can't stop.* And I'll dance for her, as if there is no one else, as if there has never been anyone else, before or after. Only this moment, only her and me. Then I'll suggest we should go someplace else, anywhere else, anywhere but here—go, go now. And when she breathlessly agrees, I'll say I need to use the washroom and I'll turn and leave her there, alone, out of breath, soaking, wet. If she follows me, I'll shoot her a look of absolute disdain. I am not a bathroom fuck. Not on the first date, anyway. When she asks where to—and she'd better ask—I'll tell her to take me to a restaurant, tell her I need something more.

Now, I want to hear what she has to say. I want to hear her voice. I want to hear what matters to her, what she wants to tell to me before we fuck. What does she offer? Politics, her-story, current events, heartbreaks, silence? If she asks me what I'm thinking, I'll tell her, "I'm thinking of your hands on me. I'm thinking of that mouth on my neck, that tongue gliding down my belly, onto my bone, that tongue parting my lips, toying with my clit. I'm thinking of those hands following that tongue's lead. I'm thinking of those hands in my hair, that hair in my hands. I'm thinking of the salty taste of that neck, the musky perfume of a woman who's danced herself into a frenzy. I'm thinking of asking you home, someday . . . but not today." I'll thank her for a wonderful time; I'll throw her my card and tell her to call me, tomorrow. I'll leave her hanging, until another day. *The game has begun.*

113

Bottoms Up

(Things you might hear and say the first time you try a little B&D)

"Ow! Don't bite so hard!"

"Sorry . . ."

"What are you trying to do, bite my fucking nipple off?"

"I said I was sorry."

"It's too tight."

"It's supposed to be tight."

"I can't move my wrist."

"Well, that's the idea."

"You're cutting off the blood to my hands."

"Okay, okay. I'll loosen it a little."

"Hurry up!"

"I'm trying."

"What's the problem?"

"I can't untie the knot. Stay still!"

"What do you mean, you can't untie it?"

"Maybe we should've used the handcuffs. These nylons are a bitch."

"Come on, already. My fingers are falling asleep!"

"Oh shit, they're turning blue."

"Stop!"

"Cry all you want, bitch."

"No, really. Stop it."

"You're not kidding anyone. You want it."

"You're hurting me, damn it!"

"Really?"

"Let me up!"

"Are you playing, or do you mean it?"

"I said stop it. Are you deaf? That really hurts."

"I'm sorry. I thought you were playing."

"I said stop it."

"I thought the word was Spam . . . ."

"Okay, bitch. Now you're gonna get it."

"What are you gonna do to me?"

"I don't know. What do you want me to do?"

"No, no! You stepped out of character."

"Sorry. Let's try it again."

"Be merciless."

"Okay."

"Make me beg."

"Okay."

"Hurt me. Don't really, you know, just make me think you will."

"Okay, okay! Stop telling me what to do."

"Well, you fucked it up once already. Do it right this time."

"Shut up, you fucking control freak!"

"That's more like it."

"I'm so damn sick of you giving me orders all the time."

"Good! Go with it."

"You think you know everything. You don't know shit."

"Teach me a lesson."

"Fuck you!"

"Hey, where are you going?"

"Play with yourself."

"Come on! Hey, come back and untie me, will you? Hey! Hello? Goddamn it . . ."

115

"Come on, bitch. Suck my big, hard cock."

"What is that?"

"Open your mouth and suck it."

"Get that thing away from me."

"Do what your daddy says, or you'll be sorry."

"Get that fucking thing out of my face!"

"Okay, Big Daddy has a better idea."

"Don't even think about it."

"Be a good little girl and spread your legs for Daddy."

"You're not sticking that thing inside me! Get the fuck away from me!"

"You're making Daddy mad. You know what happens to little girls who don't do what they're told?"

"Take that off. You look retarded."

"Hey!"

"You do. Take it off."

"That's it."

"What are you doing? Wait a minute."

"I've had about all I'm gonna take from you."

"Look, forget it. Untie me. I don't wanna play anymore. This is stupid."

"Stupid, huh?"

—Smack—

"Ow! Cut it out!"

"I'm sorry, I can't hear you."

—Smack — Smack—

"Stop, damn it!"

"How does that feel? Huh, cunt? What if I move these hand-cuffs up a little higher . . . Like that? You look so pretty standing on your toes."

"Stop it, now. Okay? You had your fun."

"Oh, the fun has just begun. . . . See if you like the flavour of these pretty little panties. . . . There, now you can scream all you want to. What's that? Gee, I can't understand what you're saying. Don't you know little girls shouldn't talk with their mouths full? You'll have to be punished."

—Smack— Smack— Smack—

"Hmmm. . . . We seem to have a little problem here. Your eyes

say no, but your pussy says yes. Look—what's this? You're all wet...
And your nipples are so hard, just like little pebbles. Want me to
suck on them? Mmmm... Like that? Am I biting too hard? Yes?
No? I can't tell what you're saying. Oh, you want me to bite hard-
er? Okay. Anything for my little girl... Why are you crying? Huh?
Stop crying, or I'll give you something to cry about."

— Smack —Smack —Smack— Smack— Smack— Smack—

"There, there. . . . Come on, stop crying. Want me to make you
feel good? Hmmm? Spread your legs. Wider. Don't make me hit
you again. That's better. How's that? Good? You like that, huh? I
knew you would. See? Maybe you'll listen to your daddy from now
on. I'm gonna take the panties out of your mouth now, okay? No
screaming, or they go right back in. There. How do you feel?"

"Don't stop . . . "

"I'm not gonna stop."

"Feels so good . . . "

"Like that? Slow like that?"

"Go faster."

"You want me to go faster?"

"Yeah."

"Say please."

"Please."

"How's that?"

"Oh yeah. . . . Suck my tits."

"What?"

"Please, Daddy, suck my tits, please."

"Good girl. Now you're learning."

"I'm gonna come!"

"No."

"Don't stop!"

"You don't have permission to come yet."

"Damn it!"

"You didn't say please."

"I can't believe you stopped. What the fuck is the matter with
you?"

"You said you wanted to beg."

"Can't you do anything right?"

"I'm sorry."

ZONNA

"Let me down."
"Where's the key?"
"You have it."
"No, I don't."

T . J .   B R Y A N

Two Bottoms in Lust

Dunno if being the bigger one, the taller one, the one that can pick your sweet self clear up off the floor, is all that. As in . . . desirable.

I mean . . . this here's a femme who does a mean Daddy's little girl and likes to serve while she's at it. So I ain't so sure why the great one made you so fine, irresistible and a bwoy bottom at that.

Can't banish you from my mind. You give off a glow that I may nevah forget. What's not to like? I've combed the hair on that head times two. Its blue-black'n' shiny curls cling like the miniscule do's of a million ashanti-descended choir boys as seen from above. And I need to mention tha eyes. Big, coercing. They contradict all that shy shit you profess and confess. Daring me to do all sorts'a dirty deeds with no regrets.

Sub meets sub. Gender fuckin' black bwoy meets diasporic femme vixen in tha makin'. Who will finally have her way? Bottom to top. Gyal, ain't you ready to play?

Two bottoms in lust . . . the universal conundrum. Can't both stay on our backs and get off. Truth is . . . I like to be taken with tenderness or force. And right about now, I'd part my thighs for whatevah you had in mind. Don't you know it?

119

Wouldn't my high heels look fine peddlin' thin air? But why should I have to make the first move?

We sit and talk . . . watch TV. Sit and talk . . . drink some tea. Sit and talk. I feel worse than the most bad behave' butch dawg for wanting . . . no . . . needing to stop you mid-sentence for an intense session of tongue-on-tongue titillation. I try to focus. Getting wetter, wetter. I fail miserably. And concede ungracefully.

With all the skill of a hard-on-crippled jock in back seat with date I grasp at tits tipped with skin the colour of roasted coffee beans. Tongue tease them out from under and into full view. Then I direct your mouth to my breast, my neck. Holding you tight as you feed on my heat. Till my passion reaction becomes your own.

I want you. Want you on top'a me. Want to coax it outta your pants and into my slit. Want your fist, your tongue, your hood. It's all good.

Moanin' and cussin' you proceed to make my all too willing black ass your own. One, two, three gloved, slick fingers slip past my sphincter. A quick intake of my breath. But . . . not . . . so . . . fast . . . I pull back, take condom to tool and suck you off like a good baby girl should. I sense, don't see your eyes half closed, rolled back in your head. Your muscles tense and spasm as latex connects to clit and cortex. Sends signals screaming. A lost limb rejoined?

No time to wonder, I take my fill. Plunge, suck, suck, plunge, suck, plunge. Cover it with my spit as you twitch and ride the inside'a my mouth. A forceful hand to the back'a my neck makes me gag. Brings tears to my eyes. Makes you laugh, drunk with the power of my gift.

Then I'm on my back. Open. You're devouring my nipples and there's pain. A myriad of tiny electric shocks assault my system. Your eyes gazing into mine speak volumes. Molten, they're as vulnerable as I've seen 'em.

You come into me with a shudder. Cock ridin' me. Pelvis grindin' and windin' me. Hitting all the right spots. Using that facsimile tool with more precision, more knowledge than a penis-possessing fool allowed to have one by accident of birth.

And as you're lungin' I'm squealin' pantin', jonesin' for more of what you've got to give. You name me size queen. I laugh and know you're right. Pulling you to me by the cheeks of your sweaty ass I taste your tongue and bite your lips.

Two bottoms in lust. Ain't that the shit? Who bottomed for who? Who topped between us two? When you fucked my pussy raw and I made you do it? Ballsy, bad butch bwoy, you please me. Damn! You pleased me.

SHARI J. BERMAN

Milestone

Bottoms up!

Hmm . . . Cynthia regarded Nani quizzically. Nani smiled. Cynthia detoured suspicions of double entendres to the nether regions of her consciousness, already overcrowded with speculation.

I've always wondered: what's it like being with a woman? Posed three months earlier, the question still reverberated in Cynthia's brain. She'd barely responded when her lover's half-sister had revealed this curiosity about lesbian relationships.

"Cheers," Cynthia managed, taking a drink. She decided to focus on the champagne. *You don't turn half a century any old day; might as well get lit!*

Lianne squeezed her thigh. "Happy birthday, baby."

"Thank you, sweetie." Cynthia covered Lianne's hand with her own, patting the pinky ring she'd given Lianne for their twentieth anniversary.

They still were sexual, but days often melted into weeks. Cynthia had told Lianne about Nani's confession and Lianne had laughed, saying, "Nani's a big talker. She'd bail if someone took her up on that!"

Nani leaned over the table to cut the lasagna. Cynthia's nose inhaled Nani's Shalimar as her eyes captured the cleavage. Nani was wearing an underwire bra—a torture device for perkier breasts that Cynthia associated with heterosexuals. Almost two decades younger, Nani had a better shot at perky breasts than her dinner guests.

As Cynthia drained the glass, her thoughts drifted back to her own early thirties. She had been wild in the 1970s. *That seems like another lifetime. Is there an official road that leads to the land of the stiff and stodgy?* Lianne winked and poured Cynthia another glassful.

Cynthia picked at her plate. Too much lasagna would deaden the buzz. She was not unhappy with her life, but she found birthdays measured in fractions of decades to be dreadfully depressing.

Lianne described "Marriage Project Hawaii" and Nani made noises of support. Cynthia pushed back her cynical voice that wanted to assure them there wasn't a snowball's chance in hell of two women being able to tie the knot in the good old U.S. of A in their lifetime. *Maybe if the native Hawaiians actually succeeded in sovereignty and made it a whole different country, it could happen. Then, of course, Lianne would be welcome to stay because she's Hawaiian, but I, the haole lover, would be bidden Aloha Oe and shoved into an outrigger canoe with "White girl go home" painted on it.* She was fighting a losing battle with her cynical side, but she managed to keep silent.

While the sisters discussed the recent granting of further autonomy to University of Hawaii, Cynthia poured more champagne. Bubbles danced around her nostrils as a half-century of kinks began to loosen. She had a designated driver and Nani's guest room, so she didn't feel particularly inhibited.

Nani loaded the dishwasher and Lianne cleared the dishes. "There's something for you in the guestroom closet," Nani called.

When Cynthia rose, the room didn't spin. *What did I expect? There're two other people sharing the bubbly.*

The closet had fancy clothing that smelled of Shalimar sachet. Cynthia fingered a gown. She imagined Nani's perky breasts filling it. She wasn't especially attracted to Nani . . . yet curious. Nani reminded her so much of herself at that age.

When she stepped back attempting an earnest search for a gift, she tripped. She grabbed at the gowns, but she landed face down, buried in fabric.

As she attempted to right herself, she felt fingers on her calves. She protested and was shushed. The woman tickled her feet. She jerked, managing to tangle her head and upper torso further in frocks.

Her shorts were inched down her thighs. "I want you, Cyn," came the throaty growl. *Did she mean "Cyn" or "sin"?* She tried to see who the woman was, but couldn't. Nimble fingers pulled down her panties. Cynthia was a jumble of ticklish anticipation, squirming and squealing, as the woman approached her exposed mound.

Cynthia felt a soft arm against her as the woman dipped into the waiting wetness and thrummed her clit. Her heart pounded as she stole breaths through the perfumed garments. A low moan grew to a muffled bleat. Her head began to rock in ecstasy.

Cynthia shuddered during the final release, biting the material imprisoning her face. "You sounded fantastic," the woman whispered, smacking Cynthia's bare ass. Cynthia tried to stand, but her captor grasped her left ankle, hooking an object around it. Partially untangling Cynthia, the woman then scooped something off the floor and left.

Ignoring the drool and sweat, Cynthia hung up the clothes. She searched for Nani's gift and gave up.

Back at the table, Nani grinned at her. Cynthia averted her eyes then glanced up. Nani looked away. This continued throughout the evening.

Riding home, they were quiet. When they got to their bedroom, Lianne pulled Cynthia against her. "What's with you and Nani?"

"Nothing."

"Don't lie to me, Cynthia. You stared at her all night."

"She stared at me."

"You're curious. If she offered, you wouldn't refuse."

Cynthia gulped.

"You thought it was her, didn't you?" Lianne demanded.

"I knew it was you . . . your arm, your ring. . . ."

"Then why were you gawking at her?"

"She was grinning at me like a fool. . . .You let her watch, didn't you!"

"Please!"

"She knew."

"I told her I gave you your present in the closet." Lianne whacked Cynthia's bottom. "I owe you forty-eight more."

Cynthia began to cry.

"You okay?" Lianne asked, wiping the tears with her fingertips.

"Yeah . . . I look at Nani and wonder where all the years went. She symbolizes Christmas past."

Lianne placed Cynthia's hand on her ankle. Cynthia removed the bracelet and read the inscription: "The best is yet to come."

Lianne retrieved it, returning the bracelet to Cynthia's ankle. Cynthia's eyes welled up again.

"I never did find Nani's gift."

"I did." Lianne produced a small bottle of Shalimar from her shirt pocket. Cynthia dabbed a drop behind each ear and allowed Lianne to resume the birthday rituals.

As Cynthia was about to climax for the fifth time, Lianne whispered. "I told you the best was yet to come."

HELEN BRADLEY

The Appointment

Haven't you a home to go to?" My boss asks rhetorically then, catching a glimpse of what I'm doing, she adds flippantly, "I'm off. Don't work too hard, will you?"

It's late. She's the last to leave. I'm alone. I'm busy building a mountain of paperclips. It's not easy work. It needs patience and a steady hand. I build a tall column, clip by unsteady clip, until its inherent instability beats the magnetic force and it totters and falls. I start over.

I am stalling. I know it but I'm powerless to act against it. My legs won't move, my energy and attention are focused on a pile of curved metal. Hard as I try I can't drag myself to leave. Well, that's not true, I could leave *here* if it didn't mean arriving *there*.

How did this happen, I ask myself. The question has been hounding me for months. I ask it to avoid thinking about the solution I have agreed to. How can it be so long since we've made love? Days have stretched into weeks and into months and, like snow in spring, the intimacy in our lives has melted away, leaving the landscape barren and bare.

I recall our early days together. We'd spend endless summer days in bed talking, cuddling, fucking hard, and loving long and slow. Days empty of everything but loving, eating, and sleeping and then waking to do it all over again.

Our days now are full. We march the treadmill of work, gym, eating, shopping, laundry, dishes, commuting, therapy . . . therapy! The word triggers activity in my legs, guilt rises like bile in my throat. I am late. I must go. I don't want to go . . . but I must.

I leave the safe haven of my office and head towards uncharted waters.

Key in hand, I stand outside our front door, unable to lift the key to the lock. I am paralyzed by fear. There's a stranger inside. She's been here for hours. I am late. She knows I am late. I know she knows. I feel the sharp edge of her tongue and I haven't even stepped inside. I berate myself for being late, for building fragile structures, for being afraid, for not wanting to be here.

The door opens from within.

Her attempt at a smile reaches only her lips and they quiver slightly with the effort. Her eyes are dry, but the redness in them tells me she has been crying. Yet she is steadfast as she takes in a shaky breath.

"Hi there, you've had a long day." She steps aside to let me in. I search her words for signs of criticism, but I hear none. She reaches out and I hand her my briefcase and keys. It would be churlish to do otherwise. I stand, hands empty, as she puts these articles away. I don't know what to do. I feel a fool just standing here but I don't know what else to do. Here is my lover of a handful of years—a stranger to me.

I have come home for sex. We have an appointment for sex. Our lives are too busy for intimacy to be a spontaneous indulgence, our counselor has explained, and even after weeks of therapy we have not yet made love. She delivers her findings with just the right amount of irony and my guilt levels soar. Taking advantage of the moment like a basketball player before an open net, she slam-dunks us with an agreement to make love by appointment, tonight. Her expertise is formidable. My excuses sound lame even to my own ears. It's do it or else, she hisses. She intimates that this is a last ditch effort to breathe life into something she thinks deserves the last rites.

That's why I am here. I am here to make love. My partner is

this person standing only feet from me. A woman so wonderfully familiar and yet so much a stranger that I don't know how to approach her. I stand immobile, incapable of voluntary movement.

Her hand stretches tentatively towards me. Her middle finger bends inward further than the others, shaping her hand into a ballerina pose, displaying her mix of softness and strength. I remember how her hand once felt stroking my cheek and how her fingers would curve to cup my breasts and her thumb would stroke my nipples to form hard buds. I remember how she would play in my slick wetness before pressing her long fingers slowly but firmly inside me. I see all this as I look at her hand stretched towards me offering so much if only I can find the confidence to take it.

I look up at her. Her eyes brim with tears. She meets my gaze. She asks me to meet her half way, to take a chance, to love her as I used to, to fulfill her needs and to allow her to satisfy mine. I cannot move.

"Please," she whispers, and her fingers touch my cheek.

This is all it takes to snap the protective band I have wrapped around my desire. It flows free like molten lava. I feel it surging through my body warming my chest and my groin.

I look at the woman before me with new eyes. I realize how much I need and want her. My lips stretch into a smile that works its way up until it creases the skin around my eyes. I reach out to take her hand, it feels cool to my touch. I pull her gently towards me, wrapping my arms around her as her body relaxes into mine. I kiss her ear lobe and cheek feeling the fine hairs tickling my lips. I reacquaint myself with her body. I sense her own need building in her, her breath shallow as she turns to meet my lips.

"Welcome home, girlfriend," she murmurs. I answer with my mouth on hers as desire fuses our bodies into one.

SUSAN LEE

Alleys

I waited in the alley by your apartment like we agreed. It was two in the morning and I was beginning to wonder where you were. I half expected your neighbours to call the cops since I'd been waiting for at least half an hour. A half-hour of envisioning what I was going to do to you. As I lit another cigarette, I caught your figure out of the corner of my eye and knew you saw me by the spark of my lighter.

You came down the steps of your apartment, looked around, and made your way to the alley. I moved against the wall, anticipating your arrival. I could hear your footsteps approaching. They matched the thumping that was beginning as the blood rushed to my ears. I saw you round the corner. You pretended not to see me as you walked passed. I stepped out of the shadows and started to walk behind you. The sound of my boots hitting the pavement echoed in the alley and you stopped in your tracks. I came up behind you and whispered in your ear.

"Move into the shadows. I want you against the wall."

You complied like a good little girl.

"Face the wall."

You did as you were told and I began to play into our fantasy. I

129

grabbed your hands and placed them above your head while you leaned the side of your face against the red brick building. You whispered something and I pressed against you to find out what you wanted.

"Do it now, like we planned."

"All right, spread your legs for me."

You moved your legs shoulder width apart with me still against you. I rested my head against yours and smelled the perfume lingering in your hair. I closed my eyes and ran my cheek down the length of your soft curly hair. I brushed it aside and saw the nape of your neck by the glow from the moonlight. I bent towards it and gave you a quick bite. You drew in a short breath; the game had begun. I reached around with my right hand while my left still kept you in place and held you by the throat. You tilted your head back just a bit and I kissed your eyes, cheek, and mouth.

I grabbed your shoulder to turn you around to face me. You had your eyes closed and a slight smile on your face. You tilted your face up to mine and I kissed you more intently, one hand wrapped in the mane of your hair and the other still at your throat. You started to push your hips and writhe beneath me, breath quickening with every movement.

"Do it now."

"Soon."

I ran my hands down the length of your body and rested them on your ass. I pulled you to me while you started to grind against my leg. I began to slowly pull up the side of your dress and discovered you had nothing on underneath. My hand traveled along your inner thigh and I could feel that you had wanted this for awhile. You took my hand with some urgency and guided my fingers in. I took over, while you found your rhythm. Back and forth, I could feel as you opened yourself up more and slowly slid in my other fingers until you could accept my fist.

I got down on my knees so I could lick your clit and pump you with more satisfaction. You supported yourself against my shoulders while I took you to the point of no return. When I felt you tighten around my fist I knew you were almost there. You cried out and fell against me. I slowly slipped out and got up. You lit a cigarette for me and asked with a smile, "Want to come back to my place?"

I smiled, nodded, and followed.

JACQUELYN ROSS

Roadside Assistance

It is a hot summer afternoon, the kind that brings back memories of ice cold root beer popsicles dripping down your fingers because it is so warm you can't possibly eat it fast enough before it melts.

I turn the radio on to my favourite station. Prince and I sing about how good we are going to make her feel tonight. Suddenly, the radio loses power. I realize my car is straining to move. Where is that cellular phone when I really need it?

Just fuckin' great, I think, as I pull my car to the side of the road. I turn the engine off and open the hood. As I move slowly towards the monster, steam rises from its bowel, like Satan smoking a good Cuban. Yep, it's broken. Willing my car to start again, I fail to notice the sound of tires spitting out pebbles as a vehicle comes to a stop just in front of mine. I turn around to see a black, dirty, dented Suzuki Sidekick.

Oh God, just my luck. Some guy with an ill-fitting pale blue polyester suit has decided to be a good Samaritan.

The door swings open slowly. I see a scruffed black boot, complete with silver buckle, emerge from the truck. The sole is well worn, and I can faintly make out oil drops on them.

The sun glares into my eyes. I hold my hand up to my brow, squinting to see who has come to save me.

She moves her body out of the truck, her shaggy blonde hair falling in waves because of the humidity.

"Looks like you might need some help," she says, a half smile playing around her mouth. She wears a white undershirt under a pair of weathered overalls.

"Yeah, I guess I do," I say.

She reaches back into her vehicle for an old cloth and walks towards me, her boots crunching in the gravel. She comes close, so close her breath feels hotter than fire, and she looks at me like she can read my thoughts.

"I'm Diane," she says, as she pushes past me, the denim on her leg grazing mine.

I can't speak. I just watch her bend over the engine. Her fingers play with wires as she explains the problem. I stare at her, watching her fingers plunge in and out of my hoses. Please let it take all day to fix, I pray.

"Should be okay now," Diane mutters. "Get in and try it."

I sit back in my car, turn the key, and the engine purrs like a kitten.

"Hey, sounds good," says Diane.

"Thanks. Please let me give you some money," I say.

"Turn off your car."

I do so, then stare into her eyes. Without a word, I slide along the seat and she gets in beside me, never losing eye contact as she closes the door behind her.

She pulls out the rag from her pocket and drags her fingers across it, leaving a smear of grease behind. Then she takes her greasy fingers and slowly touches the side of my face. I quiver. Smiling ever so slightly, she scrapes her lips over mine. Her tongue runs over my mouth as I open my lips. She pulls back. I look into her eyes, searching for some quick answers. Instead she whispers, "What do you want?"

"I want you to fuck me," I breathe.

My hands play with the buckles on her overalls, desperately wanting them undone. I snap one off, and it slides over her shoulder. I touch her nipple, feeling it through the damp cotton fabric.

Her hands are already under my bra, her fingers teasing. My concentration is gone. I moan and move back. She turns so that she is on top of me, her tongue making itself at home in my mouth. I fumble with my shorts. I feel her hand grasp mine, as her other hand slowly peels my clothing away. Her hand dives into my wet pussy. A growl escapes my throat, only to be stopped short by her persistently probing tongue in my mouth. Two fingers circle my clit, constant, perfect pressure, agonizingly slow. Her mouth detaches from mine and she looks for a response in my eyes. My hands push down on her strong shoulders and I whimper like a puppy with anticipation.

Her tongue takes over where her fingers leave off. Suddenly, the two fingers that had teased my clit glide inside me. Her mouth sucks hard on my clit as her fingers pump easily in and out of my cunt. My fingers wrap around the strap of her overalls, dig into the buckle as my body is gripped by the powerful orgasm.

She slowly pulls her face from between my legs; her wet fingers brushing on my inner thigh. She looks up at me and smiles as she brings her fingers up to her mouth and sucks on them, like an ice cold root beer popsicle on an incredibly hot day.

Shower

The coolness nipped at my naked toes that hung from under the hefty covers. I pulled them under and lodged them between your warm, hungry thighs so they could feel the wetness of your flow. Snuggled between your breasts, I couldn't help but squeeze my own nipples as I inhaled the spent aroma of our fire and your sandalwood haze. As memories of last night began to arouse me again, the fullness of my bladder became my first priority. I trudged off to the bathroom and noticed it was still dark outside. Perhaps there might still be time for us before that damned alarm clock began screaming its head off. It always seemed too soon.

I eased myself onto the chilly seat and let my head hang between my breasts. You were everywhere—in my hands, my hair, between my breasts and still-creamy thighs. I inhaled deeply while listening to the sweet sound of you sleeping through the quiet of the morning. Even when you worked your night shift, I could hear your breath sounds in my dreams and feel your fire next to me. Even though I thought how nice a morning romp might be, I figured I should just get an early start and hop in the shower, especially with our long weekend coming up. We had finally made our dream come true and bought a house up on the Cape, in

Provincetown. We were going away this weekend and had invited another couple to help us celebrate our joint venture.

The pounding of the hot water felt good beating down on my crown, massaging the rest of my body. I turned on the shower radio and my hips began to move to the jazzy rhythms. My hands traced the shower wall, revisiting all those places you had just left. As I raised my hands to begin the shampoo, a different pair of hands beat me to it.

"Thought you could have this early morning romp without me?"

I purred like a cat in heat and a slow smile crossed my lips as your long, strong fingers began to soap me down. I greeted your lips with my own and began to cover your body with the lather in my hands, feeling your nipples become erect between my fingertips. All the while, your leg was hungrily working its way between mine and your own throbbing clit moving against my other hand. Your tiny plump pearl began to swell and drip with your hot lather. I watched the feeling engulf you as you tossed your head back, then I slid down to taste your soapy mixture.

Your hips pushed into my mouth while fingertips massaged and held my head at the same time. I felt the brush of your soapy bush as I ventured to keep the succulent fruit in my mouth. I grabbed your slippery buttocks and sent my tongue as far between your lips as it was long. You began rocking faster, jerking to an eruption that left me hanging on for dear life. I cupped you in my hands and let my tongue rest on your pulsing node until you were spent.

Just when I thought you were done, I felt your hands lift me up to you and pull me close to your soapy tummy. Our lips embraced and our tongues wandered with frenzied abandon. I was as full as a harvest moon, ready to delivery a bountiful flow. Your mouth tasted me, my neck, my body, all you could swallow before I was totally consumed by your fever. I felt your thigh slide between my own and lift me, until your leg was secure on the tub's edge. My hips began to gyrate on your thigh to the beat of a tune on the radio. Your hands held me and followed my rhythm down my back to my cheeks where your fingers gripped me to join the undulation. I felt my inside winding up like a mighty rubber band about to fly. The tidal wave washed over me and I came strong but smooth and my head whipped back and was forced under the water until it felt like I was drowning.

I pulled my head from under the showerhead just in time to catch my breath. I looked around only to find my wash cloth in my hand, my own fingers between my legs, soap still in my hair, and a very throbbing clit. I washed the soap from my hair, jumped out of the shower, and peeked into the bedroom door to find you still cozied up under those damn covers, oblivious to the hot session I was supposed to be having with you. Alarm clock or no, it was time to make this shower come true.

KAREN WOODMAN

Threshold

She whispers in the middle of conversations. One afternoon at the office, we were all talking about El Niño and how warm the winter was. Someone was trying to scientifically explain the shifting plates and tidal charts when she whispered, "It's the wind." Her words made me think of how people find themselves in unexpected places.

It's not what she says, it's how. Words drift out of her. Driving me home one night, she whispered, "Quiet," pointing to a sloping, empty freeway. Just one word. Quiet.

If she wasn't my boss, I'd be in love with her.

Every morning I imagine we meet for the first time. When she's grouchy and distracted, I add a pinch of cinnamon and nutmeg to her coffee.

My friend Jules keeps trying to introduce me to new women. She doesn't understand how happy I already am, and how lucky I feel. I've been in love before. It gets so complicated. This time it's different, though. As long as she's in business, we'll be together.

"But you have to have the same goals," Jules advised. "You have to have the same values and the same vision for the future. Didn't you say she was a real estate broker?"

"Well, yeah," I replied, "but I don't care. I'm a secretary. It's not like real estate's evil, and, anyway, who cares what her job is? When you come right down to it people have to survive. She's deeper than that. She told me, once she was trekking up a ruin in Mexico and when she finally reached the top there was nothing to hold on to. She thought the wind would blow her over. She said, 'That was when I knew how precious life was.'"

"Sue, you're a dyke, she's married. Think about it."

"I know, but I can't help the way I feel."

"She might hurt you."

"I don't care."

"Listen, all that west coast free love crap you learned in Vancouver is a crock. Relationships have contexts. All actions have consequences. I can't stand all that superstitious, romantic nonsense."

"That's so depressing. No wonder it's taking you so long to finish your Ph.D. What about seizing life because tomorrow it could be gone?"

"Oh, *puh-leez*. Nothing is that simple," Jules said. "Okay, listen. Next week I want to go to the opening of the first lesbian bathhouse. Come with me, okay?"

"No way. I gave up toga parties in grade nine. I can't stand all that hip, erotic, fetish stuff. It's a circus."

"Come on. I really want to go."

I spent all week regretting that I'd agreed.

"So what am I supposed to wear to a lesbian bathhouse?" I asked Jules on the phone from my office. "Leather? Plastic? Overalls? Spiky heels? What?"

"A towel," Jules informed me.

On the evening we went, I brought an orange beach towel with bright yellow flowers and lime green leaves. Jules yanked a tiny Holiday Inn towel from her pack and grinned.

We walked down the steps to the basement, where the bathhouse was. A young, ponytailed woman beamed as she explained the system.

"The large room off to the side is for lounging. The locker room is right behind me, stocked with fresh towels, and through the locker room we have a large steam room, a whirlpool, and a bath. The private rooms toward the back are for your own private enjoyment."

"Private school girl," I muttered.

"Yes, I do believe so," Jules drawled as we surveyed the lounge. Three fully clothed women sat together on the same couch as a fourth entered and exited the room nervously.

"This is lame," I complained. "What are we supposed to do? Sit in a dark room twiddling our thumbs?"

"I don't know. Maybe. Let's check out the rest of the place," Jules suggested.

We walked past the lockers and opened the door to the steam room. One woman was lying on the hot boards while another leaned over her. "Yeah. Yeah, yeah, yeah," was all we heard. We closed the door, surprised by the sight.

Through the other door, three women chatted in a large whirlpool. The bath was empty.

"Hi," we smiled as we climbed in. The three women smiled back.

"So, when the contract came through, everything was a go, full on," a muscular woman with long curly blonde hair said.

"Make sure you get it signed," the second woman added gruffly.

"Nice tattoo," a thin woman with red short hair said brightly.

"Thanks," I replied. My black cat was showing. "I got it a few years ago on a trip to New York."

"Did ya go to the Clit Club?" the muscular blonde asked.

"No, but I went to a Dyke Ball at The Bank." I remembered Lucy dragging me to a kissing booth.

"I love New York," said the red-haired woman. "The shopping, the restaurants. It's so alive."

"Yeah, it was great," I agreed, remembering queer fire-eaters and dancing. Jules closed her eyes, concentrating on a water jet. More women entered and sat on the edge of the rectangular bath.

"I think I'm going to try the cooler water," I said, climbing out of the whirlpool.

"Water's a bit cooler over here," purred a woman with deeply freckled skin and a grey crewcut. I noticed a fine scar running from the top of her left cheekbone down her chin.

"Umm hmm." My legs dangled in the cool water. She stroked my back. Her green eyes and determined expression held me. She brushed the hair off my face.

A butterfly in my stomach fluttered. It was that free feeling. Familiar even when strange. We brushed forearms and even the soft hairs knew. An ice cube from her water glass slid up my spine to the base of my neck.

In the middle of the night, up the long flight of stairs to her apartment, her fingers lightly danced around my waist. With her front door open, we were neither inside or out. On her threshold my lips couldn't leave and hers wouldn't. In that doorway, for that moment, I was married.

What Happens If You Imagine Something Really Hard...

You are away more often than you are at home.

Late one Saturday night, I surprised two working girls trying your door.

At home in bed, I writhed with lusty dreams. I came to you unfastening my blouse, kneeling at your jeans, offering to service you sexually. You gave me money. I woke drenched in sweat and post-orgasmic fluids.

Where were you?

On restless evenings I walked through the neighbourhood streets. Your windows were usually dark. Sometimes I was rewarded with a glimpse of you. You might be working on something, wearing coarse shirts and tight jeans. Even from outside, the strength of your muscles shone in the night.

Times when I was alone I thought of you.

It was scarcely believable that the car you drove could ever spring to life, since you had patched it together with tape and loose parts. My favourite sightings were of you bent over the hood on Saturday mornings. Once you caught me staring at your ass. You blushed as if you knew I was imagining your hips thrusting against my pussy.

I saw mail piling up on your porch—science magazines about artificial intelligence, all with names that were strange on my tongue. What work did you do, I wondered.

Once during a snowstorm I was sweating over a shovel full of cold snow and looked up to find that you had materialized before me. You were so cool and calm in your parka, your eyes betraying no hint of chill or exertion. My cheeks hot and my knees weak, I blurted out, "Why don't you let me collect your mail since it spills over onto your porch?"

"I don't mind the mail," you replied, never moving your eyes away from mine, "I just wanted to ask your name."

Once I knew your name, I worried less about you returning from your mystery trips. The firmness of your body, the way you placed your hands on that car, your eyes gazing past my hair and face, were enough to sustain a lust that welled from my deepest recesses.

By last summer, we had a pattern. A short sighting of you on the street or at the store with your deep eternal stare would cause my eyes to burn for you days afterward. Just the two of us backing out of our neighbouring driveways at the same time was enough to make me feel secure in my contact with you. Once, you touched my arm in greeting me, and I bore that hot imprint for days. I grew complacent in the attraction.

I had almost forgotten my anxiety over your frequent departures when I spotted the unimaginable. A moving truck. In your driveway.

Though I walked back and forth several times that day, I never saw you.

My heart had sunk to my knees. It was as though a life force that I had come to rely on without naming it had been cut off. I took a vacation and spent sleepless nights stargazing. Did you know the night sky appears as though someone had hurled a great bucket of stars and they had stuck wherever they landed? How can people like you believe there is intelligent order in the galaxy?

When I came home it appeared that new people were preparing your house to be their home.

I tried fantasizing about you under my covers, but it seemed you had travelled too far away to be conjured like that. I fell into a sleep of dreams. In the middle of the night my body grew damp and I sensed a steady patter like rain on my skylight. Yet in my sleepy state I thought it was the sound of your heartbeat. I sensed your body close, felt you press on top of mine. Your toes dug into my calves, your pelvis was hot over my pussy, your hard tits crushed between my breasts; my fingernails scratched in desire and found smooth skin down your back. Your ass finally stretched over me as I had always yearned and your tongue plunged into my throat where I sucked hard while pushing your fingers deep in my cunt.

I came like an explosion and opened my eyes. There was nothing there. Only a quick cool exhalation of air. Then silence. I knew, however, that you had come and gone.

When I got up in the morning and smoothed my skin and hair to meet the world I had that calm post-coital sensation, as if still coated with a lover's kisses. I re-emerged to the world feeling intact once more.

How I Spent My Summer Vaction

My cousin and I have been planning this for weeks now, ever since she tried to get me to go down to the city with her to become a cop. Said she couldn't do it here. I don't know why since her daddy is a cop. Shoot. I'd be on the line like, yo pops, hook me up. But she wants to do it by herself. Go figure. What is it with Black folks anyway? You'd think we never heard of nepotism. Why do we feel we always have to do it the hard way? Whatever happened to each one up, bring one up? Well, I know it wouldn't be me down there in New York trying to crack a nut all by myself. Anyway, I better stop worrying about it and put some pep in my step if I am ever going to make it to the train on time.

Seven. I'm glad I didn't go to Back Bay Station. That train would have been mad packed. I am better off this way.

This is my lucky day. Nice looking sista. Fine, in fact. Just sat down on my left. Is the seat taken? Do I mind? Hell, no. Can I help her with her bag? It's too heavy to lift. Oh, man. She must think I'm a brotha. At five-foot-ten and 225 pounds of solid muscle, I look a little like a boy. I hate to break it to her. Let me just squeeze by her and hoist this thing on up in there. Damn, girl, what you got in here, a ton of bricks? Books. Student. Gotcha. No, I'm headed to the city for some R&R. You're headed home? Took some summer courses at BU? That's nice. Yeah. Going to New York to enjoy some of the summer fun.

Eight. Man. She's fine but all that idle chitchat can get on your nerves. Glad she finally fell asleep. It's kind of cool having her lay her head on my shoulder. I like the way her soft curls feel against my neck. And she smells so sweet. My soft brown sista. Educated sista. Eyes shining like the stars in an ebony night sky kinda sista.

Nine-thirty. Must have fallen asleep. My arm is numb. When did I put it around her shoulder? If I move it she'll awaken. Daggone she feels good all pressed up against me. This is the way a honey should feel, warm, soft. I can feel her angles and curves connecting with mine. She must like a hard body the way her hand keeps moving up and down my leg. Man what a smile. She's awake. Baby. She's going to get me into trouble. I can feel it coming. Lord Jesus help me. Yeah, I could use a Pepsi. No I can get it. Oh. Then stretch them legs, girl. Go on.

This chick is something. She's come back with Pepsis and a couple of sandwiches. Says she heard my stomach growling when she was laying on me. If she were like some of those fine sistas back home, I'd let her have my best line, You sure know how to serve a motherfucker up, but instead I give her a polite not-from-the-ghetto response, 'cause I don't know how down she is. But it doesn't take long before I know. Pepsi has washed down the sandwiches. She wraps up the trash and sticks it in the sack it came in. As we hit the Connecticut line, I feel her hand rub my chest. At first I don't think about it and then I realize this woman is a total stranger and this is no gay bar and shit, I don't need no scene on my way to the city.

I pull away and try to be conversational. The weather. Work. School. And all the while she keeps looking deeper and deeper into my eyes. The lights along the train tracks flash through the now-quiet cabin as we rock along the rails. Occasionally the light flickers and I can see the fire in those deep brown orbs flashing and fanning flames of desire. I am consumed by her gaze. Her hand grazes the cotton of my shirt and my nipple, traitress she is, smiles with desirous recognition. As the hand slowly slips beneath my shirt, I watch her face carefully for the startled realization. But it never comes. Instead I hear the coo as she pinches my nipple between her fingers. Oh fuck. This can't be happening. I'm starting my vacation early. She nuzzles her head in closer, careful to loosen a few buttons, giving her better access to the now ripened fruit bursting from my bra. Baby, whatya doing to me. Then she lets me know. Her mouth, warm and hungry, takes that little more-than-a-mouthful all the way inside and I can feel the tingle throughout. My body shakes and I am hungry for more.

She leaps up from the seat and quickly rummages through the compartment overhead. A blanket. Oh, man. This is cozy. The two of us snuggled together under a blanket on the back seat of the night train to The Big Apple. If this is any indication of what my vacation is gonna be like, I want to state for the record right now, Thank you, Jesus. Her hands feel good on my chest and I can't help but lean in and taste those irresistible lips against mine. Sweet, soft, cloud lips. She pulls closer to me, her legs reaching up and over mine. Her smooth skin brushes against my hairy thighs. Wrapping her arms around my neck she nuzzles her face against my cheek, her hot breath lingering in my ear behind each sexy sigh. She adjusts her body so that she sits squarely on my lap. Now I realize that this girl ain't playing and if she is, she ain't playing fair. Baby ain't wearing panties.

Her lips part and close as she slowly gyrates her hips across my thighs. I can feel the moistness before the scent, mixed with the sweat from our over-heated union, rises. Oh man, I want to touch the sista. But I'm no fool. I reach in the front pocket of my bag under the seat, for a little reassurance. I grin at the sound of the latex snapping onto my hand. A good woman is always prepared. And this little honey seems to appreciate it. Kiss me. First just the brush of her lips and then she parts them for me to slip in and anchor my tongue somewhere in the back of her throat. She sucks me hard and slowly strokes the stiff protrusion. I cup her cheeks with my left hand, squeezing them together, and slide one digit down the narrow crack toward the source of her moisture. She moans deeply into my mouth, and stops long enough to beg me to put it in her.

We're riding and swaying with and against the train car, being pulled into our own rhythms. I can feel her riding closer to orgasm as she pulls harder and harder on my tongue. I turn her around and pull her back up off me. Lord knows I want to taste what my nose can smell. We are in the back. I know no one can see, cause if they could, they already would have been back here. I stretch her out across the seat. I crouch down in the corner and get busy. I ain't wasting no time. If I get caught or arrested, I'm at least gonna have a healthy helping on my lips, know what I'm saying?

She spreads her legs for me. The wetness sliding on her lean thighs glistens in the flash of the passing lights. I look at her lips as I stroke them. The passing lights give ample illumination. As I brush the hairs and pull apart her magnificently red and Nubian lips for a better view, the little honey moans deeper and squirms her ass against the rough grain of the seat fabric.

My nostrils take in the scent. I lift my head to drink in long, full breaths deeply. I can feel the heat rising to my cheeks and I long to bury my face inside of her. I want to gorge her with my head and twist it and turn it and feel the wet on my lashes and on my nose hairs. I want to feel my baldness pushing up against her muscles and tickle her with the spikiness of my short, short hair. I want to fill her and feel her clamping my throat with the volcanic spasms of her head-filled pussy. And I want to impregnate her with my smile.

The taste on my tongue like tart candy dances to the back of my throat, just as the conductor announces ten minutes to Penn Station. Now we are racing with the train toward our destinations. My tongue slips inside to molten fire and darts out to taste the flowing lava. I wrap my mouth around her clit sucking and pulling, flicking its tip with my seared oral muscle. I can feel the spasms begin just as the train slows and lights come on and the once sleeping passengers rise around us and I'm thinking of that stupid old song lyric, *If I can make it here, I'll make it anywhere, it's up to you, New York, New York.* And I'm thinking, maybe I will just stay a while.

CATHY McKIM

Ms. Lonely Hearts

Monika enters the bar. Alone. Secures her dark brown leather purse over her right shoulder. Takes a deep breath. Walks into the main room.

She orders a beer. She barely looks at the lovely, young bartender as she hands her a five-dollar bill. The server brushes a dark, curly strand from her eyes as she collects her customer's change. "Thank you," Monika says quietly, leaving a tip.

Finding a space at the support pillar a few feet away, she fumbles in her purse for a pack of cigarettes. Hands shaking slightly, she places a cigarette in her mouth and lights it with an ornate silver lighter. Glancing cautiously around the thin Friday night crowd, she suddenly feels old. Monika is forty-five but her slim build, finely sculpted features, and ash blonde blunt cut easily allow her to pass as forty, or even younger. She looks at her watch, the gold band flashing as it catches the light in the dimness of the room. Ten-twenty. She's ten minutes early.

Taking a slow, final drag of her cigarette, she hears laughter to her left. A group of lesbians, thirty-somethings, are joking with each other. *God, I feel old.* Dismissing the thought, she butts out her cigarette and reaches for her beer. She looks towards the door. The music is loud. Contemporary dance music throbs throughout the bar as young women and a few men move their bodies on the dance floor. She watches them through the window-like opening in the wall that separates the dance area from the lounge. The air grows smokier by the minute. Absently, her right leg moves to the beat, ever so slightly. She takes a long drink.

Ten-thirty. She looks back towards the entranceway.

Ten-thirty-five.

Ten-forty. She peers at the women around her, briskly rubbing her right forearm. She is not cold.

Ten-forty-five. *Maybe she got stuck in traffic.*

Ten-fifty.

Ten-fifty-five. *Maybe I got the time wrong.*

Eleven o'clock. One last desperate glance. *She's not coming.* She downs the last third of her beer. *Who was I kidding? I should have known these things never work out.* Monika recalls how her friends had urged her to write the personal ad:

Attractive, professional GWF, 45, interested in music, theatre movies, long walks, good food and wine seeks soul mate for friendship, poss. relationship.

Responses had been good but something about Karen's letter had touched her deeply. Maybe it was that she'd found an equally solitary kindred spirit reaching out for someone, too. She had called Karen and, after a friendly, hour-long chat, had arranged to meet here, on Karen's request. At this very spot.

It's been over half an hour. She's obviously not coming. Monika's first impulse is to leave immediately. *Maybe she said eleven-thirty, not ten-thirty.* She lights another cigarette. *Maybe I'll meet someone else.* She looks around. Fat chance. She looks in the direction of the bar and notices a petite young woman in jeans and a red shirt ordering a beer. The woman walks past her to rejoin her group in the corner. The gang of laughing lesbians Monika had noticed earlier. *Did she look at me?*

A few minutes later, the woman in red moves to the other side of the room with a friend. They stop to chat near the chest high partition just outside the poolroom. Monika looks at her. And looks away. When she looks again, the woman in red is looking back and smiling. Mortified, Monika looks away, but only after holding the gaze for a moment.

The friend leaves for the poolroom. From the corner of her eye, Monika notices the woman in red taking regular glances in her direction. *Maybe it won't be a complete loss, coming here tonight.* Just then, another woman, entering from the poolroom, approaches the woman in red. They chat for a moment and exit to the poolroom together. *Guess I'm too old for her. Probably for Karen too.* Karen had said she was thirty-five but liked the company of older women. *Hah!*

Moments later, the woman in red emerges from the poolroom alone, but Monika does not notice.

"Excuse me," someone addresses Monika from behind, to her left.

Monika turns. It is the woman in red.

"Would you like to dance?" she continues.

"Oh! No. No, thank you. I'm waiting for someone," Monika stammers. "But I think I've been stood up." She laughs nervously.

"Can I get you a refill, then?" the woman in red nods towards Monika's empty bottle.

"I can get it!" Monika blurts, a little too defensively.

"Okay. Cheers!"

"What?"

"Good luck." And with that, the woman in red heads back to her table of rowdy friends.

Why did I say that? She's too young. A dance wouldn't have hurt. But maybe it would have.

Eleven-fifteen.

Maybe I'll have another beer. She lights another cigarette. She watches. She smokes. She can hardly hear the music for the noise in her head. Why did I come here? Why did I come here? Why did I come here?

A young, blonde femme, younger even than the woman in red, approaches her. "Hi."

"Hi," Monika returns, smiling weakly.

"Are you alone?"

"I was just getting ready to leave."

"Oh. That's too bad. I was going to ask you to dance. Maybe next time," the sweet young thing grins coyly.

"Maybe."

The girl stays in close proximity, chatting with a friend. Not understanding. Not really caring. *God, I feel like a fool.* Monika will make no more responses to replies to her ad. *It's better that way.* Stifling the urge to cry, she butts her cigarette into the full ashtray and adjusts her purse securely on her shoulder. Gets her coat.

And goes home. Alone.

In Zoe's Eyes

Has it really been twenty years? Her name alone still congeals in my belly. She still hasn't married him. Perhaps going to dinner with them, seeing them together, I will finally be able to work through my feelings for her.

He holds both our chairs and orders the wine. He dominates the conversation, in his charming male way. Occasionally I glance at Zoe and catch some far-away look. *Where are you going in that head, my friend?* Dinner finished, he orders the after-dinner drinks. He has not consulted us.

There it is again . . . that foot seeking out mine, under our table. Is this jerk foolish enough to make a pass at her best friend? Wait. It is silken and small. It is Zoe. What are you trying to tell me, little one? We lock eyes, I smoulder, I wonder if that is what I see in Zoe's eyes. Ah! There's that flash of passion I have always loved in her eyes. When he announces the end of our meal and picks up her sweater and bag, she resists.

"Robert, you go ahead and call it a night. I know you have to be up very early," she says. "I think Kay and I are going to stay and talk for a while."

With Robert gone, I curl my feet up under me and we order

another drink. I ask, "When did Roberto become Robert?" We giggle and talk and finish our drinks. Zoe and I have relaxed a bit and gotten pretty loud and merry. It is time to leave the restaurant before we embarrass ourselves. We will visit our lost youth, and take a walking tour of our old haunts. It is so natural when she takes my hand.

"Let me take you back to your hotel and we can sit in the bar for a nightcap," Zoe offers.

I am game and we proceed. Zoe sits on the divan next to me and we talk and giggle some more about our youthful escapades. I touch her face, cup her cheek in my hand. I wonder if she ever knew how much I loved her; still love her. It seems neither of us wants to be the one to call it a night. Then she picks up my key.

"Come on," our eyes meet and I melt on the spot.

We are alone on the elevator. Zoe stands in front of me, leaning into my body. I am just a head taller and I can smell her hair. I am consumed and transfixed by some intoxication. It is old but familiar. Now in the room, I hear the snap of the double bolt and my Zoe is gliding across the room to me. Our kiss is deep and transports us to a time so long ago, when this is where we would have to stop "practice kissing." This is no practice. We did all that so many years ago.

Who started undressing whom? I cannot tell you. Kisses so deep and ardent, soft sweet breasts, slightly damp down; we are all mouth and hands. This is where we become lost in each other. We come swiftly and in synch, only to slow down to savour the pitch of *the petite mort*. How many times can one arch and explode before the dream ends?

We speak of time, of undying attraction. I awaken to a pink rose on the pillow next to me and a note. "I overlooked something I had to do this morning, we'll talk."

This is nuts. Do I have to lose her again to the charade of convention? I dress for my business meeting. I am flying back to L.A. this afternoon. I know that our precious time, if it is all we are to have, will remain with me forever and never be enough.

Before leaving I check for messages, but there are none. At the airport I select a trashy novel to keep me company on the flight home. Embarking now, I am told by the flight attendant that I have been upgraded to first class. I am shown to my seat and my flight-mate lifts her sunglasses.

"I've ordered our drinks," Zoe says.

"What are you doing?"

She covers my mouth with a kiss. Our drinks arrive and we toast serendipity.

"Do you have room for a house-guest while I sort out my life and are you free to help sort?"

Knowing I will accommodate anything she wants, I simply nod my head and give my heart completely over to her.

Flowergirl

I'm lusting after my brother's girlfriend. She's got long raven hair and large tits and my cunt throbs every time she's near me.

"Wanna play tennis today, Liza? Bob won't be home till later, and there's some free court time."

I'm wearing short shorts and a t-shirt with *no balls pass here* written on it. She's wearing a black tennis skirt—and a tank top.

I'm already hot when we get to the court. It's eighty degrees out, and the net is starting to sag from the humidity.

"Better tighten it up," Liza says, and goes to crank it tight.

"Will you be staying up here for the summer, or going back to the States?" I ask. I'm acting nonchalant, hitting a ball against the tarmac, not looking at her. "I mean . . . will you be staying at our place?"

She tests the net for resistance, and then walks back to the other side of the court. "Maybe. Your serve."

We volley for a while and then take a break when a crowd assembles for spots. We didn't sign up, so we have to wait.

"I think I might stay up here, yeah. Bob doesn't want to live in Connecticut this summer, so I guess it's my turn. Why do you ask?"

I rub my feet against the tarmac. "I don't know. . . ." The fence rings as a missed ball ricochets back into the court. "I don't have a sister . . . I like playing with you. . . ."

"I'd like to stay," she says, linking her arm in mine. "We're becoming quite good friends."

It's only May seventeenth and the weather is just as hot as ever. Bob and Liza do a lot together: swimming, canoeing, jogging. It's a familiar scene: she's in the basement bedroom, Bob's in his old bedroom upstairs, and I'm in my room masturbating.

I want Liza to touch me instead of touching Bob.

My final school exams are coming up, and the next time Liza returns, she'll be here for the summer. I can't wait.

But the only time I'll get to see her is if Bob is already busy.

She's a rich girl; she doesn't even have to work. Her parents own a town or something. Bob worked on their gardens last year. That's how he met Liza.

"I just took one look at him and boom—that was it," she told me once over onion rings. "Don't you have a boyfriend yet, Cynthia? I'll bet you lots are interested."

I sucked hard on the bubbles at the bottom of my shake.

"I mean," she added, "I find you very attractive." She placed one hand over mine.

I have to make sure we get court time this week. Liza's folks have their own courts, so she's not used to having to book them.

"You have to call in Monday to save a Saturday spot," I call to her from behind the shower curtain. "If you wait till too late in the week, you won't get in."

I can hear the electric shaver through the roar of the shower spray. I'm too young to shave.

"I'll get right on it, Captain!" I hear the razor buzz stop, and Liza leaves with a click of the bathroom door.

I turn off the water.

After we get to the court on Saturday, she asks me again about boys. I just wish she'd stop. "I know this nice caddy at the golf course. I could introduce you—I'm sure you'd hit it off."

Her serve goes right over my head. I'm playing a terrible game.

The longer we play together, the harder it is to keep from watching her breasts. The game is finally over and I lose.

"We aren't supposed to be saying anything," Liza says, grabbing her bottle and towel, "but Bob and I are engaged." She tucks her racket beneath one arm and walks to where I'm standing. "Don't you think that's great? Now we'll really be sisters!" She wraps her other arm around me and walks us off the court. I take my water and dump it over my head.

By the time we reach the passenger door of her car, my stomach is feeling queasy. I'm sick from the heat and the disappointment. She'll marry Bob. They'll move away. I'll see her less than ever.

"Oh, wait," she says, eyeing my dripping hair. "Let me get those drops." She towels my head briskly, saying something about how I'll be a bridesmaid. "Flowers . . . your favourites . . . pick out something you like. . . ."

I peer out from beneath the terrycloth, seeing only her lips.

ELIZABETH   ROWAN

Bride

My best friend's wedding. If she were really my best friend she would not be putting me through this. And in a pink dress, too. I was to be chief bridesmaid to my ex-lover. She was marrying a man, in a church, wearing a fluffy white dress, and the poor maids were to wear pink. Pretty pastel pink. I hated all of it, but I still loved her enough to do it, hoping of course that she would have a change of heart at the last minute and ditch him at the altar. Then of course I would be there to console and comfort her.

The day dawned bright and clear. I dragged myself out of bed and threw on some old faded jeans and a t-shirt, picked up my makeup bag, and left for Julia's house. We were to meet for breakfast and spend the day preparing for the ceremony, which was to take place that afternoon in the local village church. All the bridesmaids were dressing at Julia's, but they would not arrive until later.

"Hello, Sam, come in," Mrs. Jacobson, Julia's mother, said. "Breakfast is ready, but Julia has not shown her face yet. I'm off home to sort the rest of the family out. Can I leave her in your hands?"

"Sure, we'll be fine," I said. "See you later." Soon she was gone, scurrying down the path. I poured two cups of tea, picked up some toast, and went up to Julia's bedroom. Julia was lying awake on the bed, pale, eyes staring. Putting down the breakfast tray, I sat on the edge of the bed and took her hand.

"Julia, what's wrong, Babe?" I had always called her Babe when she was unhappy.

"I'm not sure. Is that tea for me? It's just like old times, breakfast in bed!" Her hand lingered on mine as she took the tea. I drew away; she had pre-wedding nerves, that was all. I must control myself.

"Come on," I said, "let's go and get some fresh air. You look like you need it and we have plenty of time."

She threw on some old clothes and we left the house, wandering through the woodland until we came upon the back of the church. Julia stopped and took my hand.

"Do you remember we used to dream of getting married here?"

I remembered. How could I forget? We used to come here and talk and make love. Julia was still pale, but she smiled at me, moved close and put her head on my shoulder.

"I miss you, Sam. Make me happy?"

Gently I kissed her lips. "It'll be okay."

"No," she said, "I need you, I need you now, make me happy."

She straightened up and looked me in the eye. Then she kissed me hard and long. I could not resist that. I had dreamt of it for so long. I kissed her back passionately and pushed her against the wall of the church, my hands running over her body. She did not touch me back, but I was on fire, breathing heavy, pulse racing. I found the button of her jeans, opened it and pulled them down, pushed her t-shirt up, and then lowered her to the ground. Greedily I took a nipple into my mouth and sucked hard. I heard music and it took a few seconds to realize it was the bridal march from inside the church. We seemed to be intruding on someone else's special day. Julia turned over and wriggled her bottom at me. She did not seem to mind if we had company or not. I bit her bottom, then licked it and sucked it, pushing my tongue into her crack, trying to reach her juicy pussy. She lifted her hips a little to aid me and I tasted her. It was good. I knelt behind her, pulling her up onto all fours, one hand slipping fingers inside her, the other finding her breasts and teasing her nipples.

"Make me come, Sam, make me happy."

I knew what she liked. I pinched harder at her nipples and moved my other hand in and out, faster and faster. She pushed back at me.

"More, Sam. I want more."

It was a hoarse cry, but I heard it and responded, faster and faster, harder and harder, until I heard her pull in a deep breath and hold it. Her whole body tensed and then with her exhaled breath, I felt the ripples of ecstasy go through her, crushing my hand with their intensity. She cried out, a moan, then a sob, and then silence. I lay beside her and we kissed.

"We'd better be going," I said, looking at my watch wistfully, even though I was very horny. The last thing I wanted to do was get ready for a wedding.

Back at the house, the other bridesmaids had arrived and were worried at our absence. But we calmed them and got ready. At 3:15 our car arrived and took us to the church. Again we stood outside together.

"What will you do?" I asked.

"I'm not sure yet," she said and strode down the aisle to the strains of the tune we'd heard earlier.

L I Z A R D   J O N E S

I Can't Stand
the Rain . . .

My dear little one,

It's raining. I can hear it regular and soft on the fire escape. When I look out, the plants glisten, the chair glistens. On the street the cars glisten.

You would glisten, too, if you were here. But you're not. A week Tuesday a week Tuesday a week Tuesday.

A week Tuesday, I will pick you up at the airport. You'll be wearing jeans, a t-shirt, regular clothes. You'll look at me expectantly. Your lips will pucker for me to kiss them.

But no kissing for a long time a week Tuesday. You'll be waiting for the kiss, and I'll turn to the luggage carousel and look for your bag. You'll ask for a kiss. "Not yet," I'll say. "Here's your bag now."

We'll walk side by side to the car, me carrying your bag impenetrable between us. You'll stand beside me when I pay for parking, open the trunk, open your door. I'll feel you there next to me. It might be too much for me to bear, your sharp tense breasts, your tilted hip. But I will bear it.

When you reach for my ass I will know, and my "No" will come fast and decisive.

We will ride in the car, in familiar seats, familiar streets. The gear shift will be there between us now. You will be nervous. You won't know what to do. I will feel your eyes on my hand as I shift gears. My hand as it flexes and moves from wheel to gear shift a little like I move from air to cunt, thrusting. Just for you. For your eyes. As I enter each gear, I will moan, just a little.

I will glance over and see your hands balanced, one on each thigh, still, restless. Those hands that I dream about, those thighs that I dream about, the denim that I envy as it nestles between them. Maybe you will move your hands on your thighs, stretch your fingers back. My cunt will jump.

We will both be thinking about home, when I will let us touch. But not yet. I have plans. Someone else's house, coffee, dessert.

When I park, you will look at me, wanting me, frustrated, angry.

"Laila really wants to see you," I will say. She will be at the door. Sheila and Ray will be inside. We will sit and make small talk. You will tell them about your trip, you will bring out your presents. I will watch your body bend, I will feel my own hands longing for the fold of your stomach, for the nipples that show through your shirt, for the hair on your head that you rub back and forth. We will sit on the sofa and you will not touch me. When your hand creeps over, or you lean into me to make more room, I will stand up, dizzy with lust.

"Please," you will say when you are offered something. It is a plea to me. I will remember it.

When we leave and we get to the car, you will beg me to go home.

"Why?" I will say when we are driving away. You know I know, but I will make you say it.

"So I can fuck you," you will say.

"What's another night without touching?" I'll say.

"Please," you'll say again.

And I won't be able to pull it off. You'll be able to see the hunger in my eyes and ears and hands and lips, the hunger I have lived with for what must be forever now, and by a week Tuesday will have distended my stomach, parched my throat, made me delirious.

To see you and hear you, and be with you will be too much. I won't be able to stop. But I will stop. I will drive the car. You will say you are hot and take off your shirt. You will say you are hot and loosen your jeans. I will drive, hands clenched on the wheel.

You will laugh at me and tease me.

"I guess I'll just touch myself," you'll say.

Until my denial comes out loud and short and scratchy, crazier and crazier. I have waited so long. A week Tuesday will be longer. To have you near me, and not be touching. It will fill the car, swell my tongue, fog my eyes. Crazy.

I will stop the car. I will shove back the seat. Now will be the kiss. I will kiss every inch of you, especially your lips, raised wet and ready to mine. Your tongue, your teeth. I will bite your lip till you gasp. I will look at your flushed throat, I will feel your hands on my breasts. I will climb on top of you and ride your fingers, I will feel your nails on my bare buttocks, your sharp relentless teeth. I will turn you over and fuck you from behind, I will pull your hair. I will tell you to scream. I won't have to tell you to scream.

I miss you I miss you I miss you.

A week Tuesday, all this will happen. Till then, the rain.

She Warned Me

She warned me already. She warned me that, when she picks me up at the train station, she might just kiss me hard and then push my head roughly into her lap. She warned me that she might be packing and expect me to take her down my throat right there, in the sunny, suburban Kiss-and-Ride parking lot outside the station.

When she arrives, grinning beneath her dark shades, I throw my bag in the back seat and get into the car, a little clumsy with nerves. She guns the motor and pulls onto the highway back to her house, just glancing at me for a moment and telling me about her day at work. I'm in a state that seesaws between relief and disappointment. I'm conscious of my tongue in my mouth, though, and that swollen, thirsty longing in the back of my throat.

Jittery, I stumble behind her into her house. It's good to be back here again. The happy greeting from her big German shepherd distracts me completely from all my erotic anticipation and that's when she takes me, getting in my face, kissing me and pushing me back against the kitchen wall in one movement. A twisting movement of her hips against me lets me know she *is* packing, the hard cock under her jeans pushing against my crotch. I moan and kind of slip down against her.

She chuckles, very pleased. "Oh. You like that?"

There's a leer in her voice that puts me into the mental space that's been at the outside of my consciousness ever since I got off the train. That's what's kept me off balance all this time. But now, her cock up against me and her voice so lecherous and knowing, I just slide right into the space, whimpering a little and enjoying the feeling of my knees going weak.

She abruptly steps back. Unbuttons her jeans. Unzips the denim. I'm moaning as she pushes me to my knees and shoves her cock in my mouth.

Oh god, this is what I've thought about since she first warned me. My mouth full of her dick, my throat assaulted by it, my tongue all over it and being able to suck it as hard as I can, over and over. Her fingers are in my hair, urging me to take more and I can hear her running commentary from above, hear her saying, "Good girl," or "Oh yeah," or just groaning as I take another inch of her dick down my throat. This is what I've thought about while I masturbated alone in my bed, rubbing my clit with one hand and working a dildo in and out of my mouth with the other.

Now it's for real. She's sliding it in and out, like I like, like I've fantasized, fucking my mouth with the same mixture of ruthlessness and tenderness she uses when she's fucking my cunt. Just when she gets a good rhythm and it starts to be easy, sucking her, she changes it, shocking me and making me moan around it.

Her other hand, the one not holding my head on her cock, reaches down and squeezes my nipple through my blouse. I feel the pain-pleasure jolt in my pussy, feel myself get wetter than I am already, and I feel my throat open up. I'm inhaling her cock now, my lips all the way up the hilt. "Oh yeah," she murmurs urgently, "suck it, suck it." I can feel my eyes rolling up in my head as the head of her dick slides down my throat. A gag reflex washes over me, making my nose run and tears roll down my cheeks. It passes and I'm even wetter than I was before. I'm choking on my butch's cock and I'm going to have my first orgasm any second and her hand pinches my nipple, viciously, and I go over the top, coming *hard*, waves of contractions hitting my cunt, losing my senses and lost in my senses and for the duration of it, I'm sucking her harder than I thought possible.

Pretty soon, I know, she's going to pull out of my mouth and fuck the hell out of me, but I'm not thinking about that now. Right now, heaven is coming while I suck my butch's cock.

JEANNE CORDOVA

Cheap Gold:
A Seduction

I named my new affair-mate, Melrose, after the fleshpot boule-vard in West Hollywood, California where I live. Melrose Avenue was gaudy, slick, and sleekly adorned with shops that catered to kink and chic. My Melrose was packaged just as darkly.

I met her at the gay Lammy Writers' Award banquet in Las Vegas. What drew me to her was the way her black crepe hat arched revealingly over one eye. Or maybe it was the fact that she dared to wear a black crepe hat that arched over one eye at a P.C. writers' convention. Or the fact that she would purposefully dress like a slut at a political gathering. Or that a lesbian would dare appear as a slut anywhere. These were the early nineties. Politically correct was not just jargon, it was still code. Or maybe what turned me on were her elbow-length black gloves. Her clothed pinky finger caressed her lips when she wasn't sipping her Perrier. Her smallest finger was bound by a tiny cheap gold ring, which glistened under the banquet room's chandeliers. From ten tables away, I could tell Melrose was cheap gold.

But it was really the veil that I found irresistible. The veil that kissed her top lip like I wanted to. The black mesh veil that covered her face demanded that I stare at her long enough to make sure she stared back. Only madonnas wore veils in public, but Melrose was no lady.

It took less than a minute for her to return my stare. Her bold smile discreetly acknowledged me. Mutual climaxes satisfied me.

But presumption was running away with me. We hadn't met. There was a very large room and two hundred people between us. How to get from point A to point B and still make a soft landing? But not too soft.

Turned out Melrose didn't like soft, and she didn't like waiting. I'd been distracted by keynote speaker Dorothy Allison's insistence that writers shed blood on the page. During the standing ovation, Melrose had swept across the room. She stood in front of me now.

"The view is even better up close," she said, surveying my Jones New York dinner jacket and tie. Her blue eyes backlit her veil. She reached out and flipped my Parisian silk tie. "Nice pattern."

"You've got some pretty original patterns yourself," I managed, trying to regain my butch psyche.

"I'm glad you're not going to tell me you weren't staring at me all evening." She smiled. Her smile was like a warm wave that hits you when you're not looking. And I was looking.

"No, I'm not going to tell you that," I admitted, "but let's go somewhere we won't be interrupted. The speeches don't seem to interest you."

The hotel's cocktail bar was almost empty now, hours after the last workshop.

"Why did you come to a writer's convention?" I began politely. "You don't seem the literary type."

Melrose tossed back her head. "I'm an erotic writer, or a writer of erotica if you prefer. I went to the S & M workshop. See if I was doing things right," she said, smiling.

"I imagine you do it quite rightly," I replied gallantly.

"Thank you." Her black-gloved forearm reached across me for her drink. Her arm fell against mine, and stayed.

I watched her aluminum-studded leather bracelets clink against her bourbon. "I see you're already into S & M. Why bother going to the workshop?" I asked, fingering her metal.

"What a thing to say!" Melrose pouted and withdrew her arm.

But her lips curled into a smile. "You're putting me on the spot."

"Being on the spot is better than being on the edge, don't you think?"

"What do you know about edges?"

"What do you know about S & M?"

"They're not S & M bracelets, they're heavy metal. Everyone wears them."

"You shouldn't advertise falsely."

"There's nothing false about my advertising. I'm in marketing for a living," Melrose said with some exasperation. You'd think she'd had just been asked to make the Northwest Passage. She crossed her metal wrists over one another, encircling my ashtray. She spun it with her fingers.

"I don't know what you mean, exactly."

"Now that's false advertising," her smile drew me into her veiled eyes. "A downright lie, I think."

I speared her cherry from her bourbon and coke with a toothpick and held it up in front of her.

"You don't give a girl much room." Her lips plucked the cherry off its perch.

I eyed the two straight male patrons sitting in the corner as I put my arm around Melrose's waist. "How much room do you need?"

"Very little. And you?"

"The same. So why don't we leave and go to my hotel room?" I offered, concluding the negotiation. "I'll show you my short stories."

"No," Melrose commanded as she slid off her barstool. "Let's go to my condo. I don't travel without my make-up. A lady never brings a suitcase on the first date."

Melrose unlocked the door and we stepped into her manicured black and chrome dungeon, decorated with artificial palms and department store crystal. A white rayon couch spotted with black silk cushions sat atop a deep charcoal carpet. As I slouched against the sliding glass door of her second-storey balcony, my shoulders crushed her equally spotless vertical mini-blinds. I wondered if she ever opened them to allow in the desert sun.

Perhaps Melrose didn't need the light to market herself.

"A little light?" Her voice parted the shadows between us. She stood leaning against the couch. She peeled off her elbow-length velvet gloves.

"We don't need light," I confirmed. I watched her skirt rise as she leaned over the fireplace and stuck a long rod into the darkness. There was a flash of flame. My eyes closed.

"You can open up now," she said.

I opened my eyes to the soft flicker of chemical incandescence. Melrose stood in front of me. She purred as she reached out and brushed her fingers along the back of my neck. Our lips met. I pulled Melrose closer, and then down.

Aunt Rose

The first femme in my life was my Auntie Rose. When I was a child she was young, beautiful, glamorous, and a little crazy. One time, when Aunt Rose was first dating Uncle Marvin, she raced into our house and begged my mother to let her take me out for the day. She wanted to see what Marvin was like with children before she decided to marry him. My mother must have agreed because moments later I was sitting between them in the front seat of Marvin's 1957 Chevy convertible, my five-year-old legs stretched straight out in front of me. I looked from one to the other and then ahead, excited. I was out on a date with my aunt and her boyfriend.

Even at the age of five, I was a butch. As we drove, I studied Marvin. He sat behind the wheel with his legs spread wide, so I spread mine, too. When Marvin would turn to talk to my aunt, he raised his eyebrows and smiled at her with one side of his mouth. Sometimes he'd slick back his hair with the palm of his right hand. I tried all of his moves. My aunt laughed and ruffled my hair affectionately. The nails on her hands were long and painted red, and sitting close to her like that, I could smell her perfume. I turned to watch her as she crossed her legs, adjusted her skirt, and looked over at Marvin. They were talking about grown-up things

I couldn't understand, so I sat quietly, listening and watching.

It was a warm spring day. Aunt Rose said she was hot as she undid the top three buttons on her sweater. Marvin glanced over and stared at her open neck, his eyes wide. The car in front of us came to a sudden stop, but Marvin didn't see. I tugged on his shirt sleeve and pointed.

"Oh my God!" he blurted and slammed on the brakes.

We were all thrown forward into the dashboard. My face slammed into the hard chrome knob of the built-in radio. We came to a stop inches behind the other car. For a moment, we sat in stunned silence.

"Everyone okay?" Marvin asked, rubbing his shoulder.

"Oh my God!" Aunt Rose stared at me. "Marvin, look what you've done!"

Blood spilled from somewhere, dripping onto my pants. I tasted something salty in my mouth and my lip was tingling. Aunt Rose fiddled in her purse and pulled out a white lace hanky to wipe my face.

"Bobby, honey, does it hurt?"

I shook my head. I didn't feel anything and was enjoying the attention. As she leaned over, I could see right down her shirt. I tried to imagine what it was about seeing her breasts that caused Marvin to forget he was driving.

"Her lip is split wide open," Aunt Rose snarled at him. "We'll have to take her home now." My aunt pulled me onto her lap and, holding the hanky over my wound, she nestled me against her bosom and held me there all the way home.

M O N I C A   L E E

Hands of Clay

I stare into her world, watching long brown fingers melt into the reddish clay. The pale glow of her lamp creates a soft outline of curves, silhouetting heavy breasts leaning closer to the spiraling wheel. I watch from the negotiated safety of my perch, a safe distance for both of us, encased in our own armour.

Night chases away day's long dusk-coloured coat, and I do not stir, lured in by the fingers deep in the damp clay, entranced by the torso protectively curved over the spinning wheel. I watch, mesmerized until the moon comes out to take my place, to play witness in my absence and to recount our secrets, as we lie in the solace of our own longing. In the faint glow of the knowing moon, we prepare to shed our first layers of skin bruised by the past, to leave them to dissipate in the midnight sky.

Tonight I feel the hot rush of knowing the moment will come when she will invite me in for a drink, and I will hungrily accept with a body aching with a thirst that can be solely quenched by her smooth brown hands. She will lie patiently on the bed, which has escaped the fate of clay dust, watching as I unbutton my skirt and let it drop to the floor. I shall slide the sheer black nylons slowly down my waist, past impatient thighs, continuing down my calves

173

to let one foot out, then the other. She will watch with lips slightly parted as I unbutton my shirt to open my vulnerable body to her as each sleeve slips off my arms. Parched by my burning thirst, I will wait in turn until she pours herself into me, my head setting between her thighs like the sun that will too soon reveal our entangled bodies drunk with our own sweet wine. In that moment, her body will call my name, back arched with the same anticipation of tired eyes ready to be bathed by her.

Until then, I shall experience her world, discover this mysterious being as she spins her anticipation at the wheel, and I whisper to her from the moon.

J E A N   R O B E R T A

War Story

The once-sleepy village was in flaming ruins. Chloris (as she is known to the Greeks) and I rode between the huts, watching for snipers. She saw the young man aiming at us before I did, and dropped him with one arrow to the chest. Chloris is one of the best shots in the army. I probably rely on her more than I should; being paired with her encourages me to be reckless.

I don't like raids, but I do my duty. I would rather kill than be killed or taken captive. The noble men of Greece offer us no other choices.

A young woman with loose raven hair flowing over her shoulders came out of her hut and stood watching us. The figure of an old man lay in his own blood in the single room they had shared. She had probably been married to him as a girl, and now she was a young widow. Her eyes were dry.

The wench reached up to one shoulder. Calmly, without fear or haste, she undid her chiton and let it drop to the ground. The gesture was bold and clear. She stood naked in the bright sunlight, her plump breasts standing up like watchful animals. The triangle of hair between her legs was as black as the hair on her head.

I could no more fathom her motives than I could gossip in village Greek, but my ignorance of these things didn't trouble me at the time.

Chloris wanted to ride past, ignoring what the young woman showed to us. I could not be so rude. I dismounted and secured my horse to a post. Smiling, the wench seized one of my hands and led me to a small storage hut.

Luckily, words seemed unnecessary. I wrapped her in my arms, burying my face in her fragrant hair. She smelled like figs and oil and dust and sweat. It was a rich smell that was strongest in the curves between her neck and her smooth shoulders. Her breasts squeezed against my ribs, pressing my heart. I lifted her to feel her weight, and she was lighter than my weapons. She pushed herself against one of my thighs so that I could feel the hot moisture below her belly. When I looked into her eyes, I saw that they were dark greenish-grey, the colour of a storm cloud.

I pulled off my cloak and folded it for her to lie on. She seemed pleased, although the protection I offered was little enough. She spread her legs, raised her knees, and invited me with her eyes to worship at her altar.

I recklessly shed my war-shirt and pants, then removed the pouch that holds my little bronze wand, the thing we sometimes call "the sword of peace." I showed it to her, rubbing it in my hands, then I let her hold it so it would be warm enough for her flesh. Some women prefer being entered by cold metal, but I never assume that any woman has such a taste unless she tells me so.

I squatted between my little sweetheart's legs to part the thick black hair and peer into the wet folds within. I kissed the eager guardian at her entrance, and felt it jump in my mouth like a sleeper who has suddenly been awakened. I pulled it gently with my teeth and licked it as it grew. I explored her soft cave with my tongue, and found it as hot and tasty as any I have known.

She seemed to tremble on the edge of release for a long time, unable or unwilling to surrender. She seemed to be waiting for my wand, which she reached for as though she wanted to use it herself. Laughing, I kissed it before carefully guiding it into her warm opening. She welcomed it with her whole body.

Despite her boldness, the little widow seemed too stubborn or too afraid to let herself enjoy the climax she clearly wanted. I craved the satisfaction of outwitting that part of her which was (perhaps, who knows?) still loyal to the dead, or still committed to resistance.

I am sure it was something other than my skill at loveplay that caused the beauty beneath me to writhe on my wand in an unmistakable way as she cried out like a woman in pain. I heard the commander's footsteps before she appeared at the entrance of the hut. She undoubtedly caught a glimpse of my little lover before I managed to wrap her in my cloak. Whether the officer was moved by what she saw, I will probably never know. Those who rise through the ranks are usually those with the greatest self-control, and my own likelihood of finding glory in the army was painfully clear to me even before this episode. The commander gave me a look and a gesture, then strode away with a contemptuous swing of her cloak.

I hoped I had rewarded my companion enough for the generous gift of her body, because our idyll was over and I could give her nothing more. The commander had said we would not be taking captives in this raid.

The little widow did not seem heartbroken when I kissed her goodbye, but maybe that was a sign that she has more of the officer in her than I do.

If you can hear my thoughts, child of Aphrodite, I prayed to your goddess and mine for your protection. If my tribe seems cold or brutal to you, remember that we are constantly under threat from your brothers. If they succeed, we will be destroyed. I still don't believe that a desire to kill is part of our nature (or even part of theirs), but I have no power to end this monstrous game. I can only wage peace when I have the chance, and I treasure my memories of such subversion.

SHIRLEY WILLIAMSON

A Viennese Whirl

It is a time of Christmas fancy dress balls, of sleigh rides, of lusty affairs and hot-tempered duels. This is glittering Salzburg and Mozart has just finished *The Magic Flute*.

The virgin snow has given the city a fairytale landscape. How many people have been poisoned by a belief in fairy tale endings?

On this cold evening Elspeth has her lover lying on a fur in front of a roaring fire. Constanze is blinded by lust. Theirs is a clandestine meeting. Outside winter has a hold. Inside, it is summer. Elspeth is feeding her lover fruits gathered from far away places—strawberries, melons, quinces, pears, peaches—brought especially to please Constanze, the most beautiful *femme fatale* in the city. Constanze is married, of course, to an old merchant from Vienna, but she will kill him off with neglect.

"Johann!" Constanze giggles as Elspeth dangles a plump cherry out of reach of her lips. "You are such a tease."

"The best things are those tasted least often."

Elspeth is dressed in a man's image. She is tall and athletic enough to pass and Constanze believes her to be barely out of boyhood. She is the only surviving child of dead parents. On their demise she inherited a tutor, a cook, vast wealth, and her dead twin brother's clothes.

Elspeth looks admiringly at the slender body of her older lover. She can appreciate why Constanze is famed for her sexual prowess; the firm breasts and the curve of her hips are seductive.

Since autumn she has poured every ounce of passion her youthful frame could muster into stoking Constanze's furnace and molten it is, too.

Every social function Constanze attended with her cuckolded husband she, too, attended. Dressed in male attire, she put herself in front of Constanze until she saw no other; only the pale face with grey eyes.

There could be no indifference, nor was there, and Constanze made plain her desire for a more intimate acquaintance with the blond adolescent.

A rapier-wielding cavalry officer decided on a duel. He lost. Blood added to the intensity of Constanze's lust.

For Elspeth, tempting her is easy. Constanze thinks with her cunt.

Elspeth speaks softly to her, seducing her with words that tumble off her tongue and melt inside Constanze's mouth. Elspeth knows the slipperiness of Constanze's mouth.

She undresses her slowly, sliding her hands around Constanze's neck and over her collar bone. She lingers on her breasts, sometimes lightly pinching her nipples, before pausing to run her hands over the small hollow of her back. All of this accompanied by penetrating, passionate kisses. After this pleasure there is more to come. Constanze guides Elspeth's hand under the feminine silk, between modesty and desire, to her wetness. Elspeth's fingers dance with her clit before slipping deep inside, touching Constanze where she lives.

Elspeth indulges her, massages her skin with fragrant oils, working between her thighs until she groans and screams with pleasure.

The only thing Elspeth denies Constanze is herself. She will not allow Constanze between her legs or her secret will be exposed. She will not be seen naked nor will she cock fuck Constanze. She allows only long embraces and lingering kisses. In short, Elspeth is driving Constanze to the edge of sexual delirium; she is feverish, hot and bothered, raving and begging for that final consummation.

Elspeth pops a cherry into Constanze's mouth.

"When?" Constanze swallows. "When will you take all of me?"

"Tomorrow night." Elspeth allows Constanze the briefest grope of her false, rigid cock. She captures Constanze's thoughts and whispers into her ear all the wonderful things she will do to her the following night.

No man has ever denied Constanze for so long.

Elspeth moves away when Constanze tries to unbutton her shirt. "Tomorrow, my love, you will get what you truly deserve."

They kiss deeply.

Constanze is flushed with desire. "God, I need you so badly. I will die from wanting you."

Elspeth does not answer, but licks the drops of fruit juice that have splashed onto Constanze's belly before kissing and licking her way down to that famous cunt.

She manages not to laugh, for her plan is working better than she could ever have hoped. Constanze is ripe for picking.

Does Elspeth love Constanze? No, she hates her with a passion. Constanze has deprived her of the one thing Elspeth longs for, her Viennese lover. It was Elspeth's lover who had been destined to marry the rich old merchant. Elspeth had planned to move in with them as his young wife's companion.

Then in waltzed the beautiful and dangerous Constanze, on the look-out for a rich, pliable husband. They were married while Elspeth was away in Switzerland learning to be a lady. When she returned to Vienna she learned that her future was behind her.

The only one she will ever love has been sent to an undisclosed convent in a foreign land: obscure, forgotten, gone.

Elspeth wants revenge. She has no intention of ever seeing Constanze again.

Constanze will take other lovers, but in her heart she will always compare them to the lustful Viennese youth who vanished in a whirl of snowdust.

MARIA DE LOS RIOS

La Gaita

La Gaita is riot, grace, prayer, romance, poetry, protest, satire, revelation, celebration, invocation, magic. When the statue of Baralt witnesses Yahaira and her *gaiteras* tune their drums and four-string guitars, stone eyes look plaintively into the hot Maracaibo sky, asking passing clouds, "What did I do to deserve this plaza?"

Every Sunday morning women walk to their market stands at sunrise. Baskets overflowing with fresh ripe tropical fruit gracefully balance on top of their heads. The swing of their hips keep the rhythm of this broad plain with fertile soils and copious water bodies. The Caribbean Alisian wind arrives at the gulf from the northeast, seeps through old dirt-covered streets, smashes against thin blossom skirts, lifts them in the air caressing strong legs, proceeds along its course until it crashes against the Sierras, the Andean range. There, the suave breeze turns to heavy rain as if to comply with a prophetic mission. As these merchants with colourful flowery skirts, white cotton tops, and hip-hop moves walk in procession to their booths, *las gaiteras* park in front of *la Zapateria Alba*, unload *maracas, claves, furrucos, tamboras, llaves*, and join the perspiring parade, gathering at the corner of Fin de Siglo to take a breath. Maracaibo is the hottest land on earth.

The statue of Baralt sweats as strong mujeres carry their drums, *furras, furrucos,* and *tamboras.* These Amazonian women know how to stir centro, ancestors, plaza. They know how to play the soul, the bones of the death, with dazzling rhythm, passionate fire, iridescent strength. "*A la bella, bella, bella, a la bella, bella, bella va.*" Eleodina clears her voice.

In the heart of *la plaza,* the women vendors wait expectantly behind the fresh and vivid scenery of juicy fruits and crunchy vegetables. The rainbow of colours vibrates. The passion and intensity of the music mixes with the scent of celery, sweet onions, green peppers and ripe tomatoes, makes a salsa of bright tones, crisp musical notes, spicy poetry, irreverent wisdom, zesty flavor.

"*Que me voy, que me voy, que me voy y no vuelvo mas.*
Chiviri, chiviri, chiviri Caballito blanco veni pa'ca."

When Yahaira sings, plays *la furra,* the melody vibrates, she glorifies her protest, a rally which rises from her underside with gusto, arrogance, self-respect, *como debe ser.*

I recall how the fire travelled from my chest to neck, cheeks, ears, down my spine, to my crotch, the first time I watched Yahaira's muscular arms bang the furra stick up and down the tight hole in the centre of the drum's dry-pressed skin. The sexual encounter between her hands and the drum provoked urges I repressed for months. The crave to bite her protruding cheeks, suck her sweaty lips, savour every inch of her roasted-almond, wildflower honey-covered skin, possessed me. Every week, I played hide and seek, fantasizing about this hot, spicy, and juicy *mamacita.* That late afternoon at the plaza, I desired to eat her alive, digest her rhythm, absorb her intensity. Like grandmother Chepa used to say, ask and you shall receive. "*Ay mi patrona de La Chichinquira,* let this hot *mami* notice me."

After a few seconds, she looked in my direction. Yahaira smiled, stroked the surface of the drum, pushed the stick into the hole, made love to it. It dove deep into the dry skin. Sin *despegar los ojo,* she slowed the beat. Her hands stopped fondling the stick, caressed the skin, grabbed *la charrasca* from her partner's hands. As she approached me, she raised the instrument over her head, keeping the beat, lustfully electrifying the dancing crowd with charged hips, taking my breath away. Her hands made the *charrasca* weep, screech, scream. My imagination fled.

My hunger transformed into prayer. My prayer evolved into lust. In that portal of sweat and passion, the door into a juicy, steamy world opened as her pelvic bone rhythmically banged mine. We danced, taking each other in public, *como quien quiere la cosa*, no shame, no apology. Her soft voice whispered in my ear. *"Que rica mami."* Deyanira released a scream. *"Menealo mi sangre."* Eleodina joined. *"Asi, cosa rica."* A state of carnival trance, street fiesta, erotic mardi gras radiated from the core of this plaza.

At this point, women vendors left their merchandise behind, joined the comparsa. Eleodina jerked the *furra*. The drum's heartbeat penetrated folds, mouths, vaginas. The musical notes had lips, tongues, hands. The melody nuzzled hips, asses, legs. Its beat pinched, bit, sucked erect nipples. The *gaita* transposed from celebration to riot, and from riot to collective orgy. When the music, *el coje culo*, ceased, we embraced ecstasy, shared sweats, grins, kisses, and returned temporarily satisfied to our thing, lo nuestro, with renewed energies.

The sun hid behind the temple of Our Lady of Chiquinquira. Pulled by Yahaira's strong heavy hand, I followed the swing of her wide tight ass to the old *moriche* house with the uneven boardwalk. Its angled legs stood firm above the coffee-coloured surface of Maracaibo Lake. We made out with our clothes on, then again naked as we came to the world, with teeth and tongues, suavely and roughly. As night fell, the tide rose, the dark of moonlit waters slapped against my womb. For the next three days, the sun sprang from the waters of the lake as her agile fingers and trained fist pumped fire into my depths again and again. My rim sucked her wrist. The scent of mangrove dew, coconut milk, my sweat, her sweat, her juice, my juice constantly licked my brain.

This *gaita* lasted three nights and three days under the Alisian rains. On the third day, Yahaira left me a taste of her beat, rhythm, song, riot, grace, prayer, romance, protest, poetry, satire, revelation, celebration, invocation, magic and took a piece of my soul with her.

Notes

La gaita is a type of Afro-Venezuelan rhythm that originated in the State of Zulia. The music is accompanied by lyric that is poetic, satirical and revolutionary. It is played in open plazas, especially during Christmas seasons.

Gaiteras are women who play *la gaita*. For many generations, Venezuelan women were not allowed to play *gaitas* in a public plaza (*sinverguenzas* did it, anyway).

Plaza Baralt hosts the largest flea market in the region and is located in the old downtown, in the core of *Maracaibo,* capital of the state of Zulia.

Claves are two sticks played by beating them against each other.

Cuatro is a small four-string guitar, also, the typical instrument of Venezuelan folk-lore.

Furruco is a type of drum also used in Brazil that produces a very sensual sound as a stick is moved up and down through a tight hole on the drum's skin. It requires very special skill to make this instrument sound properly, the reason why it is high-ly eroticized.

Furra and *tambora* are different types of drums.

Our Lady of Chiquinquira is the goddess/matron of the region.

Corn Fed Gal

S adie Lou!," Irma shouted loudly from her end of the phone. "Can you hear me, girl? I just phoned to warn you that trouble is coming your way. She left from here in South Carolina over two months ago. We hear she stopped for a few weeks in Savannah, Georgia and now she is continuing her journey south. She likes small towns and cozy little cities. This town of ours ain't been the same since she came and went.

"She confused and misled all the men folk, played with their minds. Left this town without looking back, leaving many of them still fantasizing about her. Messed with their heads she did, and then she ran off with their wives.

"Men around here nicknamed her Corn Fed Gal. In the beginning she hated that name. She asked old man Joe, who owns the corner garage, why he and his friends insisted on calling her Corn Fed while they knew that was not her true name. Old Joe would take a step back and look her up and down, he would wink and say, 'Gal, it may not be your true name but it sure *is* your situation.'

"You know how the men around here like voluptuous women, Irma went on to say. They feel that women with well-built bodies must have been raised on fertile farm land and fed plenty fresh

185

corn. Corn Fed loved teasing Old Joe and his other old friends who hung around his garage. When she would shop at the general store next to Joe's station, she would be sure to park her car up the street so that she could walk past the old men and make them plenty happy, especially Old Joe. Joe would stand up every time he saw her walking his way. He would arch his back as straight as possible so that he would look taller than his five feet eight inches would allow. She always wore skirts or pants that would accentuate her well-rounded figure. Time would stand still when she walked past that garage.

"Old Joe loved seeing her in tight skirts," Irma continued. "It was a shame how she sexually upset that old man, yet would not show him the time of day. I saw her give him a seductive smile once as she walked by his garage with a bag of groceries, allowing her behind to wriggle loosely in her short black cotton skirt. She had on a halter top which embraced her large firm breasts, showing the impression of her luscious nipples. Old Joe looked as if he wanted to run to her and touch that beautiful brown midriff that was bare and exposed down to her navel.

"Joe maintained his composure and called out to her, saying, 'Gal, if I was just thirty years younger!'

"Corn Fed looked over her shoulder and smiled at Old Joe before getting into her blue station wagon. She sized up the old grey-haired man standing there with a huge grin, wearing immaculate blue overalls kept clean by his second loving wife of twenty-eight years.

"Corn Fed placed her grocery bag in the passenger seat, then straightened up and said, 'Old Joe, I bet you was some smooth play-boy in your day, with your flawless black skin and that sly smile. A couple of decades ago you would have truly given me a run for my money.'

"The young girl threw a kiss to Old Joe and made sure that she gave the old man a glimpse of her strong, shapely, brown thighs as she lifted her legs one at a time to sit behind the wheel of her wagon. 'Don't let your wife catch you staring at me like that Old Joe,' Corn Fed called out to him as she drove off, 'you'll be in the dog house again for sure.'

"When her car could no longer be seen, Old Joe turned around and faced the three men sitting in the shade on crates in front of his garage. They had been amusing themselves watching the entire scene between Old Joe and the young girl. Old Joe kicked one leg as high in the air as his old age would allow him, laughed and said, 'I know that young gal got the hots for me. Couldn't y'all see it? I still got it,' he bragged, 'I still got it.'

"Sadie Lou, are you still listening to me?" Irma didn't even give Sadie a chance to respond; she herself seemed as infatuated by Corn Fed an Old Joe was. "I'm telling you, Sadie, she is heading your way. She targets small communities. When she first arrived here she would hold meetings at the schoolhouse and the local church. She even held a couple of meetings in the back room at Lucy's beauty shop. She was teaching and talking to us about Sisterhood, Black Awareness, Planned Parenting, Herbal Medicine, and Safe Sex. The several months that she was here she gathered up quite a following. At first, the town's women were suspicious of this newcomer, but soon they too were taken in by her charm.

"From day one, the men in town adored her, although the only thing she did was tease their minds. Within weeks the entire town began to dress better, became neighoubourly toward one another, and many of them began to make trips to the drugstore buying those things called condoms, I just call then rubbers. She gave us quite a scare educating us about that sickness called AIDS, and how to prevent its spreading.

"Many of the townsfolk took her leaving real hard, especially the men. and word has it that quite a few women ain't taking it too easy either. People still look down the road toward the junction expecting to see her smoking blue station wagon coming toward the centre of town.

"Some are glad she's gone, 'cause she surely was not a saint. There was talk going around that she sometimes got too intimately close to certain women. The men vehemently defended her by saying this was only jealous female gossip. Yet not one male in town could boast about being intimately close to her. She only made love to their minds and ran off with their wives. Sadie, I am telling you, three married women left town with that gal, leaving notes to their husbands saying they may or may not be back. One of the wives called from Savannah. That's how we know they passed through there. She told her husband not to wait up for her. They're not in Savannah anymore. I'm telling you, Sadie, she is heading toward your town. Beware of her. She drives a blue station wagon that now carries five passengers. She picked up two more women in Savannah. You will know her when you see her. She's a beautiful brown-skinned woman, about twenty-eight years old, built like a brick house, and they sometimes call her Corn Fed."

Until that point Sadie had remained quiet, allowing Irma to carry on her usual one-sided conversation. Finally Sadie broke her silence, saying, "Thank you, Irma, for the warning, but it really ain't necessary. I hate to rush you off the phone, but I have got to continue packing, for we'll be leaving town very early in the morning. She is no longer driving a blue station wagon, she traded it in last week for a brown van. She needed more space because we now number nine. The three women from your town are still with her, also the two from Savannah, and she picked up three more in my small city, one of them being me. We will drive to a town in northern Florida, spending time in new cities along the way. We shall continue to educate the townspeople about Sisterhood, Black Awareness, Planned Parenting, Herbal Medicine, and Safe Sex. We are all now devoted followers of that Corn Fed Gal. And by the way, Irma, Corn Fed is not her true name. It's just her situation."

SHARON HANNA

Naughty by Nature

Okay. Hold your horses. I set the Windex bottle on the table. My right arm moves in big circles, rag in hand, against the glass of the big sliding door. She couldn't care less about my clean windows. Her timing is generally impeccable. In fact, you could say she invented it. But, it is always like this. On her time.

Come to me.

The Windex bottle hits the old pine table with a dull thud. She wraps herself around my waist, bypassing what little cerebral cortex I have left, and begins to knead me all over. Eyes glazed, I am being moved, zombie-like, out the door.

In the garden, fecundity explodes from everything. Drifts of perfume waft by, luring the innocent into sin. Newborn bees are tempted by brazen red and white parrot tulips, nipples budding softly at the ends. Lift themselves up shamelessly, into the salivating mouths of the little bees. I brush by the tulips and a slender stem scratches my ankle.

She loves me best.

The warm golden heat of the morning sun penetrates through my white flannelette nightgown and onto my skin. I pad, barefoot, through the cool green sparkling grass. I am naked under the nightgown. She prefers it. She loves all my smells, but especially one, which she has compared to that of a honeydew melon.

189

I kneel down and notice the weeds. She stops inhaling me, pulling away sharply. To her, there is no weed. All of them are her babies. Her darlings. I squat over the soil, which warms with her breathing. I feel it on the only curly hair I have on my body. Between my legs.

She thinks pretty highly of herself, naturally. Well, she doesn't actually think. It's more like knowing. I don't get away with anything. Ever. I remember last night. We were in the bathtub together. With my thumb and forefinger, I twirled that hair into little Shirley Temple ringlets, hoping to tempt her but . . . she only yawned. Later on in bed, it had been an unsatisfying night, what with me pressing myself every which way to no avail. She was preoccupied with one of her projects.

Two can play at this game.

She flinches hard as I rip the tiny dandelion out of the dirt, quickly suppressing the thought: *Fuck you.* I stand up, holding the dandelion by the root hairs, step forward, and feel the stab as the thorn plunges deep into the sole of my right foot. *You bitch.*

I am getting so turned on. Now she wants me, there is no way to resist. She moves up inside me from underneath. Like heavy marshmallow energy, pushing upward. She is moaning low down in me, her moans make my whole body vibrate, but particularly the part below the waist. Between my legs. The slowly warming soil has turned into a damp tongue which remains poised a couple of inches away. She doesn't move it.

What do you want me to do?

As if she does not know . . . I look down and see my hands. Blistered, from dealing with her. I am getting angry now. My hands make me remember every fall, how she flings maple leaves everywhere. And just when I finish raking she does it again! I feel the anger in my chest and throat. I feel so used by her. She never seems to notice how much work I do.

There, I'm glad I said it. She loves it when I get angry. It turns me on, of course. Just another thing we love about each other.

Then I feel what I have been waiting for. Her tongue touches me lazily. She just lies there, so calmly, with all the time in the world. Okay, I forgive you.

I just think it inside my head and her damp, slithery, hard

tongue is underneath me, where it counts. It's like she is holding me up with her tongue. Everything slows down, and now I am only aware of my breathing, and the sound of the earthworms moving, underneath, inside of her. She begins to lick me in slow motion. I gasp, and my nipples go like rocks under my nightie, as I squat there, wondering if anyone can see me through the knotholes in the fence.

The wind chimes clang. *Drama queen.* She stops moving her tongue. *Bitch. Stop teasing me. I haven't got all day. It's easy for you, you can lay around like this, forever. Can't you?*

She tells me to be still. I squat there, staring at the newly emerging candytuft and violets. When I spot the asparagus tips pushing their way up out of the soil, I am right on the edge. They poke out lasciviously at me. I feel them mocking me. That sad wave moves through my stomach. It's true, I do get jealous. She loves everything, after all. I guess I always knew I would never be the only one. She reads me like a book. Her tongue enfolds me, and feels like God, as she says:

Come.

The garden vibrates, turning silvery-black in my eyes. I can't hold on to myself any longer. Shaking, I fall over the edge. Fall into her. Afterward, I stand and brush the dirt from the hem of my nightgown. Three deceptively innocent black-capped chickadees flit around near the asparagus, snapping up the early aphids. They have perfect vision, so I know they have been watching us. Dirty birdies.

She has her eye on them, I know it. She is so easily distracted. Luckily, I stopped taking it personally a long time ago. She could have them for breakfast any moment, if she wanted to. Innocent, like most of her creatures, they have no idea how she works.

But I know.

Whispers Getting Fainter

The other night I dreamed that Patsy Cline's ghost was wandering up and down Prior Street. Eventually she went into that greasy spoon I took Madge to last August, the Eat Here Kitchen.

None of the tired, sulky regulars in the restaurant would talk to the great singer—they left her alone as if they knew she was not supposed to be there.

When I awoke I felt a sense of peace instead of my usual sadness. If I had called Madge and told her about that dream she would have said, "Anyone can have a dream about Patsy Cline. Big ruddy deal."

Or she might have said, "You dream about a Patsy because that's what you are—a patsy, like a chump."

Last August, Madge would have said something like, "You have the coolest visions, my little commando. Come closer."

Madge used to be so positive and enthusiastic, and she always wore white so you could see her from afar, shimmering like a visitor from some other world. That was last summer.

I wrote down my dream about Patsy Cline because I felt my unconscious was telling me something important. It was telling me not to shut myself in the apartment, lip-synching to "Leavin' On Your Mind."

Madge broke up with me last fall, and I have not moved forward since. We were together only three months, but it felt like a year-long holiday. Was it the heat?

It was such a blazing summer, we would keep her bedroom window open as wide as possible. When the moon was visible we'd lean out and watch it shine on Madge's wind-blown hair. Then I'd whisper about how heaven must look, and say her name like a subtropical breeze: "Madge. *Ma chere.*"

The weather turned, and Madge found someone she liked better. She turned against me when I wouldn't evaporate.

I tried to visualize a woman I would like better than Madge. Someone not too young and not too old, not too prosperous but with enough money to pay the bills, careworn features with a bit of eternal youth, hunkered over a motorcycle. I had to stop. I was describing myself, and I was describing Madge.

I've been through this end-of-affair feeling enough times to know the emptiness will go cloudy and then disappear, like the dreams I try to remember each frosty morning. I'm counting on it anyway.

I know to phone people every day, to keep away the demon called Isolation. It's a healing thing to check in with someone else every twenty-four hours. But not Madge. I call anyone but Madge once a day. I read a bit of the paper first so I can begin a conversation.

I can't just tell people I'm floating away. Hello, I'm floating, yes, and I'm only going to sad places.

Covetous

I like to linger in the women's change room after my weekly swim. Slowly, methodically, I dry between my toes, wring and re-wring my bathing suit, and comb out my hair in front of the dryers—always artfully positioned with a direct line of sight into the open bank of showers.

It's true, I admit it. I am the one who causes fundamentalist Christian girls to awkwardly clutch a towel around themselves with one hand while they try and slither their panties up with the other. It can't be done, but they keep trying, just in case there are sneaky, horny eyes like mine crawling over their breasts and licking at their thighs. For a woman living a straight life—home by six, him in the apron your aunt gave you, depositing a casserole on the table with a flourish—it's one way to keep sane; a little something to keep you going long after he's turned away and fallen into sleep.

I met Moira when she joined the advanced swim class in January, putting her slim, twenty-something body on the New Year's resolution fast track. We stood outside before class, smoking our cigarettes in the cold.

"It's more a preventative thing," she explained, with that particular mixture of pride and guilt strong-limbed women feel when they talk fitness with soft-shouldered women like me.

After that we ran into each other every week. My lingering dragged on longer and longer so that I could be there when she wriggled out of her suit and stepped into the shower. The smooth curve of her tummy and the unruly dark curls that blossomed under it, her shoulder smudged by a birthmark shaped like Vancouver Island. I took to leaving my long hair for last, standing under the dryer and combing it forward into a curtain that concealed me as I watched her shift back and forth under the hot spray.

On the day of her last class, Moira was already ploughing back and forth in the fast lane when I began paddling along in the slow one. When I reached the end of the pool she was standing on the deck above me.

"Have you ever thought of doing the breast stroke?" she asked, eyebrows pinched together earnestly. "It would be a lot easier than, well, what you're doing." From my perspective, I could see all the way up the inside of her legs to where they met in a royal blue Lycra-wrapped mound.

"I never learned how to swim," I said, embarrassed by my dog paddling. "But it would be great if you could show me."

She slid into the pool next to me and demonstrated the stroke. Her smooth legs pushed off the wall and disappeared. She cupped the water in her fingers and pushed it back past her hips. Her narrow shoulders rose up and water streamed off her back.

I hit the water like a walrus in its death throes. I got water up my nose and wanted to quit. She stood behind me and held my elbows, moving my arms through the stroke. Her breasts, snug and full in her wet bathing suit, brushed against my back.

"Well, maybe if you keep working on it," she said finally with a sweet smile.

Moira went to her locker while I pulled off my suit in the empty shower room. She came back naked, carrying a towel and a bar of soap.

"I remember now why I gave up swimming. The chlorine is so hard on your skin," she said. I smiled, and busied myself adjusting the hot water. Flushed out of my hiding places, this close to her wet skin, I didn't know where to look.

She put her towel on the wooden bench across from the

showers and stepped under the nozzle next to mine. She tipped her head back, let the hot water run over her face, and pulled her hair into the spray until it was a dark streak hanging straight down the centre of her back.

Humming a little, she picked up the soap and began washing her arms, stretching one over her head and slowly drawing the soap down over her forearm and nuzzling it into her armpit and around the muscle of her shoulder. She switched hands and smoothed the soap evenly down the other arm. A lifeguard's whistle echoed against the wet tiles. I held my breath.

One at a time she traced the curve and weight of her breasts with slippery palms, circling her nipples gently until they puckered like kisses beneath her fingers. Shifting her weight to one side, she moved her hands down over her ribs, hips and ass in looping, graceful circles that left a thin, slick sheath of soapy water on her flushed skin. She bent over, the curve of her ass hovering inches from my thigh, her spine floating like a lane-rope in the muscle of her back, and worked her hands down the insides of her legs. Voices arrived in the change room behind us, three or four, emphasized by the slamming of locker doors. I shook out my hair under the water then turned back toward Moira with half-closed eyes. She stood up and languidly worked one soapy hand back and forth between her legs.

Then she turned, blinking water from her dark eyelashes, and saw me watching her.

She glanced at the doorway to the change room, then raised her hand, palm up, and let the soap hover in the space between us. Hot water needled at my back and streamed over her shoulders and belly. Steam shrouded us. I reached out. Took it.

"I told you before Satya, you've got to give him the gears." Their laughter burst between us just before the two women turned the corner into the shower room, mincing careful on the wet tiles. I spun red-faced into the hot spray; Moira disappeared from beside me.

When their voices finally echoed out of the shower room and into the pool, I turned to find Moira wrapped in her towel under the dryer, watching me soap the wet away from between my legs, and plucking at her brown curls until they retracted like springs beneath her fingers.

LASHONDA K. BARNETT

Breakfast With Dinah

There are many splendid forms of first love experiences: the first glance, the first hand-holding session, the first kiss, the first time you hang up the telephone knowing the woman on the other end has won your heart. These experiences with Dinah are imprinted so indelibly on my mind and heart that I scarcely remember the women who came before her. The first time I had a clue our relationship would bear such fruit was the morning after we'd made love for the first time.

I like to recall the first breakfast I prepared for us. Out of nervousness I pull everything out of the refrigerator. Happy that I'd found the world's last meat-eating lesbian, I proceed to rip open a package of bacon and start to brew my secret blend of coffee: Guatemalan and Ethiopian beans. Dinah enters the kitchen wearing a fresh shower scent and a rejuvenated air. My nose slightly tickles at the lilacs, roses, or some other floral scent coming from her short hair. She smiles, rubs her tummy like a two-year-old, kisses me on the back of the neck, and starts searching the cupboards for the coffee mugs. I admire her for making herself at home. She volunteers to help, but I want to prepare this breakfast for her not, with her. I explain this and she resolves to read our horoscopes while I

197

cook. Both of us, Geminis, are promised a four-star day.

I turn bacon, flip French toast, and sprinkle cinnamon on it, and begin to scramble eggs.

"Mmm . . ." Dinah begins. "I love cinnamon, baby. I can't believe you're cooking like this. This is so nice. No one, other than my Mam-Maw, has ever cooked this way for me."

Eating has always been one of my favourite pastimes. In a matter of seconds, I conclude that Dinah and I have this in common. She is ravenous. I watch her savour every bit of food that I've placed on her plate. I grow warm watching her eat. My eyes follow her willowy hand as she allows her fork to skate a piece of French toast through syrup speckled with cinnamon.

"You are such a good cook," she says, in the voice she used the night before to thank me for the pleasure I'd given her.

Dinah pauses. She is sitting near the only window in the house that welcomes sunlight's northern exposure. Looking at her, I begin to feel some of the old pain from being mistreated, misunderstood, and taken for granted, dissolve. I relay this image of us onto the canvas of my memory. I am aware now that I had it all wrong. The notion that I'd fall in love in some grandiose vacation spot or in any scene comparable to that of a Hollywood drama was wrong. Nothing could have prepared me for the amount of love I feel during breakfast with Dinah. I place the last bit of food into my mouth. Syrup trickles down my chin. Dinah uses her napkin to lightly rub it away. I feel cared for. Quietly, we stand and clear the table.

We carry the dishes into the kitchen and place them on the counter. I put my hand on the kitchen faucet and she places her hand over mind. I do not turn on the water. I feel wanted. Dinah carries my hand away from the sink and leads me to the bedroom.

I look out from the bedroom doorway at the table where we've just shared our first breakfast. Our two chairs stand abandoned—away from the table. Somehow I know I will never be able to look back on that room without loving her and loving us. She closes the door. Maintaining my balance is a challenge, for my heart and head greatly anticipate this reunion. I stand near the bed. She walks over to me, kisses me softly.

"I hope you don't have any plans for this afternoon or this

evening," she whispers, as we break away from our kiss. I shake my head no.

"Good. Because I want to thank you for making such a wonderful breakfast," Dinah sings into the cleft of my chin and neck.

I close my eyes, knowing that she will love me even better than she did the night before, as we lower each other onto the bed.

My First Time

You want to know about my first time? That was years ago. I was twenty, stuck in London. Alone. I had just had the baby—she was just two months. It was freezing cold in England that year.

I had been living in a squat with an English guy. The baby was just part of all the chaos and an effort, I suppose, on my part to get some sort of stability or love or something out of the situation. He was too busy being stoned and looking for his next hit to know I was there most of the time. I was young, a lost soul.

Anyway, here I was, a kid alone in a foreign country, no money, in freezing cold, soggy old England with a new baby. The guy split for Amsterdam—where the junk was better and cheaper, and he didn't have to share—as soon as I got big enough to embarrass him. As a lover he was as dull as toast. I have always thought that it's nature's cruelest joke on the human female that she can produce another being, an amazing act, without sexually achieving even the slightest pleasure. So I had the baby alone and waited for something to happen. I think I was too spaced out to think I might do something to change my situation.

I had taken to wandering the West End department stores

to stay warm. I loved the fresh new clothes and warmth. The purposefulness of shoppers, normal people. It was right before Christmas and the decorations and music gave me that confusing combination of sensations: warmth, sadness, hopefulness, joy, that spacey dissociation and languor—just strong and confusing enough to drag me out of the flattened existence of waiting. I noticed things. I could feel.

That day I stayed in the store longer than usual. I was exhausted and the squat was freezing so I wanted to hang out in the warmth as long as possible. The baby started squawking, demanding a feed, so I went to the ladies room where they had this wonderful and big mother's room. I made myself comfortable in a soft, classy wing-backed chair and settled down to nurse her.

It was the end of the day, mid-week, quiet. I had the room to myself. As the baby sucked on my breast I felt myself relax into the chair and begin to enjoy the near erotic pull on my nipple. I must have fallen asleep or drifted off because I remember waking up to the door opening and seeing a man walk in. He was thin, not too tall. He had a leather jacket on and ripped jeans. He glanced at me and I knew that I was really looking at a woman, one of those butch dykes I saw from time to time in the city.

She looked at me and I could see her catch her breath and almost say something, and then she caught herself and moved quickly to the toilets. I looked down to where she had dropped her eyes and saw that my breast was bare and a single drop of milk hung waiting on my nipple. The baby was fast asleep in my lap.

My heart was beating hard when she walked past me again. As she was about to open the door and leave, she stopped, turned around, and looked at me. At my face and then my breast. She had a cocky smile, and I felt myself blush. I knew I should say something, or at least cover my breast, but I couldn't move. I was frozen in place and burning up. And she knew it.

She dragged a chair over and blocked the door with it. She came to me, lifted the baby from my lap, placed her gently in her carrier, and covered the carrier with the baby blanket.

She stood in front of me and looked down. My heart was beating so hard I'm sure she heard it and I realized I was terrified. She dropped down in front of me, pushed my knees apart roughly, and leaned forward and licked the milk off my nipple. Then she bit me. It was like being hit with a lightning bolt. I gasped and grabbed her jacket. The leather was cold in my hands. My legs tightened and my pelvis pushed against her chest.

She pushed my dress up and stroked my inner thigh. She dropped her head into my lap and nuzzled my thigh with her nose and lips, biting once in a while.

Her head in my lap, the warmth of it—her breath like moths on my skin, her tongue gently tasting my thigh, moving up and taking forever.

I gazed at the back of her head, her back. The leather coat. Feeling the cold and hardness of the leather against my legs as she breathed me in. I was beyond self-consciousness as my hips lifted up to her. She pressed her mouth hard against the crotch of my panties—pushing and breathing against my cunt. I melted into her face and lost myself. Her finger slipped behind the fabric of my panties and into me.

My hips began to move on their own, reaching for the single finger. She slipped two, three, and then four fingers into me. Her head was back at my breast, biting and sucking hard.

My hips were pushing, forcing me out of the chair and on to the floor. She slid down with me and pressed against me to keep me in place as her finger probed me, pushed into me. I rocked against her fingers.

Her teeth held tightly on my nipple, dangerously tight. It made me drive my hips harder onto her fingers. She began moving her hand differently and then I could not move and I held my breath. It took me a minute to figure out that she had her whole hand in me. Her fist.

I forgot to breathe. I couldn't move. I was held in place by her fist inside me. Her breath was short and hot against my breast. She rubbed her pelvis, hard, against my leg. And I realized she was coming over and over again. She moved her fist and I screamed and opened more to her.

I was laying flat out on the carpet and she was above me moving her fist in and out of me while I cried, my hips lifting on their own, wanting more. She watched me and then moved her mouth to my clit and licked me and sent shock waves to my core. I screamed a final time and sank back into the floor.

When I opened my eyes I saw her smiling down at me, that cocky smile. She reached up touched my forehead—wet fingers, got up off her knees, moved the chair back to where it belonged and left.

My first time.

Last Time

I found my way back to her apartment without directions. Rebecca's sheets were cool against my skin, but I couldn't sleep. I studied every crack in the ceiling, my mind racing. Soon I switched the light on and tried to read, but my eyes circled the same paragraph over and over. I stared at the words. At four a.m., Rebecca's keys jingled in the lock, her boots made two clunks against the floor, and then the faucet ran in the bathroom. I didn't look up as she entered the bedroom. I heard a drawer open and then shut. When Rebecca crawled into bed beside me, she put out the light, though I was still staring at the page. Crossly I turned my back to her. But soon I felt her on my side of the bed, her lips against my neck, her hands everywhere.

Something was missing. Her touch was as tawdry as my middle school boyfriends and their rush to reach the bases and score. Her finger prowled sentiments that meant nothing anymore. As her tongue lingered on my neck I felt as if she was leaving her insignia, proof that she had entered this terrain. Rebecca's lips were soft against my skin, and thrilling. I savoured her touch like dessert before a fasting. Her dark eyes both loathed and caressed me. My fear pricked up my body's responses. She coaxed me to build and build like a hallelujah chorus swelling to reach the rafters, and then there was only silence.

The next morning, Rebecca's cool veneer rose again, like a wall. She watched television in the next room as I struggled to close my backpack; the harsh noise droned through the thin wall. She didn't even look at me as I lugged my bag to the door. When I saw her messy scribble in my mailbox three days later, I knew what the letter contained.

Denouément

I undress and slip under the covers. The familiar feel of her flannel sheets caresses my skin, and as I burrow beneath the covers, the smell of wool, and the musk scent that she wears, invoke waves of memory. I can feel the tears prickling behind my eyes, before I force my mind away from the past, away from the future, and bring it back to now, to this moment.

I can hear her moving in the bathroom, turning off the shower. I imagine her standing in front of the mirror, running her fingers through her short wet hair. She will be inspecting her face while she brushes her teeth. The towel will be wrapped around her waist, and there will still be droplets of water on her shoulders and breasts.

I hear the water shut off. Then she is standing next to me, her skin looking even more tanned in the flickering light of the candles. For an instant I think I might shatter if she touches me, but I push that too from my mind and wait, frozen. It is no longer possible for me to reach out to her and she knows this. She stands, looking down at me. She does not smile, but she does not have to.

"Let me see you."

I push the blankets from my body, my skin prickling at the almost tangible caress of her eyes.

"Put your hands above your head, spread your legs."

I do, the sticky lips of my cunt peeling apart for her. My breasts, belly, ribs feeling vulnerable and exposed.

"Close your eyes."

And I do, aware now of the sound of her breathing, the cool touch of the air on my skin. I have lain like this for her, vulnerable and open, more times then I can count, and still my body responds —my skin tingles, warm with excitement.

"Don't move."

She reaches out for me but does not touch. Her open palm so close to my skin that I can feel its heat. Her hands that know me so very intimately, yet have never become blurred with familiarity. They move slowly along my body, tantalizingly close. Up my thighs, cupping the air above my bush, then moving on, brushing a single hair, sending shock waves through my cunt. She moves up my belly, over my breasts—my nipples grow hard in anticipation. When she finally touches me, it is to reach out and cup my face in her hand, tracing the line of my cheekbone with her thumb.

"What do you want?"

I flush red. It does not matter how many times she asks me this, it is still just as hard to answer. I try to turn my head away, but she holds me still, fingers around my jaw.

"Look at me!"

My eyes fly open.

"Tell me."

I know she will not touch me until I've spoken, but I squirm, feeling it impossible to get the words past my lips. She waits: patient, still, strong. Her eyes say she wants me, but I know from experience how great is her self-control.

I try to speak, stumble, try again, and manage a whispered, "I want you to fuck me." My body is burning, there is a touch of a smile on her lips.

"I can't hear you, slut. Tell me what you want. Tell me exactly what you want. Convince me."

"Please," I manage, my voice a little louder, "please, I need to feel you, I need you to fuck me, I want your fingers in my cunt, I need you, please, I need you." I stop then, unable to continue, the edge in my voice a little too close to the surface. But she's heard it and her face softens. She reaches for me, sooner then usual, and draws me into her soft embrace, into her strong arms. Her hand moves down my body, pressing into me, kneading my flesh.

The towel slips from her hips as she pushes her fingers into my cunt and her tongue into my mouth. I keep my arms and legs wide, but cannot stop myself from moving, frcm thrusting toward her, reaching for the depths of her mouth, the length of her fingers. Now, in her urgency, she reveals her passion. Her arms tighten around me, pin me to her. Her teeth find my neck, and she bites, just hard enough to catch my breath, to create seconds of stillness. Her fingers become more demanding as she reaches toward my core, exploring me, opening me. Then her thumb slips in next to her fingers and in one exquisite movement she pushes her hand into me, her fingers curling into a fist under my heart. My breath catches in an almost-scream as I fold into her, curl around her fist and into the circle of her arms. I am consumed by her; she is all around me, and she fills me. Her fist moves and I feel her presence in every cell of my body.

She hurts me just enough to sweeten the pleasure to almost beyond bearing, and when I come I lose myself, forget where I end and the world begins.

After, her cheeks are wet with tears as she holds me. I had not expected this. My face is dry. I have shed all my tears lying in my own bed, shaking with the agony of loss.

"I love you," and I believe her, know it to be true. This woman, who has made the decision to pledge herself, exclusively, to another, loves me.

"Thank you," I whisper.

Thank you for the gift of consciousness, of awareness. To be so lucky as to know it to be the last time, so that we can hoard the memory of each glorious touch, of every word. So that we can say goodbye in this most intimate of ways.

"I'm sorry." Her voice is gentle, loving. I slip into sleep, treasuring the feel of her arms around me.

Penetration

Y ou think I'm going to tie you down and fuck you, don't you. You think I'm going to strap on a dildo, and do this intercourse thing, play butch boy for you, and let you scream and carry on, indulge your rape fantasies and all that good stuff, that stuff that gets you so hot, that makes you drip wet . . . I can see you dripping now, from the way I grabbed you by the hair and forced you into the bonds, spread-eagled on your bed. Maybe it's the bed, especially, that makes you think we're going to fuck, and maybe it's all the hints you've been dropping to me about the way you like it, the things you've done . . . you're a smooth bottom, practiced, you've been with badder bitches and butches than me. So if I'm going to give you what you want, I know, I've got to give you something you don't know you want. I'm going to start with my finger. I pull off my leather glove and toss it away, and work my index finger right between your wet lips, right into the hot spot, and into you it goes. I can see the look in your eyes—*What, no foreplay? No clit action?*— but as my finger slides as deep as it can go, your eyes close and you gasp with deep pleasure. Then two fingers. You don't need foreplay, you don't need lube, sweet thing, your cunt is hungry and I'm going to feed it. Next, I pull a dagger from my pocket. It's not a dagger, it's a letter opener, but you don't know that. I see you gasp and flinch and squirm—you think I'm going to pretend to cut you, run the tip all over your flesh, across your nipples . . . I see your eyes go wide as I dip it between your legs. Have you figured it out yet? I slide the dull metal into you, using the flat blade like a tongue depressor, to peer into the folds of your flesh. Your vagina convulses as you realize what I'm doing and you strain against your bonds, helpless to stop me. I know if you really want to stop me you'll say the word. But you're too interested, wondering what I'm going to do next, to stop now. I pull a Magic Marker out of my pocket and write my name in flowing script across your belly, then cap the thing and hold you open with the fingers of one hand while I slide the hard plastic cylinder into you. Your legs are shaking as I move it in a wide circle . . . what are you thinking, darling? Have you ever put a Magic Marker up your cunt before? Is this something you used to do when you were a kid, under the sheets at night, terrified of being caught, but unable to stop yourself—what did you turn to when your fingers weren't enough? The marker is not large, but it is hard and foreign, is that what's making you shake? The thought of this thing protruding out of your body, probing into places it was never intended to go? You almost laugh when you see the kielbasa, a thousand phallic puns half-remembered flicker across your face as your eyes take in the curve of sausage in my hand. No, I wouldn't, you think. But I will, and I do, rolling a condom onto the end for full phallic effect, and pushing the thickness against your lips until they give way and then inch it inside. You whimper, a sweet sound. It feels big, I know it, I see you clenching and relaxing, trying to take it in. Good girl. It's too soft to fuck you with so I settle for burying it a few inches deep and then lean down to bite off the end. When my nose rubs your clit I stop my nibbling and pull the meat out of you, toss it away. Too late I realize I should have made you eat some of it, should have let you taste your own juice on it. No matter, there is more in store. The unlit end of a burning candle. You twitch as you feel the heat of the flame, although I'm the one who gets wax on her hands as I move it from side to side in you. A pair of black lacquer chopsticks, so thin you barely feel them at all, until I split then like a speculum and widen you side to side, top to bottom. I let you lick them when I'm done. What else can we stick into your cunt, my girl? I've used up the things that I brought with me, so cast about your apartment looking for more. You've got dildos galore but they don't interest me, cunt girl. I roll a condom over an Idaho potato I find in your fridge, cold and fat and wide, and I push the tip of it in as far as it will go. I fuck you with it until it is sliding in up to its widest point, and you are moaning and thrashing. Have you ever been fucked with something this big, cunt girl? You probably have, I don't kid myself after all the hints you gave me. Have you ever slept with a man? The potato is getting slick and hard to hold onto, but I'm shoving it with my palm into you now. I bet you have slept with men before, even if you haven't said anything about it to me. How could that hungry cunt resist? A pole of hard, hot flesh, that fits snug and twitches in response. I'd love to have one myself, love to have one to ram into you and feel your wetness on every nerve ending. But there's no use wishing for things I don't have, and what I have is you, wide open before me, your cunt is my cunt, and I can put anything into it that I like. The potato slips out onto the floor and your head jerks up, your vagina gasping like a fish, so empty, so needy. A bottle of shampoo. The handle of a hairbrush. Pinking shears. Yours is the cunt that ate Tokyo. When I'm done with you there won't be a phallic object left in your apartment that doesn't smell like your desire. Everything will remind you of me. I am just beginning to wish I had a crusty baguette to go with the kielbasa when I decide maybe you've had enough. You sense the hesitation and look up, hope in your eyes. No, I'm still not going to fuck you. You realize it when I pack the harness back into my bag. You want to ask so bad, I see you holding back, you want to beg me for something, but you aren't sure whether you can abase yourself that way. Silly girl, you'll let me stick anything into your slit as long as you're tied up. Maybe next time I'll sit and watch while I order you to stick things up into yourself—a flashlight, a fake rubber dog bone, the old standby: the cucumber. Maybe I'll take photographs of each of these things sticking out of your cunt to horrify my politically correct friends with. You're biting your lip with impatience—I'm sorry, my sweet. I get this way sometimes. For now, what kind of a top do you think I am? Don't worry, I'll get you off. After all, I've brought a whole array of things to try on your clitoris—fur, sandpaper, chains, a nail file, macramé rope, a hairbrush, a braided thong—and when I run out of those I'm sure there are more things here I can try. I'm not tired in the least.

Complexities of Desire

Desire and childhood wounds equal passion for me. A continuous rerun of old pain. The hard slap on the face. Rejection and grief. Trying again and again to be loved by the unloving.

When I was a little girl, my body felt good when I touched myself. I walked around feeling hot desire all the time, not knowing that part of my lust was born from the countless unwanted hands that had touched me before. Before I could speak my own name or write arithmetic.

When I wanted Johnny to have sex with me, I didn't know what it meant. I just knew I wanted him to pull down his pants and put his "car in my garage," as someone had said to me earlier. Johnny was scared and pulled away from my lust. We were seven.

When my sister and I had sex, she would tell me I had to pretend to rape her. I felt guilty, but also turned on. She was thirteen and I was eleven. I didn't know then that the intensity of our desire came from a need in us to repeat what had been done and to make sense out of what was senseless.

It didn't feel good to be hurt when I was little. I was always, always, scared and in terror of the darkness and what came out of it.

Yet in my adulthood I fantasized about being dominated, enslaved, tied up, and tortured by women.

A big dildo sliding in and out of my ass as I screamed in pain would give me a near instant orgasm when I masturbated and fantasized.

Face slapped hard. Nipples pinched. Big butch woman's hand brutally fucking me in the cunt.

To be able to tell a lover, "This is what I want." To spill honesty from a mouth that wanted hard kisses was difficult when my lover would say, "I don't want to hurt you! Your face is beautiful! I don't want to slap it!"

"But this is what turns me on," I screamed at her softness and at her concern. "I like it. I need it. Otherwise boredom takes over."

I have had to teach my lovers how to make love to me. I've needed to be unashamed, assertive and clear. "Yes, touch me there! Harder! No, harder! Bite harder! Don't stop!"

Not a romantic version of lovemaking. I've tried other ways. Softness, for a while. Sweet women. And it would be good, for a while. Yet my lust for more always haunted me with shame. What was wrong with me? I didn't like the sweet softness of lovemaking.

Romantic and gentle, the way it's shown in movies.

It's not who I am. It's not where I want to be.

I like hard sex. Hard and passionate. Intensely sharp. Razor-edged pain that brings me back into my body. Again and again.

Riding Sally

I gently sucked her nipples as I caressed her buttocks and slender thighs. I had been so lonely since Mel's death, but now I had Sally. I felt her soft, pliable breasts while I whispered loving thoughts in her ear. I climbed upon her and pushed my body against hers and said softly, "Would you like to try my double-ended dildo?" I pulled the toy from its box and lubed it up before inserting it into Sally's soft cavity. I could hear Melissa rocking on the stereo and I began to sing with her as I climbed up onto the dildo and slid it into my cunt. "Does she move you like I move you!" Melissa belted it out on the stereo. My thoughts flashed back and I pictured Mel and I making love with the stereo blasting. We would have supper and then we would have a long hot bath with a special erotic blend of essential oils that Mel would concoct. We would tell each other how our day went while sipping on glasses of Chardonnay. I had never known a woman as erotic as Mel. She loved having sex at any time of the day or night. She was never shy about wanting it or asking for it. I would find her masturbating on the couch when I got home from work sometimes. I found it a real turn-on and Mel knew it.

I started panting loudly as I thought of Mel masturbating. Her large breasts would fly about as she moved up and down and all around the bed. I grabbed Sally's breasts hard and said, "I love fucking you, Sally, and I wouldn't know what to do if I didn't have you in my life at this time." I sucked her nipples as hard as I could and moved slowly on top of her.

Mel knew me like no one had ever known me. She accepted me totally, everything about me. She was so easy-going, so loving and kind. When she was diagnosed with cancer I thought I would die. For the first time in my life I had felt alive, and then it was being ripped away from me. Now I felt like one of the walking dead most of the time. I promised Mel I would survive and go on without her, but now I wished I had never made that promise. It has been a year now and it feels like yesterday. I don't believe the person who said time heals all wounds. This wound will never heal and I will never forget my Mel.

My mind returned to the present and I started riding Sally wildly. I knew I was not going to have an orgasm, but I furiously continued fucking her. What would I have done if I hadn't had Sally for my sexual pleasures? Mel sure knew what she was doing when she brought Sally home for me just before she was admitted to the hospital for the last time. Finally, I collapsed with fatigue on top of Sally and fell asleep.

I remember when I first met Sally. Mel found her in her favourite sex shop downtown. One day while perusing in her preferred store, the manager Jez approached Mel, excited. She'd held back a new item for Mel to check out, before letting the public see the latest in blowup dolls. Her skin was so soft, her nipples erect and life-like, and her eyes a beautiful blue. When Mel first brought her home I was reluctant and didn't want to think about having sex without Mel, so Mel suggested I watch while she made love to Sally one evening in front of the fire. Mel talked to Sally as if she were real. Her touches were gentle and precise as if she were trying to arouse Sally. With her gentle touch, she slowly undressed Sally while at the same time undressing herself. If I didn't know better, I would think Sally was real, except she never made any noise, so Mel did Sally's talking for her. "Please stick your fist in my cunt," Mel whispered for Sally. It was like watching live theatre in the comfort of my home. Mel stared at me and began slowly riding her. It was like she was fucking me and I began feeling hot all over. It was all I could do to sit and watch Mel and Sally without joining in, but I wanted to know how it could be so sexual, erotic, and real. Mel screamed loudly as she came, then she collapsed on top of Sally. A few minutes later she jumped up and then said to me, "Okay, now it's your turn."

My cunt was dripping wet from watching, so I thought I might as well give her a try. Mel sat naked on the chair, teasing her own cunt, as I began to make love with Sally. I couldn't get over how real she felt. Her nipples felt real, which got me going as I sucked and played with her breasts. Mel reached over and poured some of her Grand Marnier over Sally's breasts and I quickly licked it up. I couldn't contain my orgasm any longer and came with a sigh as I pulled Sally toward me as hard as I could.

I can't say that Mel bringing Sally home that day made me feel any better about what was happening, but it did take my mind off things for the evening. We discussed our lovemaking with Sally as we sipped our Chardonnay in the bath that night.

I never saw Sally after that until a few months after Mel's death. Then I brought her out of the closet and I haven't been able to bring myself back to the real world ever since.

Fisting Sally

Her white lace bra, its frayed edges, the eyelet unraveling. The damp cotton had lost its brightness, its elasticity, and it held her loosely in its fragile cups. How little we had in way of accoutrements. I didn't own a single sex toy. No straps or paddles. No plugs or dildos. That night it was only the weight of our own bodies, the pressure of our hands, and that old white bra that pulled us into each other.

I had a job as a line cook at a shoddy Mexican restaurant. Sally worked the prep table. All night, we were pressed up against each other in that narrow space behind the counter. The heat rising from my grease-slick grill curled her braided red hair. She palmed the vegetables, pressing her fingers into their tight skins. The onions made her cry. She wiped the tears away with the back of her hand, the knife's silver handle gleaming against her palm. She had a loose, rangy look about her and I thought she was beautiful. Every flaw on her slouched, agile body felt like an opening, an invitation: the crooked front tooth, the mole on her left forearm, that long S curve of her back.

A small, all-night bathhouse stood at the edge of town. For an overblown price you could rent a tub in a private room by the hour.

I asked her if I could take her there sometime. She tested the knife's sharp tip, shifted her weight toward me and said no, then yes, then tonight. After work. I plunked down forty-four dollars that night, spent a day's pay for a roofless room, two flights up. I kissed her and we pulled off each other's clothes, but she would not let me take off that bra. That was the one thing she would not give me. She folded her tan arms across her chest and shook her head.

It was October and the frost had already begun to creep into the grass at night. Smoke from a pile of smouldering leaves in the yard next door curled into the wind and wafted up to us. A street lamp curved out above us toward the long road. It caught the shape of that old bra. Her mother had bought it for her on a trip to the Eastside Mall in Algona, Iowa years ago she said. She'd had it since her sophomore year in high school. It's the one real thing I knew about her, that bra, the one piece of personal information she allowed me. She clung to that bra. I think she enjoyed the perversion of it. I think it made her feel safe. It brought her mother into the room with us that night. Her eyes shifting back and forth between my face and that tired bra.

I had never done it before, never the whole hand. She pulled me into her, from the first finger to the fourth, from the thumb past the palm. We ran out of lube just before the knuckle, but she did not want to stop. Her nipples hardened under that thin, cotton weight. My hand cramped. The empty bottle of lube floated away from us across the pool. Her stomach muscles tightened. My hand formed not a fist so much as a cup, a shallow bowl inside of her until that last moment when I kissed the heel of my palm as it slid into her and my fingers folded in on themselves. The way it felt to hold her with my fist, palm empty, the way she closed around me, sweat beading on her upper lip, forming a fine, thin moustache. I stayed there, quiet, unmoving, watching as she trembled beneath me.

"It's in?" she asked and I nodded. She looked distracted for a moment. Her braids fell down her back. Sweat dampened the fine hair around her temples. "It's in," she whispered again, the soft edges of her midwestern accent slipping into her words. A hunger grows in you when you put your hand in a girl and I could not get enough of her, could not press far enough into her. My biceps warming with the effort, my knuckles against her cervix, my heart in my throat. Her feet slipped off my shoulders and hovered weightless in the air behind me. She held the edge of the pool, her voice rising with my movement. Harderharderharder she said again and again until I shook with the effort. I pressed my mouth against her thigh. Her back arched. My fist found a steady rhythm. She let out a cry and pulled me down on top of her.

The next day she was gone. She just didn't show up for work. The owner's wife filled in at the vegetable table for the rest of the month. Her wide hands hovered over the tomatoes, the onions, touching them gingerly. Her face softened with the sting of the onions, but she never cried and I never heard from Sally again. Sometimes, when I smell the acrid, sweet smell of fresh onion, I remember those last moments with her as she leaned back onto the cedar deck, her tanned skin disappearing into the darkness around her. That white bra glowing, caught in the light from the street as her breathing slowed and the night stilled. Then Sally pushed herself up on an elbow and stared at my wrist where it disappeared inside of her, searching for a glimpse of that lost hand.

Faux John

She said I had an attitude about sex workers. So to prove her wrong I put on my dick, slipped on my quido t-shirt, paid cash at the front door, and walked into her place of work.

Nobody flinched. Nobody moved. Except her when I stepped through those swinging doors and there she was all laid up on some man, giving him her pussy for cash. She was shocked and thrilled . . . or so it seemed. She took me by the hand, a hand so soft, a hand I'd never held, and led me past her johns with *their* pricks.

As we walked, she introduced me to her fellow lap dancers. We stepped over cum-filled tissues, carefully maneuvered past tricks and their cocks. She guided me onto a bench, next to a man with a woman showing him her cunt for his cash. Then she rubbed her pussy in my face and I kept trying to strike up a conversation with her, but she was way too busy rubbing her twat in my face. I fell into her soft flesh, knowing the meter was running and she had to go back to her tricks and their dicks. For cash.

Me, foolish me. Neither of us understanding that underneath my bad-ass bravado amidst my tricks and my dicks I was really just standing there holding not my prick in my hand but my heart. I merely wanted to say hello, to kiss her one more time and show her I was willing to do anything to keep her around.

Me, foolish me.

She excused herself and headed back to ply her trade but asked me to stay. For a while. So I sat in the rows of the cinema and watched the woman I'd fallen in love with rub her cunt on men's dicks for cash. Then for a few dollars more she guided them back where she gave them her tits—for more cash.

Me smiling, acting cool as I always do. Me broke, as I always am. Too poor to buy the woman I loved from the men who didn't. Me with my dick in my hand, hoping I wouldn't cry, knowing I was at that moment living a lie.

Later that night she did her kiddie porn strip, dressed in a little girl's dress. Me? I slipped her the few dollars I so desperately needed for groceries and she came down and sat on my lap, rubbing my rubber dick against her nice tight ass. Me so in love, trapped by my desire to make myself okay with what I was not.

When she got up, I slipped a tiny bunny into her g-string and said I had to go. Within days she dumped me . . . and my bunny, too. Two softies. Two strays. In love with a lap dancer.

Who threw us away.

Lonely Doesn't Always Mean Alone

For my dancing bear

The woman upstairs is a screamer and a giggler. On rare occasions, Amanda trills out her pleasure, singing wordlessly to the rhythm of the bed banging against the wall. Each time I hear her, I find myself wondering about her partner Josh and the effect of her constant noise on him as he moves silently to his own grunting explosion.

We live in an old building, and my bedroom is directly below theirs. In the early mornings and at night, when my apartment is silent, I become an unwilling witness to their every sound, every movement, everything. Occasionally, I run into Amanda in the elevator or the laundry room, and she reminds me to phone if their music gets too loud. I just nod and shrug. No way I want to be the one to tell her exactly how much noise passes through their floor and my ceiling.

Last Sunday morning, Rebecca and I tracked Amanda's bumpy road to orgasm together. We were half-awake, savouring the all too rare pleasure of curling around each other in the same bed. The curve of Rebecca's ass snuggled against my crotch, my breasts pressed against her back. Her long dark hair had escaped its confinement under her shoulder to tickle my nose and eyes. We listened to Amanda for a few minutes, letting our imaginations fill in the spaces between sounds, then started snickering at exactly the same time. We do that every so often. Neither of us are sure if it's a good thing or not.

"Sshh." I put my hand over Rebecca's lips, giggling harder as I tried to quiet her. "They might hear us."

"You think they can hear anything right now? I think they're a little too distracted." She sucked one of my fingers into her mouth. The wetness curled around my belly, weighing me down with heat. Rebecca released my finger and twisted around to face me. A wicked smile lit up her face. "Maybe you need a little distraction."

My response was lost in her mouth, stolen when her tongue played with mine. We closed the tiny space remaining between our bodies. Skin touching skin. Arms trying to pull the other even closer, to merge us into one being. My leg slipped between hers. Our nipples rubbed against each other, sending tiny bolts of lightning shooting downward, leaving the skin puckered and hard.

Our hands moved constantly. Mine slid down her spine, teasing the damp crack at the base.

Rebecca pushed me away slightly. She caressed and toyed with my breasts, leaving them aching with need when her hands travelled down my stomach to play with my navel.

I stretched my arm just a little and stroked my fingers across her moist, swollen labia. She moaned and shifted her hips to give me better access.

The alarm clock erupted in loud beeps, reminding us why we'd set the damned thing.

"Fuck!" Rebecca slammed her hand on the button and pulled away.

"Please?" I dragged her back down on top of me. My teeth captured her lower lip, and she surrendered, at first reluctantly and then with enthusiasm. Foreplay disappeared, replaced by fierce determination. We had no time for games, not if Rebecca was going to catch her plane.

My fingers spread her folds and were sucked into the depths. I pulled them out, slid them back in. In and out. My other thumb rubbed her clit, around and around, up and down. Again and again until she moaned, her back arched, and her muscles convulsed.

A moment to breathe, then she was between my legs, and all I knew was her mouth. Electricity sparked through me as she rimmed my labia. Her tongue traced patterns, flickering in and around. Sucking and licking. Over and over until I screamed and gripped her shoulders, detonating in painful, shuddering bursts.

Minutes later we were taking turns under a hot shower, erasing the lingering musk of sex. We have a fast, workman-like interchange that we've perfected over the years. All spray and soapy lather without any of the playfulness and laughter of the day before.

She left before lunch. We sat outside my apartment building, her carry-on bag on the ground between us. We waited for the taxi that would take her to the airport, talking about nothing at all, just wanting to hear the other's voice. Once my hand stole across the space that separated us and stroked the denim encasing her thigh. Once she leaned over, her body hiding the fingers that tweaked my nipple.

The taxi came too soon; we weren't ready to say goodbye. Then again, I'm not sure we could ever be ready for that. It's just something we have to do. Over the long months of our cross-border relationship, we've said goodbye in airports and bus terminals, train stations and car parks. At the beginning, we tried to tell each other that it would get easier, that we'd grow accustomed to the rhythm of coming together and pulling apart every three or four weeks. We were lying. Any couple who claims that saying goodbye gets easier is either lying, or has fallen apart, victim to the pain and pressure of hello and goodbye.

That was last weekend. Tonight, Amanda is humming and giggling. Their bed is creaking over my head as I sprawl out on my stomach, trying unsuccessfully to fall asleep. For some strange reason, I always take up more space in my suddenly enormous bed when I'm alone than Rebecca and I do when we sleep together.

Amanda sings out in triumph and a shaft of envy slices through me. I want Rebecca's arms around me, want her to ease the pain of our separation. A stupid thought really, because if she was here, if she could hold me, there would be no pain.

JOHANNE CADORETTE

Lesbian Sex

Excuse me, I'm looking for lesbian sex!"

I shake my head as a perfectly witty comeback is sadly relegated to an imaginary thought bubble above my head: *Oh, try the lesbian brothel, two doors up. This is a bookstore.*

I look up from my inventory sheet to respond to the query. A woman, dripping wet and wearing a yellow rain slicker, is looking at me with a hint of desperation in her large, grey eyes. Her hair is a matted, soggy mass of sand-coloured curls. A droplet slowly runs down from the tip of a curl, down her slightly upturned nose and over a sensuous pink mouth to finally plunge off a broad chin.

For this I get up, leaving Simone de Beauvoir and friends to be counted later.

"Lesbian sex?" I ask, arching an eyebrow.

Slicker Girl blinks her luminescent greys at me, her jaw dropping slightly. She slowly turns an intriguing shade of red, obscuring her freckles. I imagine Doris Day getting mad at Rock Hudson ("Oh, you!").

"Uh, I mean *Lesbian Sex*, the book," she stammers, "by Joanne Loulann. It's a book."

She crosses her arms and bites her lower lip. A little pool of water is forming around her rubber-booted feet.

Making an effort to look sincere, I grab my clipboard and head to the right shelf. I won't find the book, having sold the last copy yesterday, but I am compelled to pretence. I blame the freckles.

"Gee, sorry, we're sold out. Would you like us to call you when it arrives?"

I turn around. She looks stunned, shocked, her pink lips making a small O shape.

"I . . . no! How soon can you get it?"

"Maybe next week," I answer, shrugging.

"But I need it now!"

Her voice has risen an octave or two. She is wringing her hands and her eyes are filling up with tears.

"It'll be here soon," I repeat flatly. "We'll reserve one for you."

Tears are flowing now, blending in with the raindrops. She sniffs, using the back of her hand to wipe her nose.

Oh, this is really too much. I look around the store, and thankfully, we are alone.

I soften my tone.

"Listen, I'm very sorry. Is it for a gift?"

"No," she sniffs. "It's for me. I need to read it today."

The intensity radiating from her gaze becomes nearly unbearable. What does she want from me. I don't have the goddamned book!

"Well, I'm sorry I can't help you," I say curtly, heading back to Simone. An annoying customer, after all, is an annoying customer. No matter how cute.

I am suddenly stopped dead in my tracks by a wet hand gripping my arm like a vice. I turn around slowly, counting to ten in my head.

"Listen, lady. . . ."

"Sorry," she says, no longer crying. She shakes her head a little, spraying me. "Maybe you can help me anyway."

Her damp, soft hand lingers on my arm.

"It's just that . . . I've never been with a woman and I have a date. Tonight."

My annoyance with her has now been replaced by intrigue. I

want to see what exactly she has in mind.

"Maybe you can tell me . . . ," she ventures, and then stops, looking at the floor.

"What? You want me to tell you how to have lesbian sex?"

The blush returns, but when she speaks, she looks me boldly in the eye.

"I just need to..." she pauses, and takes a breath. "Would you mind if I kissed you, you know, just to see how it feels?"

Not waiting for an answer, she shoves me, albeit gently, into the *Études féministe* shelf. My clipboard drops to the floor as she grabs hold of both my hands. Her face very close to mine, she breathes softly against my cheek.

She plants a big wet one on my mouth.

"Ugh!" I spit out after she backs off. "What's the matter with you? Too much saliva."

"Sorry," she says with a smirk as I wipe my mouth with the back of my hand.

As bizarre as the situation is, I figure, what the hell. I am, after all, pinned here against a shelf.

"No," I say. "It goes like this."

We are still holding hands and I lean slowly into her. I nuzzle up to her neck, brushing my lips against her damp skin. Her scent, a heady mix of wet earth, vanilla, and sweat, is intoxicating. Her body relaxes, her head tilting back as she moans softly. I move my mouth up to her earlobe, feeling its delicate fuzz with my tongue, and then move to her lips. I kiss her quickly once before moving on to a longer, open-mouthed kiss.

Her mouth is silky soft and warm. She is breathing rapidly, exhaling little puffs of air through her nose and onto my face. The wet slicker is dripping all over me and is making her skin damp. The kiss goes on for some time before I realize that her wet, eager little fingers are inching their way up my t-shirt. She places one hand on my bare waist, while the other searches for my breast. I feel myself getting wet as she finds it. My nipple is hard, and this encourages her to slip her other hand inside the waistband of my jeans. She is in my underwear quickly, and suddenly I want nothing else but to be on the floor with her fingers deep inside of me.

But, I am at work. I clear my throat. She snaps out of a daze and looks at me.

"Should we still call you when the book arrives?"

"No," she says, zipping up her slicker. "That won't be necessary."

She strolls confidently out the door, brushing past the UPS guy, who carries a single box. He plunks it down on the floor in front of me, the packing slip face up: ten copies of *Lesbian Sex.*

"*Bonjour, mademoiselle. Payez-vous comptant ou par chèque?*"

R O B I N   B E R N S T E I N

How Emma Lost
Her Bra

Emma is wearing her pink jogging bra.

And socks.

We should be in French class. Instead, we're in the locker room. Not Frenching.

Here, strictly reported, are the events that led to this moment.

I intercepted Emma on the way to homeroom and suggested we skip our first class of the semester. Emma nabbed the idea, which suited her taste for wickedness. Besides, we'd barely seen each other during the summer. Emma was busy with her boyfriends, and I was . . . not.

"I want to tell you something," I said.

"Me too!" she said. Then she looked at me sly. "Maybe it's the same thing, Tammy."

"I doubt it." We slunk down the metal stairs to the basement, to the locker room. It was deserted in the middle of the period.

"I missed you all summer," Emma said. I couldn't answer that any more than she had answered my phone calls.

Alone in the locker room, Emma spun me into a hug. She

pressed the pads of her fingers up and down my spine.

"I love hugging you," she said. "You're so soft." I reached my arms around her, and she slipped away. "What did you want to tell me?" she asked.

"Uh . . ."

"Maybe I should go first."

"No, then I'll chicken out. Uh . . ." I had rehearsed, but now the words weren't coming. I wanted to tell her everything—how I spent my summer taking long walks, ten miles or more. I had walked quickly, keeping rhythm for miles. And the whole time, I thought and thought. Until I was sure.

"I want you to know that . . . I'm gay."

"You're what?"

"You know." It was the first time I'd said it out loud. The sound made me breathless, like a gong.

Emma looked worried. "Are you in love with me?"

Not anymore.

"No," I said, "I love you as a friend."

Mostly true.

"Good," she said. "Because I'm straight, you know. I mean, I like guys."

"I know what straight means."

"Oh!" Emma leaned back and expelled a huge sigh. "I thought you might be. I'm glad we're talking about it. It makes me feel so . . . liberated!"

I laughed. Emma clasped my arms and stood before me, looking level into my eyes. "I want you to know how much I love you," she said. "Right now I feel closer to you than I've ever felt to anyone. Ever." She dropped to her knees. "You are my spiritual sister," she said. She looked so solemn, I tried not to laugh. She took my hand and kissed it.

"I honour you," she said.

"Oh, for God's sake."

"I mean it. I am humble before you."

"Yeah, me, too."

"How can I let you know how I feel?" Emma twirled in a circle, arms wide. "This is how! I'm full of love!"

"Dizzy?"

"Honest! Primal! Naked!" She stopped twirling. "Primal!" A gorilla, she pulled her sneaker off, tore her teeth into the leather, and flung it aside. "Primal!" Her other shoe came off, then her shirt and jeans. "Feel the energy! Physical nakedness meets emotional nakedness!" She threw her underpants over her head. She almost ripped off her socks, but a glance at the locker room floor changed her mind. She hooked her fingers under her bra, about to tear it away, when she froze.

"No," she said, raking her fingers across her breasts. "I have to keep this on, because it covers my heart. I can't show you my heart yet, because I still have a secret."

And that is precisely how Emma came to be standing now, in the locker room, wearing only her jogging bra and socks.

"What do you want to tell me?" I ask.

Emma's fingers comb languidly through her pubic hair; her eyes close halfway.

"I lost my virginity."

I'm not in love with Emma. Anymore. Still, when she says it, my heart plunges six inches. Emma has joined a new world, earned an adulthood that will never be mine. She has slipped from my side, and now she's far away.

"Lost your virginity? Who was it?"

Emma slides her head back and shivers.

"Paul."

"Paul? I thought he was in Nepal."

"He is," Emma says. "We did it over the Internet."

I am, I remind myself as my hands tense toward her neck, a non-violent person.

"Oh, Tammy!" she says. "We've each told our secret. There's nothing left to hide. Now I can truly stand naked before you."

And the bell for second period rings as Emma flings away her bra.

Why do I feel so guilty in the changeroom at Britannia Pool?

After all, I'm a swimmer, I have a Speedo, I can do a flip turn and a shallow dive, and I can say "breaststroke" without smirking. I even know that spitting in my goggles will reduce the fog, that baby powder in my cap will stop it sticking to itself. It should be clear to anyone who sees my flipping and diving and spitting and powdering that I am legitimate. That three times a week I mingle with a bunch of naked women and it's all on the up and up. I've been doing it for years, starting at six when I routinely showered at the Y with my mother and her swimming buddies.

I lost sleep over those shower scenes back then, due to the parasite problem. In retrospect I can identify tampon strings as my troubling fixation, but at the time I suffered over how to break it to my mother that she and her friends had worms. Athlete's foot wasn't the only thing you could catch at the pool.

You would think after twenty-five years, I could feign a little nonchalance. But instead I sneak more peeks, get more flustered when I read that sign "Inappropriate behaviour will not be tolerated in the changerooms," and forget more quarters in the coin-operated lockers as every season brings me closer to my scatter-brained sexual prime. Sometimes, particularly when I'm low on cash, I scan the lockers to see if other girls have left quarters behind. Nobody else has this problem. These are women who gossip in the showers while soaping up their gleaming thighs, then smile calmly into the wild scream of blow-dryers wearing nothing but plush coral pink towels wrapped around their waists, chlorine dripping languorously from suits on hooks. Where did they learn to be so blasé, and why don't they ever forget their quarters?

I learned a while back not to go to Adult Swim on weekends. I took "Adult" to mean that I could do some lengths in peace, without being blindsided by an innertube or looking down at my legs later and saying, "Hey, these aren't my Band-Aids." But I found that some guys interpret "Adult" as in "Adult magazines sold here." They lounge in the shallow end. You try to keep your head down as you approach their creepily billowing trunks and the flash of a medallion nestled in chest hair. Beefy arms span the length of the wall and you have to stop short and, in the time it takes you to suck in a breath, one's nabbed you with an irresistible "Lookin' good," or "Can you teach me the breaststroke?"

I'm no better. While I usually breathe right, stroke stroke, breathe left, stroke stroke, today I breathe right, stroke, breathe right, stroke, breathe right on the way up the pool, and breathe left, stroke, breathe left, stroke, breathe left all the way back, just so I can keep my foggy goggles fixed on the red suit in the next lane. I'm a creep, too.

She's faster than me. She's plump and shiny and slick. She's like the sea lion in the AquaWorld tank, oblivious to me as she undulates past, her nostrils collapsed into slits. I kick as fast as I can, stroke without splashing, imagine I have long, wiry whiskers, trying to catch her notice. I want to be in the sea lion club. When she stops at the end, I stop, too, and take off my goggles. I spit in them, eager to prove I'm très cool. But instead of hitting the mark clean and sharp, the gob remains slung from my mouth, bobbing like a tiny bungee jumper. She looks over and I forget my lips and smile. Then she's off again like a shot, leaving me and my spittle hanging.

I rest my weary AquaWorld tourist muscles in the sauna. I brought the paper so I don't have to concentrate on where to direct my eyes should any naked women come in. I flip to the personals. The straight section is full of older gentlemen seeking slim ladies

233

and affectionate ladies seeking generous gentlemen. I find the usual chasm between genders in the queer section:

> *Wimmin to Womyn*
> *GF wants to meet someone who likes music, laughter,*
> *animals and quiet walks. If you're looking for*
> *someone to share with, let's make friends and then,*
> *who knows?*
>
> *Men to Men*
> *My 8-inch uncut dick needs a hungry hole to pump into*
> *oblivion. Do you have a bubble butt and shaved balls?*
> *Shoot me a message and let's see who's more oral.*

Why don't lesbians have a genital aesthetic? Are we too skittish about objectifying each other? Or could the problem be, as Mr. Rogers explains, that boys are fancy on the outside, while girls are fancy on the inside? Is it true that men are just hornier? Do I even know what kind of pussy I like? Have I ever met one I didn't like? Is it in fact the lesbians who are so horny we don't have the patience to be discriminating? I press my back against the hot cedar, close my eyes and compose a proper personal:

> *My full breasts need some hard sucking* (Okay, they
> aren't "full," but 8 inches? Please.) *and my long*
> *tongue hungers for a wet snatch with plenty*
> *of meat to grab on to. Can you give up music, laughter,*
> *and animals for a chance to fist me all night,*
> *taking breathers only to receive explosive*
> *comes under my busy lips and fingers? Would you*
> *rather have a quiet walk along the seawall, or my*
> *thumb jammed into your lubed-up ass as I . . .*

"Hot today, eh?" Sea lion girl.

"Oh hi. Yeah," I check to make sure my hands still hold the paper. She isn't wearing her red suit. As she sits across from me with one leg bent up to her chest and the other swinging off the bench, I note that her fanciness is not completely on the inside. I swallow and wonder if inappropriate behaviour would be tolerated in the sauna.

"You're a Leo, aren't you?" she says knowingly.

I gasp, amazed. "How did you know?" I'm a Capricorn, but I want to please, and besides, her confidence is so dazzling, I've begun to doubt my birthday.

"You have a calm about you, you seem comfortable in your body." Suddenly it's too hot. Why didn't I realize it before? Saunas are unbearably hot. Comfortable in my body? Does that mean I look like an old quilt or a one-eyed teddy bear? Are my legs crossed or uncrossed? Do I have worms? I can't remember. I can't breathe. I could pass out. She's still looking at me. The romance novel phrase, "Her eyes are limpid pools," comes to mind. Now I know what it means. What if I passed out right this minute? I should plan for it, so I can tumble gracefully to the floor without breaking my nose or hip. The tiles down there look nice and cool, a great big ice cube tray. She's cute. When I come to, I might find her hovering over me, a concerned look on her face, as she fans me with her flipper. I need to run out, take a cold shower, or move down to the lower bench. At least lose this newspaper, which is about to combust in my lap. But I sit still, comfortable in my body.

"Have you had your Saturn's return?" she asks.

"I don't know, I'm . . . I'm from Calgary."

Is "What's your sign" making a comeback? Did it ever stop working in Vancouver? It's clearly working on me. Why is she so cool? Why don't I put down my paper? I could just put down the paper in a really beyond comfortable way. She's smiling. I'm evaporating. She takes a swig from her Volvic bottle. With a sudden rush of bravado, I toss the paper aside. But with all the heat, it's become affixed to my fingers, and I can't shake it. I'm still trying to peel myself off when she gets up to leave. Cool air rushes in as her glossy butt swishes out. The newsprint has made an impression on my sillyputty skin, so now I have "raunchy action" on one thumb and "social drinker" on the other.

I wait a couple of minutes so it doesn't look like I'm following. Slink down to the lower bench with arms extended so I can break my fall if indeed I pass out. Finally I make it to the shower and wash off the sweat, careful also to scrub my thumbs, since she's probably not into labels.

I approach my locker naked, less because of being comfortable in my body than because I don't want her to see that I stole my towel from the Holiday Inn. Her locker's next to mine. She's about to leave. Her boots are all laced up and she's putting on a black rainslicker. I'm buck naked, but I don't care because I'm a Leo. I put my key in and my quarter pings to the floor. While bending over I glance up, look her straight in the limpid pools, which are discovered dilating and travelling over my skin. She turns pink and bolts for the exit. The door to her empty locker swings open, and I pinch the quarter peeking out of her slot.

Got Milk?

Ginger Snap was one tough cookie but lately she'd been feeling crummy. Her nerves were raw and she'd grown thin as a wafer. And it was all because of Sara Lee. That girl had burned Ginger Snap one too many times. Why did I ever get mixed up with her? Ginger Snap asked herself, as she sat on a stool at the local greasy spoon. Sara Lee was kind of flaky, and nutty as a fruitcake. Not to mention a tart. But she was sweet, too. When she called her Honey, Ginger Snap practically dissolved. But they hadn't had vanilla sex in a long time, and according to Sara Lee, Ginger Snap was toast.

I should just ask someone else for a date, Ginger Snap said to herself, even though she thought it was a half-baked idea. Who'd go out with me, a Spice Girl? Ginger Snap smiled at her own joke. There was always Apple Brown Betty. She was easy as pie. Or Susie Q. She was always a piece of cake. But somehow, those girls grated on Ginger Snap's nerves. She wanted a girl who was more than a trifle. A girl who would melt in her mouth. A girl who would make her smack her lips in ecstasy. A girl like Lorna Doone.

Now Lorna Doone was one hot dish. She looked good enough to eat, with those hot buns of hers and those creamy thighs. . . . But she was a bit too crisp, like she had a chocolate chip on her shoulder. But maybe that was just a Charlotte Russe. Ginger Snap knew that she herself was kind of crusty, but underneath she was just mush. Lorna Doone was probably one big marshmallow, too. Ginger Snap was sure she could make her melt. All she had to do was butter her up. But how?

Lorna Doone was in a jam. Her last relationship had gone stale. Lately she'd been seeing a cute Danish, but she was kind of cheesy. Melba Toast was after her as usual (and had been, ever since they were Brownies) but she wasn't exactly Lorna Doone's cup of tea. And now, to top things off, she had a wicked crush on Ginger Snap. Lorna Doone had plenty of dough and she really, really, really wanted to be Ginger Snap's sugar mama. She wanted it so badly she could taste it. But why would Ginger Snap go out with her? She didn't have one good raisin. Sure she was rich, but she was also kind of square. Granted, her plate was full, and didn't need to be anyone's girl. But to go out with Ginger Snap . . . why, that would be the icing on the cake. And didn't she deserve her just desserts?

Cherry Jubilee was in the mood for a treat. Why not throw a party? She rented out a dance hall on Rocky Road for the following Sundae and called all her friends. Lorna Doone dressed in layers. Ginger Snap hit the sauce. Neither of them were big mixers, but eventually they found themselves sandwiched together. Lorna Doone struck a cheesecake pose before Ginger Snap could waffle.

"You look delicious, Sugar," Lorna Doone smiled. "You from around here?"

"Born and bread," Ginger Snap replied, her eyes glazing over.

Lorna Doone felt frozen to the spot. "I knead you," she whispered.

"You don't mince words, do you?" Ginger Snap asked.

"Why fudge it?" Lorna Doone replied. "I've dreamed of you whisking me away."

Ginger Snap didn't stir. Then slowly she reached out her ladyfingers and whipped Lorna Doone out onto the dance floor. Lorna Doone felt light as a cocoa puff as they swirled around the room.

Just then Cherry Jubilee announced the dance contest. Ginger Snap and Lorna Doone really started cooking. "May

I dip you?" Ginger Snap asked.

"Well done!" a batch of girls cried. They knew when they were licked.

"It's boiling in here," Lorna Doone said to Ginger Snap as the band took a break.

"My temperature's definitely on the rise," Ginger Snap agreed. "Would you like a drink?"

"I'd rather have a little bite," said Lorna Doone. "How about you?"

Ginger Snap smiled. "I could use a nibble."

Our two heroines slid outside. They were both hot and moist and so excited, they simply devoured each other.

And that's the way the cookie crumbles.

CONTRIBUTORS

Nilaja Montgomery-Akalu is a 20-something African-American lesbian. She's an aspiring filmmaker-writer-photographer currently living in the San Francisco Bay Area where she is pursuing a certificate in American Sign Language.

Donna Allegra has been published in *Hers 3: brilliant new fiction by lesbians, Best Lesbian Erotica 1999, Lesbian Travels: A Literary Companion,* and *Does Your Mama Know?: An Anthology of Black Lesbian Coming-Out Stories.*

Sarah Van Arsdale's first novel, *Toward Amnesia*, was published by Riverhead Books/Putnam. She has taught at California State University, Vermont College, and the University of Vermont. Her book reviews appear in the *San Francisco Chronicle, Lambda Book Report,* and *Publishers Weekly.*

Wendy Atkin lives in Ottawa with her partner and two children. She organizes ideas and people by day, and reads and writes erotic stories because it creates a fun space in the world.

LaShonda K. Barnett resides in Virginia where she is a Ph.D. candidate in the American Studies Program at the College of William & Mary. She is the author of *Callaloo & Other Lesbian Love Tales* (New Victoria Publishers, 1999). Her works have appeared in several lesbian anthologies. Her favourite past-time includes "breakfasts with" her partner, Kate.

Russel Baskin divides her time between her own art practice, writing, and teaching creative process to youth and adults. Her writing appears in *Queer View Mirror 2* and *Hot & Bothered.*

Wendy Becker is a Ph.D. student. When she's not writing about lesbian desire for anthologies like this one, she's studying it in her seminars or enjoying it in her bedroom. Equally drawn to fiction and fact, she is also a columnist for a queer newspaper.

Shari J. Berman is a writer, educator, Japanese translator and entrepreneur. She writes an Internet lesbian fiction serial called *The SelenaStories* (www.wow-women.com). Her fiction also appears in anthologies from Alyson, Elles and Robinson.

Robin Bernstein is an editor of *Bridges*, a journal of Jewish feminist culture and politics. Her books include *Terrible, Terrible!,* the first picture book to feature a Jewish stepfamily, and *Generation Q*, which was a finalist for a Lambda Literary Award. In 1999 she earned an Honourable Mention in the Astraea Emerging Lesbian Writers Fund Award for Fiction. Her work appears in *Friday the Rabbi Wore Lace*, *Best Lesbian Erotica 1997*, *The Oy of Sex*, and many other books.

Persimmon Blackbridge is a sculptor, performer and author of six books, including *Prozac Highway*, finalist for a 1997 Lambda Literary Award; *Sunnybrook*, winner of the 1996 Ferro-Grumley Fiction Prize; and *Slow Dance* (with Bonnie Sherr Klein), winner of the 1998 VanCity Book Prize. A new novel, *The Truth About Ramona* with Lizard Jones, is forthcoming in 2000.

Helen Bradley is an Australian-born cybergrrl, journalist, and writer who met the butch of her dreams in a lesbian chat room. She currently lives and writes in California. Her non-fiction is published internationally and her erotic stories have appeared in *The Lesbian Erotic Cookbook* and *Cosmopolitan*.

T.J. Bryan is a 31-year-old out, exhibitionistic/voyeuristic, bajan-born, femme, capricornian dyke, and recovering feminist. Her work has been seen in *Tessera*, *Matriart*, *Fireweed*, *Fuse*, *This Magazine*, *Absinthe*, *Canadian Women's Studies*, *At The Crossroads* and in eight Black/dyke/queer/young women's anthologies.

Johanne Cadorette of Montreal would like to say that even though she did work in a gay and lesbian bookstore for six years, she makes up all the stuff she writes about. If she were to venture into writing about her actual experiences, the result would be far from sexy. Ask anyone who works in a book store. Her first French-language short story will be published in 1999 in a special gay and lesbian edition of the literary journal *Moebus*.

Connie Chapman is a lesbian feminist who lives with her partner, five cats, a dog, and two horses at Stonewall Guest House, a bed-and-breakfast she owns and operates outside Ladysmith, B.C. on beautiful Vancouver Island.

Jeanne Cordova is a Mexican/Irish publisher, author, and journalist who lives underneath the "D" of the Hollywood Sign in Los Angeles. She is the former founder/publisher of *The Lesbian Tide*, *Square Peg Magazine*, and *Spirit of Todos Santos (MX)*. Her last memoir, *Kicking The Habit: A Lesbian Nun Story*, is available from Amazon.com.

MR Daniel is an African-American writer and spoken word artist. She has performed her work at clubs, galleries, and performance spaces throughout the San Francisco Bay Area.

Robin Dann is a bisexual Jewish pagan writer/painter who lives in a turret in Brooklyn with her cat, a bike, and a laptop. She shares her hopes/fears/joys with her many wonderful friends, both real and imaginary. Currently she is between partners and working on a novel—perhaps no coincidence.

Maria de los Rios, born in Cuba and raised in Venezuela, is a writer, poet, composer, story teller, and performer. Published in *Revista Mujeres, Conmocion, Hot & Bothered, Tongues on Fire,* and *New to North America,* and served as member of the Advisory Editorial Board of the Latina lesbian magazine *Conmoción.*

Donna Dow is currently living on the oceanfront of Vancouver Island in a small community just outside of Victoria. She has been retired for six years and loves the island and its energy. She hikes, gardens, writes, woodworks, and generally keeps busy.

Elana Dykewomon has been a lesbian cultural worker and radical activist for thirty years. *Beyond the Pale,* her Jewish lesbian historical novel, won both the Lambda Literary and Gay and Lesbian Publishers' Awards for lesbian fiction in 1998. Other works include *Riverfinger Women* (one of the first dyke novels of the '70s), and *Nothing Will Be As Sweet As The Taste* (poetry, Onlywomen Press). Currently teaching English at San Francisco State University, living happily with her partner among friends, she tries to make trouble whenever she can.

Gale "Sky" Edeawo is an African-American freelance writer and story teller who writes mostly for and about women. She has been writing since 1972 and has been published numerous times. She has received several awards for her prose pieces and short stories, and recently completed her first novel. She now lives in Savannah, Georgia, where she contributes articles to several of the local papers, and coordinates writers' workshops.

Deb Ellis, of Dunnville, Ontario, has published a novel, *Haley and Scotia,* and a children's novel, *Looking for X. Women of the Afghan War: An Oral History* is due out soon. She works at Margaret Frazer House in Toronto, travels when she can, and has fun where she can find it.

Sandra E. Fellner is a writer and performer in Vancouver. Primarily a comedian, Sandra is also a veteran sex show producer. She's a dirty girl from way back when.

Karen Galbreath is an author, mother of four, and a published poet. She is currently compiling her short stories and poetry with photographs by her daughter, Amanda, into a book. It is to be an autobiographical journey of a woman coming out, after marriage and motherhood. Born in Buffalo, N.Y., the author resides in Los Angeles and Chicago with her life partner, Joanne.

Gabrielle Glancy's work had appeared in numerous journals and anthologies including *The New Yorker, The Paris Review, The Harvard Gay & Lesbian Review, Sister and Brother, Queer View Mirror 1* and *2,* and *Hot & Bothered.* She lives in London.

CONTRIBUTORS

Jewelle Gomez is the executive director of the San Francisco State Poetry Center and Archives. In addition to the acclaimed *Gilda Stories*, she is the author of *Don't Explain, Forty-Three Septembers,* and the poetry collection, *Oral Tradition.*

Erin Graham lives in Vancouver, where she is a writer, an actor, a mental health worker, and an artist's model. So far nothing like this has ever happened to her.

Florence Grandview's story title "Whispers Getting Fainter" was inspired by the Jackie Wilson song "Whispers (Getting' Louder)." She has previously published a story in *Tidelines: Stories of Change by Lesbians*, edited by Lee Fleming (Gynergy Books, 1991). She lives in Vancouver.

Terrie Hamazaki is a Barracuda Femme living in Vancouver. She is a writer and performer whose signature piece, "Furusato (Birth Place)," appears in *Mom: Candid memoirs by lesbians about the first woman in their life.*

Sharon Hanna is obsessed with how gardening mirrors life, and writes to the sound of Norway maples in front of her vine-covered home in Vancouver. She is a master gardener and works in the field of urban and rural agriculture.

Quade Hermann has finally given in to the seduction of the written word and is pursuing an MFA in Creative Writing at the University of British Columbia.

Lou Hill lives with her partner of seven years, their son, and a houseful of pets. She has written several short stories, which have appeared in a number of anthologies. She is also awaiting the publication of her first novel.

Susan Holbrook wrote her story while living just around the corner from Womyn's Ware in Vancouver. She currently writes and teaches in Tuscaloosa, Alabama, where it's illegal to sell sex toys. Her first book, *misled* (1999), is published by Red Deer Press.

Elisabeth Hurst is a lesbian living in Vancouver who has been making up stories for as long as she can remember. This is her first published work of fiction, but one day she hopes to have a list of them so these bios don't feel quite so daunting.

Lizard Jones is a writer and artist living in Vancouver. She is a member of the lesbian art collective Kiss & Tell, creators of *Drawing the Line* and *Her Tongue on My Theory*, as well as performances and videos. Her novel *Two Ends of Sleep* came out in 1997.

Sook C. Kong is a survivor of the wordless. Poetry and fiction writer. Cultural critic. Sook's writing has appeared in several publications, including *Herizons* and *Kinesis*. Co-author of *Your Everyday Health Guide: A Lesbian, Gay, Bisexual and Transgender Community Resource* (1998). She lives in Vancouver.

Marlys LaBrash is single and lives in Vancouver. She can usually be found on her motorcycle or hanging out at the beach.

Annitsa Laitman is a working-class Croatian lesbian who counsels women who have been abused as children. She lives in Vancouver with her dog, Kayla. She believes that women reclaiming and loving their bodies and their sexuality is the ultimate revolutionary act. This is her first published story.

Monica Lee is a Korean-Canadian, born in Montreal who has been busy living, working, and being in love in Vancouver, and finds most of her writing time on the number 20 bus and the 99 B-line.

Rosalyn S. Lee has previously been published in *Hot & Bothered* as well as poetry in the Library of Congress Poetry Series. She is currently working on several short stories for future submissions. She shares her New York apartment with her well-pampered pug.

Susan Lee lives in Toronto. Her first published short short story appears in *Hot & Bothered* and her poetry appears in the anthology, *But Where Are You Really From? Writings on Identity and Assimilation in Canada.*

River Light is a 31-year-old dyke living in Vancouver who started writing porn for her first leather lover to remind her of how much ____ loved her and loved what she did. She is still writing because she wants to see as much good erotica out there as possible.

Rosalind Christine Lloyd's work has been included in *Pillowtalk II, Skin Deep,* and various gay and lesbian publications. Currently the travel editor for *Venus Magazine*, this lesbian of colour, native New Yorker, and Harlem resident is working on her first novel.

L.M. McArthur is currently living in the Vancouver area with her partner. This is her first piece of published fiction. She is currently researching and writing for future stories.

Liz McKenna is a writer and editor living on the east coast of the United States with her attack cat Fredo.

Cathy McKim's work appears in *Countering The Myths* (Women's Press) and *Letters to our Children* (Franklin Watts). In addition to the occasional voice-over gig, Cathy is currently co-writing a stage play and hopes to someday publish a collection of her own short stories. She lives in Toronto.

Mary Midgett resides in San Francisco. She teaches elementry school and lectures on human sexuality at a university in the Bay area. Her experiences include lecturing on sexuality, ageing, human relationships and parenting. She is the author of, *Brown on Brown; Black Lesbian Erotica.*

Heather Mitchell, a native Vancouverite, now lives in Toronto, where she slings coffee and tends bar. She graduated from Mills College in Oakland, California in 1997 and is currently studying comparative literature at the

University of Toronto. She sends kisses to all deserving grrls—you know who you are!

Shani Mootoo is the author of *Cereus Blooms at Night*, which was shortlisted for the B.C. Book Prize for Fiction, the Chapters/*Books in Canada* First Novel Award, and the Giller Prize. She is the author of *Out On Main Street*, and a multi-media visual artist and video-maker whose painting and photo-based works have been exhibited internationally.

Joan Nestle is the author of *A Fragile Union*, a nominee for the 1999 American Library Association Gay, Lesbian, and Bisexual Book Award, and *A Restricted Country*. She is the editor of *A Persistent Desire: A Femme Butch Reader* and co-editor of the Lambda Literary Award-winning *Sister and Brother: Lesbians and Gay Men Write About Their Lives Together*, and *Women on Women 1, 2,* and *3*.

Lesléa Newman is an author and editor whose thirty books include *Pillow Talk: Lesbian Stories Between the Covers* (volumes I and II), *The Femme Mystique*, *The Little Butch Book*, *My Lover is a Woman: Contemporary Lesbian Love Poems*, and *Out of the Closet and Nothing to Wear*. Her newest book, *Girls Will Be Girls: a novella and short stories,* has just been published.

Carol Queen has a doctorate in sexology and takes every opportunity to stay atop her field. (Or on the bottom.) She authored *The Leather Daddy and the Femme, Real Live Nude Girl*, and *Exhibitionism for the Shy*, and co-edited *Best Bisexual Erotica, PoMoSexuals, Switch Hitters*, and *Sex Spoken Here*.

Jean Roberta was born in the United States and moved to Canada with her family in the 1960s. She teaches English at a university in Saskatchewan. One of her stories appeared in *Batteries Not Included*, an anthology edited by Alison Tyler (Diva Books). Another story will appear in *Tears on Black Roses* (Anxiety Publications) in 2000.

Jacquelyn Ross is a high femme with no mechanical aspirations. She lives and cruises in Vancouver. This is her first published story.

Elizabeth Rowan was born in Nottinghamshire, England and lives in Milton Keynes with her cat where they have made some good new friends. She has always wanted to write and this is her first published work.

Lisa Sheridan was born in 1969 in Lincolnshire, England. She graduated 1993 from Aberdeen University in English and French, and currently resides in Aberdeen with her two cats. She is a self-confessed lesbian-feminist and practicing Buddhist and a lover of words, women, and warm beer.

Alison L. Smith's writing has appeared in *Best Lesbian Erotica 1999* and *Curve*. She lives in Northampton, Mass. She is writing a novel.

Wickie Stamps work appears in numerous anthologies, including *Flashpoint,*

Close Calls, Brothers and Sisters, Doing It For Daddy, Leatherfolks, Queer View Mirror, Switch Hitters, Once Upon a Time, Sons of Darkness, and *Strategic Sex.* Wickie is a prior editor of *Drummer* magazine and current editor of *Socialist Review.*

Jessica Stein is a senior at New York University and an editor of *Bridges: A Journal for Jewish Feminists and Our Friends.* Her work has appeared in *Hanging Loose, Sinister Wisdom,* and *Sojourner.* Her story is from her novel, *Now You See Her,* which is looking for a home.

Zara Suleman is a basic brown girl who writes, speaks out, and stands up for what she believes in. Her work has appeared in *Rungh, SAMAR, Canadian Women's Studies Journal, DIVA* and two anthologies, *Aurat Durbar* and *The Journal Project.* She lives in Vancouver.

Cecilia Tan is the author of *Black Feathers: Erotic Dreams* (Harper Collins) and *The Velderet* (Masquerade). Her stories have appeared in Susie Bright's *Best American Erotica, On a Bed of Rice: An Asian American Erotic Feast,* and in magazines as diverse as *Penthouse* and *Ms.* She is the founder and publisher of Circlet Press and lives in Cambridge, Mass.

Shoshie Tornberg is a poet who enjoys expounding to the unconverted on the attractions of her neighbourhood of Jamaica Plain, Mass. She is an erstwhile Canadian with a passion for subjecting her friends and family to spontaneous poetry. Shoshie's work has appeared in *P'Town Woman* and *Best Lesbian Erotica 1999.*

Jules Torti is currently entertaining thoughts of writing *Chicken Poop for the Lesbian Soul,* but may keep her day job as a registered massage therapist instead. Her true ambition is to become a Carole Pope roadie. Jules lives in Dunnville, Ontario, home of a Bick's pickle factory . . . and that's about it.

Jess Wells' ten volumes of work include the new novel, *Price of Passion* (Firebrand Books). Her previous novel, *AfterShocks* (Third Side Press) was nominated for the American Library Association Gay and Lesbian Literary Award. The anthology, *Lesbians Raising Sons* (Alyson), was a finalist for a Lambda Literary Award. Her five collections of short stories include *Loon Lake Duet* (currently seeking publication), *Two Willow Chairs,* and *The Dress/The Sharda Stories.*

Robin G. White, an African-Brazilian-American, has published in *Best Lesbian Erotica 1999, Dyka'tude, ButiVoxx,* and the forthcoming *No Guest List.* Her play *Pantyliners* and other spoken words have been choreographed, performed and recorded nationally by The Theatre Offensive, Sweet Black Molasses and Drag Kings, Sluts & Goddesses. She lives in Georgia.

L. Wilder is the pseudonym of a shy novice Canadian queer writer with not enough time on her hands. She is currently working on a novel while juggling the demands of work that pays the bills, kids who don't and a lover who makes it worth while. She sculpts, writes and walks her dog.

Shirley Williamson is a writer and photographer. She has contributed to *On Our Backs*, *Diva*, and *Lesbian Short Fiction*. She has just completed her fourth novel.

Phoenix Wisebone's writing has appeared in *Queer View Mirror 2, Ante Up*, and literary publications in Canada. She's also a singer-songwriter, gigging with her guitar in and around Vancouver.

Karen Woodman is a visual artist and writer. Her work has appeared in *Queer View Mirror 2*, and more recently in *She's Gonna Be*. She lives in Toronto.

Zonna lives in New York. When she's not writing lesbian vampire stories, erotica, or novels, she performs as an out musician. Never one to keep a low profile, she refuses to write the story of her life in invisible ink.

ABOUT THE EDITOR

Karen X. Tulchinsky is the award-winning author of *Love Ruins Everything*, a novel, and *In Her Nature*, short fiction. She is the editor or co-editor of numerous anthologies, including the critically acclaimed *Queer View Mirror 1* and *2*, the bestselling *Hot & Bothered: Short Short Fiction on Lesbian Desire*, the Lambda Literary Award finalist *To Be Continued* and *Friday the Rabbi Wore Lace*. She has written for several magazines and newspapers including the *Vancouver Sun*, *Curve*, *Girlfriends*, *DIVA*, *Quill & Quire*, the *Georgia Straight,* and the *Lambda Book Report*. She lives, writes and teaches creative writing in Vancouver, Canada.

Credits